Station in the Sky

Station in the Sky

Caye Marsh

Space Wizard Science Fantasy
Raleigh, NC
www.spacewizardsciencefantasy.com

Cover art by MoorBooks
Editing by Heather Tracy
Book Layout © 2015 BookDesignTemplates.com

Station in the Sky/Caye Marsh.— 1st ed.
ISBN 978-1-960247-36-0

Author's website: https://cayemarsh.com/

CONTENTS

I conceived this story during many late nights nursing my first child. So, this is for my two children, who taught me what it feels like to be a mother.

Peace in the Sky

Part One

Greasy gray dark. Slippery, smeary confusion.

When I open my eyes, shapes coalesce. Metal clinks against metal. I sway, suspended above the ground.

Across from me there is a shape, and I see it move. Something alive.

I don't know why but I reach up to touch one side of my head. Violent nausea. I retch, and see blue everywhere, and I can't tell which direction is up.

When the feeling fades and everything is real again, I open my eyes. It's a girl that's across from me. I don't touch my head.

The girl is sitting on the floor like I am, her back against rusted metal bars. I feel them at my back, too. She is in the dark, but I think I see her eyes moving. She is watching me.

Later, there is a little more light. A man is outside our cage, looking in. His brown cheeks are rough with a patchy beard.

He speaks to the girl. He's smiling but it's an ugly smile. He opens his pants and gestures at himself, thrusts suggestively at the girl. I look at her face, and she squeezes her eyes shut and turns her head away.

"Stop it," I say.

Both of them look at me, startled.

"Leave," I tell the man. He looks at me, both angry and scared. And he leaves.

I look at the girl, and she looks at me. Her eyes are wide now. She's waiting for me to do something.

Her long arms and legs are bony, but her face is still round and sweet. She must be young, on the cusp of her body changing. One of her sleeves is torn and there's some caked blood on her arm.

How long have I been staring at her? Three men come, their faces and arms covered with patches of calloused, horny skin. They bring water and we drink it while they talk. I hear their voices, but I can't understand them. They walk around the girl's side of the cage and grab at her through the bars. They don't come to my side at all.

I hold out my arm and say, "Come here," to her.

She looks at me for only a moment, then she scoots across the small distance between us and fits herself into the space I make for her. The men's eyes grow narrow in their crusty faces and as they leave, they shove the cage. It swings on its chain and knocks once against the wall.

The shock sends me spiraling into that greasy limbo again and when I come to, the men are gone and I'm holding the girl tightly against my side. She smells like sweat and urine. But the skin of her bare arm under my hand is smooth and tender. When I touch her, I'm overpowered by some unrecognizable feeling that sends me sliding back to the edge of that gray chasm, and I fight to stay conscious.

She buries her head in my shoulder. "Momma," she says.

* * *

I think she sleeps for a while. Maybe I sleep. I'm thirsty and I try not to drink all the water so she can have plenty.

"Why can't I remember your name?" I ask her.

"Your head," she looks up at me. "It's cracked open. What happened to you?"

I don't know. I don't know anything. "But what is your name, daughter? Remind me just once."

"Anissa."

Quietly I whisper, "Anissa," and stroke her temple. She relaxes into me. I feel her fear fading.

The men come back determined. They have poles with them that have metal crooks on the end. They pull the cage door open and reach in to hook Anissa. There is struggling and curses and Anissa cries out and I won't let her go so they end up pulling us both out. But they won't touch me. They give me a little prod with the poles, but they won't hook me. They want Anissa and they try to separate us.

I still can't understand them. I can't focus. I hear their words, but they don't seem to make any sense.

They have her now. Away from me. They are holding her arms and blocking me with the poles.

"Momma!" she screams, reaching out for me. "Momma! Call the pillars-of-flame!" They are dragging her away. "MOMMA!"

I push forward and reach her. One of the men puts a firm hand on my arm. As if in response, a needle of cold lances through my head just above my ear. I feel Anissa throw her arms about me as columns of blinding white engulf each man. Anissa and I hide our faces against each other, the roaring in our ears drowning out all else.

Just as suddenly, it is terribly quiet. My ears are ringing, and my eyes see strange after-images. There are no corpses. Three piles of smoldering carbon lay in a semi-circle around us. Above each pile there's a hole melted through the roof, the edges still smoking.

Anissa makes a strange little sound. She's quiet for a moment, then makes it again, then dissolves into laughter. Manic laughter. She goes limp. I catch her in my arms and carry her out of the building and see how crudely it's built, with stacked rocks and mud slathered in the cracks. The streets outside are rutted dirt and gravel. There are some sickly-looking trees with only a little foliage, and there are smaller huts in the distance, not far. They are all topped with flimsy hammered metal sheets. Even the parched gardens and some of the paths are shaded with them.

The sky is overcast but as I stand there holding Anissa the clouds slide by and the sun glares down. Heat breaks over me and my skin prickles uncomfortably. The squat bush at the edge of the path curls its leaves into tight rolls. I rush to stand under a metal shade and my eyes scan the area. There are miles of arid nothingness all around us. And all of it under the cruel eye of the sun.

Poor Anissa. I let her stand, but she is still weak. I breathe evenly, deeply and hold her to my chest so she can feel my calm. A ways off, there's a dip in the landscape and a row of trees. As soon as the clouds blow overhead and shade the ground, I set off across the yard, supporting Anissa. It's a long way to go and the edges of my thoughts begin to gray. I focus straight ahead and push on, step by stumbling step.

We make it. I find a spot in the shade of the trees on a ridge and look down a crumbling bank to a shallow river running orange with dirt. I take Anissa's arm and we scramble down the bank. The chalky silt at the river's margins is ankle-deep. We slog through and begin to splash our arms and legs and necks to clean off everything we accumulated in the cage.

"Don't drink it," I tell Anissa.

"It's probably what they gave us to drink," she says in a teary voice.

"Who are they?" I ask.

She looks over her shoulder up the rise. "They are the Intha, Momma, you know that."

The clouds drift by and the sun bakes us again. Anissa whimpers and we rush back to the trees. But they have curled their leaves and no longer provide much shade.

"We have to hide from it!" Anissa shades her eyes, but the light doesn't bother me. "We'll be burned."

Behind us there is noise. We squat low and turn to peer over the ridge. The sun on my neck, even in the shade, is searing. Men and women are gathering around the hut we were in. They peer inside, though they don't enter, and scan the paths around them. Their roughened brown skin and brown clothes fade into the landscape.

"Where can we go?" I whisper to Anissa. "Are we far from home?"

"Far," she says in a small voice. "So far."

Quickly I say, "It will be dark in a few hours. We can travel easier then and find a place to shelter in the day. We will make a plan, Anissa. I will take you home. Our home." I remember nothing about it, but already I'm longing for it.

She moves closer to me, both of us watching the group of Intha carefully. I hate that she is exposed to the unfiltered sunshine. I know, somehow, that it is harming her subtly. It's not just the heat of it. I have to get her away.

Clouds cover the sun again.

"Come on." I lead Anissa back down to the water.

She drinks some and I can't tell her not to because she must be so thirsty, but it floods me with worry to see her do it.

"We have to follow the river," she tells me. "That will lead us home."

I look upriver and see that in places the bank is undercut and there are shaded spots. It's not enough to conceal us for long but it's better than being in the open.

We start walking quickly against the flow of the river. When the sun breaks free of the clouds we jog until we reach the shaded bank. We squelch through the silt as long lizards slide away from us under the water, abandoning the shade for opaque water. We sit, and water soaks through our pants and wicks up our clothing.

When we're resting, I can feel just how tired I am, how thirsty I am. I'm more aware of the ever-present ache in my head that makes clear thinking so difficult, that makes the world spin if I exert myself. There are thoughts swimming around in back of the gray. But I can't reach them.

"What do the Intha want with us?" I ask Anissa.

Her eyes lose their vacant look, and she lifts her chin.

"Me, they want because I'm Riches, from the Tribes-under-the-Dome. We live there in bounty and our babies are so beautiful. You know, Momma." She smiles at me, so happy.

I'm not sure what she means by all of it, but seeing her glow with pride and love affects me deeply. I reach out to put my hand on her thin shoulder and feel an ache in my chest. Whether it is pain or pleasure I can't tell. Maybe both.

When the clouds block the light again, we move further up the river until we reach the next overhang of bank. And so on and on, sometimes breaking into a jog when the sun catches us in the open. The shadows are growing longer now as we turn away from the face of the sun so it's easier to find cover. And though we find cover, I know it's not enough. It doesn't yet show on her dark skin, but I am keenly aware that Anissa is slowly burning.

Finally, the sun is eclipsed by the horizon, and we slow to a trudging walk. We're exhausted.

"Stay here, Anissa." I find her some deep shade in the gray light. We haven't heard another person, and all we've seen is the banks on either side of us and sometimes thorny trees lining the ridge.

I walk up the ridge and scan the darkening landscape. It's so empty. There are ridges and shallow valleys and stands of scrub. There's chalky dirt, and hard-baked clay, and rocks. But no soil. And no more huts. No signs of people.

We need fresh water and a place to shelter from the sun, but I see no options. I make my way back to Anissa.

"Can you walk farther?" I ask her gently. Her head jerks up. I've caught her just as she is falling asleep.

Now that it's dark we could really cover some distance. But instead, I sit beside her and put my back to a stretch of bank that isn't so muddy. Anissa leans against me. I wrap my arms across her chest and hold her close. My legs are weak with so much walking, my throat is dry, my head throbs with the pain that never leaves me. But holding her brings peace. I bury my face in her curly hair and breathe deep. Under all the grime and sweat I can still detect her smell. The scent of my daughter.

We sleep.

* * *

I wake to Anissa shaking my arm.

"Momma? Momma?"

I force my eyes open and take deliberate deep, slow breaths. I know that I was dying, and I push away panic. I feel certain that if she hadn't woken me, I would never have woken.

I look to Anissa. Her eyes are wide in the dark and she points to something at the water's edge that's rooting through the silt with its long snout. It's like a boulder with short legs. Plates cover its humped back and a long scaly tail extends toward us. But it's not paying attention to us, so its size doesn't worry me. It's not hunting. It's foraging.

I get up and stretch and walk down to the water upstream from the animal. The animal snorts and startles. But after watching me for a moment with small black eyes, it shuffles off away down the bank, leaving deep depressions in the muck with its feet and dragging tail.

Anissa runs to me, and we both kneel and drink water. It tastes like clay and metal, but I can't stop myself drinking. I drink until I feel uncomfortably full. Anissa has finished and is touching the skin of her arms gingerly.

"Oh! My girl." I go to her and touch her softly. Her skin is so hot. I turn her and sit her in my lap and take the softest silt from the water's edge and dab it gently over her burns. I wish her clothes covered more of her. She's wearing a wrapped garment held up with only a thin strap over each shoulder. It was once red, I see, but is now so stained that it just looks dark. Underneath she has on the wide leather pants the Intha wore.

When I finish covering her shoulders with mud, she turns to me and takes my cheeks in her hands, tilting my head down until she can see my wound. She shoos away the little winged insects that are swarming it. She looks for a moment, then releases me and looks away.

"Don't let it worry you, Anissa. I will take care of it later. It's fine for now." But she doesn't say anything, and she won't meet my eyes.

"I won't leave you," I tell her. "I'll see you home. I'll see us both home."

We get up to walk again. Though we don't jog it feels like we're covering more ground. Every so often I ask Anissa to take a break and I climb the ridge and scout the area, though in the dark I can't tell much.

Hours pass by and I know dawn can't be long off. We still haven't found a place to shelter during the day.

When we stop to drink, I look up and see—floating on the surface of the lazy water—a rounded shape. I watch it as it passes. An eggshell? A few moments later, I see another. I look upstream and see a thin line of gray smoke against the dark sky.

"I smell food," Anissa says.

I start walking upstream. Anissa follows. After a few bends in the riverbed, we look up to see a shack on the edge of the bank. I start to scramble up the bank.

"Momma," Anissa hisses. "You can't!"

"Why?" I turn back to look at her.

"They'll catch us again."

"It's not the same people," I say.

"It doesn't matter! They'll know us."

Her distress is so plain that I slide back down to her.

"Anissa, you need to eat something. Maybe they won't know who you are."

"But they will," she says. "Look at my skin, Momma. They would know me anywhere. The Inthas all want girls from Tribes-under-the-Dome. Any one of them would catch me and sell me to the traders who deal in girls, too."

"Could I go alone? What will they think of me?"

She thinks for a moment and answers slowly.

"They will know you, Momma. Of course they will. Even the Intha know Peace-in-the-Sky when they see one."

"What?"

"You." She smiles slowly. "They wouldn't even touch you in the hut, Momma. They know you can call the pillars-of-flame."

I remember doing it. Strangest of all I remember it not feeling strange that I could do it.

"Can anyone do that?" I ask.

"No one!" She laughs. "No one can do that. It's impossible. Only Peace-in-the-Sky can do it."

"I'll go up there," I say, "and you can stay here."

She nods but looks uncertain. I crest the bank of the river but stay low. There's a hut with metal scraps patchworked over the roof. A fenced and shaded yard encloses a flock of some plump birds, streaked brown and gray and white. There's a dusty garden with short bushes growing red and orange and yellow fruits. I creep closer to the side of the hut and circle around back.

But behind are two large beasts that bring me up short. They have their heads down at first, but raise them, funnel-shaped ears rotating, as I come into view. Chewing slowly, they watch me carefully with brown eyes shaded by wide bony ridges. Short leathery wings are folded alongside a large hump on their back.

"Camels," Anissa whispers behind me. I turn to see her close by.

Before I can question her, she whispers, "I came to help, Momma. I know what to do." She looks so brave and determined that I don't disagree. And I like it better to have her with me.

We can hear people inside talking and moving around, and we tuck ourselves into the deep shadows by the wall. Through a small window I glimpse a man and a woman busy around a table. In the hearth burns a fire with a pan over it. There's a dirt floor, and on every wall of the hut are hung tools of cooking and of gardening, coils of rough rope and strips of brown leather, and in the corner a big metal drum.

We creep around to the door, and I raise my hand to knock, but Anissa shoves it open with a bang.

I stand startled in the doorway, and Anissa shouts out, "Behold Peace-in-the-Sky!"

Man and woman both jump and spin around, their mouths open in surprise. The man moves toward us, but Anissa stops him in his tracks with a mad tirade.

"Bow down! Bow before the godshard! Dare not touch the sacred person or pillars-of-flame will erupt from the ground and swallow your flesh! Get down! Get *down*!"

They do not get down, but they do step back, glancing at each other. I don't think they are afraid, exactly, but they are stunned. I take two steps in, just watching them, and Anissa squirms around me and grabs both plates from the table. She grabs things off the wall, too, but I can't watch her. I'm watching the man and woman.

He is broad-shouldered and dark-haired. The woman's eyes are nearly concealed by her orange hair. Their features are marred in the same way by thick scabrous patches, and their clothes are the same plain brown.

Very quickly Anissa is done, and she disappears through the door behind me. I step back slowly and note two things in the moment I am closing the door. One is the naked look of lust on their faces as they watch Anissa's back disappear. And the second is a pair of dark eyes in a distorted face, just at knee level beside the woman. A child.

Anissa is already halfway down the bank, and as I follow, I hear clanging behind us in the hut. I assume they are going to give chase. So I run, clamping down on the nausea that brings.

There's a hint of pink on the horizon which shows me Anissa's form sprinting along the riverbed. Her long legs propel her, so effortlessly athletic, that I nearly forget our pursuers and just follow, feeling joy in her health and strength.

I'm not sure how long she can maintain the pace, but my glances back show nothing but empty landscape. I don't think the Intha could run like her, they're built more for long plodding distances than fleet bursts, but our tracks would be easy enough to follow. I let Anissa keep the lead. Running is difficult for me; I have to cushion each step so I don't jar my head. I see the swirling gray at the edges of my vision as it is.

The first rays of sun come lancing over the horizon, and I catch up to Anissa in the shadow of a wide tree trunk. She has already drunk from the river and is now sitting on the ratty swath of cloth, eating the eggs from one of the plates. I drink from the river, too, and sit by her. She offers me the other plate. I take the dry, flat bread, but leave the egg and boiled greens and strip of salted meat.

The bread is thick and stale, so I chew it at length, just watching her eat. Seeing her eat so heartily eases some of my sense of wrongness at stealing.

"Aren't you going to eat more?" she asks after an audible swallow.

I look at the plate for a second and take half the strip of meat, and push the rest back at her.

"Momma, you have to eat," she says.

"You first, Anissa-my-Daughter."

"What did you call me?" she asks, reaching for my eggs with a guilty glance at me.

I pause to recall my words.

"Can I not say it like that?"

"No, that's not a word. You can't put my name in word like that." Anissa is smiling though.

"It makes sense to me when said like that. Do I use words the wrong way?"

"Sometimes. And you use words I don't know."

"How can it be true that my own daughter does not understand my words?" I ask her.

"Oh." She waves a hand, chewing for a moment. "You know different things, same way you know about calling the pillars-of-flame. That's something about being a Peace-in-the-Sky."

"You called me a 'godshard,' too. Is that the same? Am I not from Riches as my daughter is?"

"You don't remember anything?" Anissa asks wonderingly. "Really, not even one thing?"

I try to think of what I remember. But my memories are impressions, not things I can put into words. Nothing seems clear. And it makes me feel empty and painfully removed from my own daughter, so I put it aside. I watch her finishing up the food on my plate.

"Anissa, that family had a child. The things we took will be missed. Why didn't you tell me you were going to steal from them?"

There's a flash of defiance across her face.

"They stole *me* from my family, from my home, they brought me out here into the drylands to steal my babies..." She draws an angry breath to continue but I interrupt gently.

"That family did not steal you."

"What were you going to do?" she shoots back. "*Ask* them for stuff?"

"Yes."

She laughs. "That's foolish! They wouldn't have given you anything."

"But Anissa you have to give them the chance. Maybe we could have exchanged work for the food. We could have asked for shelter for the day."

"They wouldn't have done it." She sits back against the tree trunk looking sulky.

The memory of the pure greed on their faces when they looked at Anissa makes me stop pressing her. Because I think she is right. But that doesn't change the fundamental wrongness.

"Next time, Anissa," I say, "we will try to come to an agreement with the Intha we meet."

"*You* can," she says under her breath, not meeting my eyes.

"Anissa, I don't want you to do that again."

Her gaze flickers to me and away again. "Alright."

The sun is just beginning to show, and I feel the early heat on my skin. Anissa is wrapping her tender shoulders with the ratty, scratchy cloth. But I take it away from her.

"Don't put that around you." I take off my own shirt and hand it to her. I wish I had thought of it sooner. It's made of strong yet weightless cloth and the sleeves cover to the elbow.

She starts to object but then she focuses on my naked torso and freezes for a confused moment. I put the shirt over her head, and she obediently slips her arms through the sleeves. While she's busy putting it on I look down at myself, but I don't see anything wrong.

I take the cloth and drape it over her head and around her shoulders so that it forms a shade. It's not densely woven enough to completely protect her. And I know that it doesn't block any of what is most harmful. That type of harm passes straight through cloth.

"We have to find shade," I tell Anissa. I climb the ridge of the riverbed and look up and down. Behind us I look for the Intha family. But if they are following, they aren't visible to me. Upstream I look for cover and spy another hut deeper into the landscape. From this distance it looks nearly collapsed. I hope that it is abandoned.

"There's shelter ahead," I say. "Are you rested from your run?"

Anissa nods. "Should we run again?"

"No, but let's set a quick pace. The Intha may still be following. I think they can be more active during the day than we should be. Especially after all your exposure yesterday."

We begin to walk. I lead the way.

Anissa says, "I called you 'godshard' because that's what Inthas think of Peace-in-the-Sky. They think there was once one big powerful god, but he died, or broke into pieces or something. And all that's left are tiny shards. That's what they think a Peace-in-the-Sky is."

"Is that why our captors wouldn't touch me?" I ask.

"Maybe. But the main reason is because if you touch a Peace-in-the-Sky, they flame you to a pile of ashes."

She sounds resentful. It feels hypocritical to have lectured her about stealing when I have killed and the Intha kidnapped her.

The sun is becoming unmercifully hot, and we walk the rest of the way in silence. Anissa struggles in the heat, but I struggle with my thoughts. I probe the gray murkiness for something concrete and come up with only: that I can control the pillars-of-flame. But also, that it can take over for itself. So that I have to take care not to let someone touch me, grab me unexpectedly.

I listen for Anissa's steps behind me and think of her. I know—somehow I find the answer in my head—that if my daughter were to grab me, take me utterly by surprise, that I would not call the pillars-of-flame on her. Never. Never never never.

We jog the last stretch to the hut. I know Anissa's already-burned skin is hurting in this heat. The roof is not covered by a metal plate, and it's not even whole, but there's enough shade, deep enough shade, that we can hide. I'm worried about the radiation damaging Anissa, but I can't think of a way to escape it.

We settle down to sleep the day away, and I think to myself that I have to find a way for us to shorten the trip. Walking through this empty country won't work. We need to move faster, and we need more protection, and we need safe, regular food and water.

* * *

Anissa wakes me. I gasp and sit up quickly, struggling again with the feeling of having been dying. Anissa's eyes are wide and dart back and forth between my face and the door of the hut. It's full light in the late afternoon, but I see nothing around us. Then a moment later, I hear a sound. There's something coming slowly across the rocky, dusty ground.

It could be anything, a person, an animal. I stand up and walk out into the sun. It's painfully hot on my bare back.

A man is crossing the distance from the riverbed to the hut. I wait and watch him come. When he's closer he looks up and sees me and stops. He sends nervous glances to my hair, my face, my naked chest. His matted hair covers his head and shades his face, but he is looking at me with fear in his eyes. I recognize the Intha father from this morning.

We stand watching each other for a moment.

"Why have you come?" I ask.

After some hesitation he mumbles something to himself.

"Leave us," I say.

He takes a half step back and won't meet my eyes. His gaze skirts around me to the hut behind.

"Leave," I repeat.

He looks down but he doesn't go.

I go back in the hut.

Anissa says, "Momma, send him away! Make him go!"

"I asked him to go but he won't. He is only one. He has no weapon that I can see."

Anissa groans and watches the door anxiously.

After a moment it begins to creak open slowly on its leather hinges. I cannot see the man, but his view inside must show him Anissa. Suddenly he darts through and lunges for her. She screams.

I flinch, waiting for the pillars-of-flame, but no one touches me, so nothing happens.

Instead, I step between them.

The man halts. Anissa scrambles behind me and I feel her thin fingers tight around my arm.

"What do you want?" I ask him.

"Momma, he wants me," Anissa hisses.

"What do you want?" I repeat.

He mumbles something.

"Anissa, what does he say?" I ask. His accent is strange to me. I wish he would speak clearly.

"I think he wants his stuff," Anissa says.

In the corner is a pile of some of the things we took. I point to it.

"Take it. Go."

He gathers it up, but he doesn't leave. He sneaks furtive glances at Anissa.

"Don't try to touch me," Anissa warns. "The godshard will call the pillars-of-flame!"

The man retreats a few steps.

"Didn't come here to die," he grunts.

Something falls into place in my head and I'm relieved to finally understand him.

"I won't kill you," I say. "Take your things and leave us."

"Pretty 'shiny out," he says almost to himself. "Might rest away from the heat here."

"You came here under the sun," I say to him. "Already it is starting to set. You can bear it. Go."

He meets my eyes briefly and then settles back in a shady part of the hut.

"Make him go," Anissa says to me in low voice. "Get him out."

I sit down, too, keeping Anissa behind me.

"You know this area," I say to him.

"Yeah."

"Where's the nearest large settlement?"

He shoots me a strange look.

"Follow the river a bit. Cross it and strike off into the flat." He waves with his hand. "Two days maybe, then cross a ridge of rock just at the right angle, there it is."

"Do you have coordinates for any of those turns?"

A blank look.

"Will you guide us?"

"Nah. Can't be gone so long."

I lean back a little. He won't help us.

"What are you talking about?" Anissa asks. She is still struggling to understand his dialect, it seems.

"I want him to guide us," I tell her. "But he doesn't want to travel so far."

"Momma," Anissa whispers. "Those camels at his house. They're for riding, right?"

I ask the man, "How long is the journey riding one of your beasts?"

He scratches at his neck before answering.

"Might do it in a night. Long night. Gotta take some 'shine."

Anissa starts to ask me something, but we turn to him when he starts to mumble to himself.

"But can they pay, though?"

"No." I answer as if he directed the question to me. There's nothing I have. Right now, I am not even wearing a shirt.

He leans around me to look at Anissa. I resist the urge to gather her in my arms to be sure he can't grab her.

"She is not for you. Touch her and I will kill you," I say.

Anissa speaks slowly and distinctly to him. "Guide us there. We can find a trader that pays for girls. I'm Riches tribe. Worth a lot."

I'm not prepared for her to offer this, but I don't betray my surprise. The man is not so coy. He studies us both with narrowed eyes, quite obviously suspicious.

To Anissa I say quietly, in her language, "Why would you make such a bargain?"

She whispers back, "We'll wait until he gets paid. Then we'll get away. Because they can't touch us, right?"

"Anissa-my-Daughter, I may have to kill them for us to get away."

"I'll threaten them, like I did in the hut. And then we'll run."

I look at her for a long moment. She meets my eyes, her own so full of life, so proud. I am filled with admiration for her boldness, though there are so many ways the plan is a dangerous one. It's not likely to happen the way she hopes. And I'm not sure I can protect us among so many who wish us harm. I have the wound on my head to attest to that. I am not invulnerable.

Anissa mistakes the reason for my hesitation.

"Momma, that way this man will get money. It'll cover all the things we took from him and more and more. Only the traders will get cheated. And that's good! If they have less money, then maybe they won't be able to catch another girl."

"They won't," I agree. "Because likely they will die in our escape."

Anissa stares at me still. And underneath the boldness in her expression I see a hardness. Maybe she is thinking, "even better." It wounds me unexpectedly to see she's grown this way so young.

"Anissa-my-Daughter," I murmur sadly.

She turns to the man and speaks loudly again. "Don't be suspicious. Of course, we cheat the traders. But you get paid first."

He looks back and forth between the two of us and his gaze settles on Anissa.

"Make it say it won't fry me where I stand."

I realize he's talking about me.

In his language I say, "If you try to harm my daughter or myself, or separate us, or threaten us, I may. But if you treat us fairly, I will do the same for you. Take care to whom you lead us, though. I cannot promise their safety."

"Don't care about them if I get paid," he says. "That's what this Riches says, yeah? I'll get the money, even if you run off?"

"Yes," I say.

We all look back and forth among each other and it seems an agreement has been reached.

"Need a day to get the animals in order, square away my family. It's coming on dark now. But before the sun sinks again I'll be back. Be ready to start before the 'shine goes."

"If you can, bring us something to cover ourselves," I say. "And food. We have nothing."

He shakes his head. "Look after yourselves."

"Bring my daughter food, then. If she collapses before we arrive, you won't be paid as well."

He scowls, collects his things, and turns to go. We watch his back as he disappears in the direction of the river.

Anissa sighs loudly. "What are we going to eat now?"

"It's nearly dark," I say. "I will see what our surroundings offer. You can rest."

* * *

Although she doesn't want me to leave, I convince her to stay while I forage. Once I am out of sight of the hut, though, I feel a persistent tug of worry and half of my focus always remains on her behind me.

Not only do I want her to rest, but I want privacy for a necessary but indelicate task. I go through the scrubby country pulling a few leaves from every gnarled bush and chewing them. Automatically and without tasting them, I grind them with my teeth and swallow them. I grub roots from the chalky soil and gnaw them without washing or cooking them. Animals appear now in the cool dark, and I snatch lizards from rocks and crunch them whole. Always my eyes are sharp for something that Anissa could eat.

A nest. With tiny eggs. I hold them carefully in one hand and carry them back for her.

Obediently she swallows their contents raw, with an awful grimace, and we drink water from the turbid river. Then we scavenge the yard, picking over the debris left behind when the inhabitants moved. We construct a shade using the cloth Anissa stole. We hope to attach it to the animal's saddle. Back at the river I forage again for Anissa, catching a fish with my hands from which I tear strips of flesh. She tells me the taste is fine and eats as much as I can get for her. And then the sun comes on hot and terrible, and we retreat to the hut, huddling in the shade and sleeping the day away.

I try to sleep lightly so I can wake before the man surprises us, but it feels more as though I lose consciousness than fall sleep. I am useless as a guard.

* * *

"Momma, he's here."

I shake off the weight of death and sit up. The sun is setting, and two camels are crossing the dry land to us, one with a ragged rider. We get up and collect our things. The Intha arrives and hands Anissa a canteen of water and a wrapped packet of food.

We go outside in the early evening and the beasts reach down with their broad noses to snuffle in our hair. Their coat is thick and tangled. The twin leathery sails on their backs open and close slowly in time with their breathing, perhaps to cool them. We sit on a folded mat tucked into the crook of their necks. There is no way to attach the shade, so I strap it onto myself. Anissa sits in front of me, and I can tell she is excited to be traveling. She is alert and full of energy.

We don't have to guide our beast—it follows the other. Their pace is not as plodding as I would have thought. I watch the land sail by. The sun sinks the last few degrees and finally it is dark. The bright moon transforms the surface of the turbid river to silver. We turn from it at last and strike off through the stark landscape. My attention fades in and out and it's possible I sleep for small stretches despite the camel's uneven gait. We stop once or twice to relieve ourselves but otherwise travel steadily through the night.

Anissa is shifting around uncomfortably when I wake for the last time. I notice the moon has sunk and the sky is that dull gray which precedes dawn.

"I don't see any city," Anissa says quietly. "I'm so sore. When can we get off this animal?"

"Are we near?" I call out to the Intha. His beast drops back even with ours.

"Still more time," he says. "Didn't go as quickly as I'd hoped. Maybe turned away from the river too soon."

"Are we lost?" Anissa asks me with an edge to her voice.

He understands her. "Not lost. We'll get there one way or another."

Anissa looks at me pointedly.

"We don't know the way," I say to her in her language. "We have to follow him."

To him I say, "What is your name?"

"Why would a godshard care?" he mumbles to himself, not looking at me.

"What is your name?"

"Rill." He shrugs.

"Rill, will we arrive by sunrise?"

"Not likely."

There's nothing else to say. His beast takes the lead again. I pass on what he said to Anissa, who groans and tries to get comfortable. My eyes scan the horizon over and over, watching for some promising sign. Hours pass.

The sun is halfway to its zenith when I call Rill back.

"We have to stop and take shelter," I tell him. Anissa is huddled into me and my arms are wrapped around her. Our constructed shade is doing little to spare us, and the passing clouds offer only occasional relief.

"Told you we'd have to take some 'shine," he grunts.

"We've had enough 'shine," I say.

"We're close now. Another couple hours."

"We cannot be out at noon. Find us a place to pass the daylight."

He doesn't like it, but he doesn't argue. We've been traveling along a rocky ridge over which we cannot see, and he finds an overhang with some deep shade. I pull Anissa from the camel's back and carry her over. Her eyes are squeezed shut and she clings to me.

I cradle her in my lap and tip water from the canteen into her small open mouth. I feed her crumbles of stale bread with my fingers, then tuck her behind me in the deepest shade I can find, blocking any light that might reach her with my own body.

I look to Rill and he's watching us closely. He sits at the other end of the shaded overhang, but it still feels too close. I don't take my eyes from him. When I feel Anissa's body relax against mine, I know she's asleep.

"Keep your distance," I say to him.

He endures my gaze more confidently than before. His smile is not friendly.

"Get some sleep yourself," he says. "I'll keep watch."

"I will not sleep," I tell him.

"Godshards don't sleep?"

"Not in your presence," I say.

"Of course not. Godshards love best Tribes-under-the-Dome, yeah? All that about not taking sides is shit, isn't it?"

I've never heard him say so much. Something about what he says stirs some memory in me, but I can't grasp it.

"Rill, I don't have answers for you. But don't make the mistake of thinking I am helpless out here because we are far from everything."

I recall being threatened by our Intha captors, that cold, sharp feeling deep inside my mind that produced the pillars-of-flame. I reach for it deliberately this time, and find it, and keep my attention hovering over it in case I should need it.

"Not helpless? But half dead. 'Too broken to be useful. Too useful to be broken.' That's what they say about godshards."

He nods at my wounded head. "But whatever did that's broken you for good. Just a matter of time now."

"And yet for now I still live," I say. "I've enough use left in me to end your life."

"Sure, sure," he says and looks away with an angry scowl.

We sit in silence. Our beasts crowd against the rocks, trying to get some shade, their leathery wings pumping continuously and stirring little swirls in the dirt. They've drunk nothing since we left the river, and I wonder how much longer they can go. Hours pass.

Rill dozes, though he wakes occasionally to check on us. He's looking down at his own hands when he speaks again. I find it concerning that he often seems to be speaking to himself though others are present.

"Following her through the world like her own little personal piece of god. No one following me. No one following any Intha."

I watch him carefully.

"Giving them all the sweet water. All the food. All of everything. A dome full of plenty. And all the children she can bear."

"Rill, you have a child," I say.

He startles and jerks around, as if he wasn't aware I could hear him.

"You have a child," I repeat.

"Oh, he's alive," Rill says carelessly. "He eats half the food, yeah? But will he ever make his own kids?"

"Intha offspring are sterile?"

He gives me an odd look. "Sometimes. Or they don't even live long enough to try. Why don't you know anything? That whack knocked half your brains out."

"I have some memory loss," I say.

He makes a scornful noise. "Maybe you remember why Tribes-under-the-Dome get paradise and Intha get shit."

"If it's so favorable where Tribes-under-the-Dome live, why don't you move there?"

"Won't let us in! Damn. You know nothing. Maybe you'll get there, and they won't let you in, broken god. Think of that? Maybe an Intha godshard not welcome there, neither."

I don't answer. I cannot reconcile what he says with what Anissa has told me. I'm her mother. Haven't I lived there with her all my life?

"Look," Rill leans in. "Come follow me, godshard. Make my family grow. Let me quicken my wife with healthy babies. Make my land green."

"If I give you babies like Tribes-under-the-Dome have, they won't live. Only Intha can survive in this habitat."

His face is contorted with anger. For a moment it seems he can't speak, and I'm worried he'll attack me, and I'll call the flame on him.

"I'm not your godshard, Rill. I'm Peace-in-the-Sky. I'm not here for the Intha or the Riches. I belong only to Anissa-my-Daughter. And I am taking us home. Guide us and get your money and be content with that. It's all I can do for you."

The day passes so slowly: Anissa breathing softly behind me, Rill restless across from me, glancing our way with hooded eyes. I'm forced to take a sip from Anissa's canteen when the sun's heat becomes intense. I feel like my flesh is baking. But my skin shows no sign of being damaged.

When night falls, I wake Anissa, and she looks at Rill and me suspiciously. It's as though she knows we talked of important things while she slept. She eats and drinks, Rill calls the camels, and we mount again and start off.

Rill keeps his eyes up on the ridge we follow. I take this as a sign he thinks we are near some important landmark, and I hope he spots it.

While we ride, my tired mind thinks about what Rill said.

"Anissa-my-Daughter, how did you come to leave your Riches tribe?"

"I was stolen! Intha are always prowling the edges of the dome, looking for girls or anything else they can get. I was visiting the trade spot in Sas Tabo just before my birthday to pick out my present." She shudders with the memory. "I was so scared when they grabbed me!"

"And did they grab me, too?"

"No, you weren't there. You were training? Or whatever you do to learn all the stuff you know. I don't know how someone becomes Peace-in-the-Sky, Momma. I wish I knew. I wish I could be one." She looks back over her shoulder at me for a moment. "Will you teach me how, someday? But not if I have to leave Tribes-under-the-Dome. I never want to leave again. Ever!"

I reach forward to cover her hands with mine and wait for her to calm.

"But we were together in the hut of the traders," I say.

"Didn't you come to get me?" she asks. "I thought you had come to rescue me, but you were so hurt I thought maybe you'd die. I didn't recognize you at first. But when you spoke, I knew I'd be safe."

I wrap my arms tightly around her. And I don't speak for a long time. Because her story opens my mind to doubt. What if she is mistaken? What if I am not her mother at all?

I close my eyes and focus. I know the girl in my arms is mine. This tender feeling—the truest I've felt—cannot be a lie. I am attached to her by some invisible force in a way that is strong and inseverable. Anissa-my-Daughter.

* * *

The moon begins its descent. Ahead I see a glow that is not the sun. It is lights. The town must be illuminated in the evenings.

"We leave the camels here," Rill says, dropping back. "They can't cross the rocks. Have to be back for them before light, or they'll wander looking for shade."

I pat our beast's neck as we dismount and ready ourselves to hike. I know Anissa is glad to be away from the camel, but I'm grateful to it. How could we have made the journey without them? And Rill. I watch him load up a pack for himself. He swallows gulps of water and then, surprisingly, offers me some.

"Drink up," he says gruffly. "Got to be ready for trouble. And I can refill there."

I drink deeply while he watches.

"Remember that. Haven't I been good to you? Didn't put my hand on either of you, not once."

"Thank you, Rill," I say. I mean it sincerely, but he doesn't smile.

I dismantle the shade we constructed and wrap the cloth of it around myself, looping it over my shoulders and drawing it tight under my arms. I am not ashamed to be unclothed and I do not need the protection for my skin, but it is better, I think, to be clothed more like those we walk among. We wait for the clouds to blow by and uncover the moon. We need the light to pick our way among the rocks and make our ascent.

I was worried about walking into a large town, but this settlement is not so densely populated. There are some permanent-looking homes, public squares, and shops in the town center. Paddocks for beasts and small garden plots are interspersed among the outer, more primitive huts. And at the far end of the settlement, I see larger buildings by roads leading into the land beyond. Off in the distance I see the river.

"What is this place called?" I ask Rill.

He mumbles, "What does it matter?"

Anissa and I follow him down a rocky path on the other side.

At the bottom he tells us, "We keep to the outskirts. Soon as anyone sees you there's going to be trouble. Far end of the town we find the traders and sneak up on them."

"Are they near the roads?" I ask. "Are there vehicles that run on those roads?"

"Yeah, the trucks run from there."

"Where do they go?"

"Deep into the drylands to Salvage for scavenging. Or toward the dome, to trade."

"Or to capture girls," Anissa says angrily.

"If they're stupid enough to be out where someone can see them, then yeah. They grab them."

I don't think she understands Rill's reply. "I'm sure I was here," she hisses to me.

"Then we can get back home from here," I tell her.

"Steal a truck?" I can tell she is starting to plan.

"There's a way," I say.

We skirt the town like Rill suggests. It's busy. Lamps burning some noxious substance light the pathways with a yellow glow. Houses crowd up against the shops. Despite the commerce, there's still a feeling of poverty to it. Everything is dirty and in disrepair.

Intha walk the streets and from afar I see children among them. Most of them are scabbed with the thick patches Intha have, but others have darker skin which is clearer. Not as dark or as smooth as Anissa's. But I assume these children have both Intha and Tribes-under-the-Dome ancestry, however that may have come about. It is wrong to think of Anissa as superior, but I can't help imagining what a lovely woman she will be.

Rill steals out onto the streets and comes back laden with water from a public well. We drink and drink. It feels so clean.

We near the far end of the settlement where the buildings crowd against the high ridge, and we're forced to travel the streets. Rill is so obviously nervous, I wonder if I have underestimated the danger to us. I walk closer still to Anissa, and she slips her hand in mine. We're taking her into a place where they are desperate for the money that someone like her can bring. But I trust that they won't willingly hurt her. She's valuable. I also believe they will do everything in their power to separate her from me. My hand tightens around hers.

We slow as we come to an intersection and Rill leans forward to scout around the corner of a stone building.

He jumps back and throws out an arm, sweeping Anissa and me behind him. His arm strikes me across the chest, and the familiar cold lances through my skull just above my ear. I know that I can't stop it. I'm foundering...and then I withdraw from my own body. I am within myself, flattened, dimensionless, blind. After moments of confusion, I haltingly reach out and turn off the agitated cold sliver like a switch.

And I turn and look through my own eyes again. I'm still with Rill and Anissa in the alley, my back hasn't even hit the wall.

And I'm angry.

"Rill!" I shove his arm away from me.

He gives me an irritated backward glance, but his attention is on whatever is around the corner.

"Don't do that. Don't touch me. I warned you. I can't control...I may not be able to control..."

Finally, he turns.

"Shut up, shard of a god! I'm putting myself out for you, and this rich burden you're dragging around. This wasn't in our deal, but I'm watching out for you. And you're pissing about whether I knock into you?" At this point his speech deteriorates into mumbled curses, and his scowl couldn't hold more contempt.

"I am dangerous, Rill," I say. "Don't forget that."

We wait in simmering silence as a group of serious looking men pass us. Then we proceed. I keep Anissa and myself back an extra pace from Rill. He is in a bad state, whispering angrily to himself and moving his hands like he's arguing with someone. Since seeing the group of men pass, Anissa's breath is coming quick and shallow. If I'm going to help them, I know I need to hold on to calm. Every so often I reach out tentatively for that dimensionless space, without leaving the present, and it gives me a more removed perspective.

At the next intersection we encounter a few Intha leaning against the walls. Here the buildings are more permanent, constructed of stone and mortar. We've run out of hiding places and back alleys. There's nothing to do but press on confidently. As we approach, the men stand and watch us come. I put my arm around Anissa's shoulders and pull her in tight to me. The men fall in behind us, talking low to each other. We push on, but as we proceed, we encounter more people. The twin spectacle of Peace-in-the-Sky and a girl from Tribes-under-the-Dome walking through the streets is enough that many of them follow along in our wake. Some bolder children reach out as if to touch us, but they never quite do.

As we enter a more open space among buildings, I look back to see worn clothing of faded colors, tangled red or tatted brown hair, dark eyes, open mouths showing yellowed teeth. Faces shift in and out the crowd and I can focus on none. I struggle to see them as people, but they remain a sea of faceless threats.

As we walk, more than one man falls in line with Rill, offering him money or asking him questions.

"A Riches girl and the tame godshard that follows her around," I hear him say. "Mine, and I intend to sell them. Don't want nothing off you. Shove off."

An old man we pass catches my eye, and he narrows his eyes angrily.

"Dictum 3!" he shouts in a shaky voice. "I remember! Even if you don't."

But I'm focused on watching for sudden moves from the crowd and I firmly put aside his words for later. I need to be in the present.

The warehouse that Rill leads us to has a sign outside that depicts a simplified truck, and I take it to be a shipping warehouse of some kind. It's squat and sprawling, with rocky concrete walls and a flat metal roof that seems to weigh it down. We slip under the overhang to enter at a double set of doors. The crowd we've drawn presses close behind us. So close that I pull Anissa inside to escape them before I see what we're walking into. Their voices—curious or questioning or angry—follow us inside.

The walls of the big room are lined with crowded shelves. Crates and boxes, empty drums and wheels make the space feel tight and close. The only light comes from two glaring white lanterns on a stone counter at the back of the room.

There's a man leaning on the counter talking to someone out of sight, but the sound of so many people causes him to turn.

Rill rushes up to talk to him, trying to draw his attention, but the man only has eyes for Anissa. He calls for someone in one of the small rooms behind the counter, and a broad-faced, sour-looking woman appears. Her eyes fix on Anissa, and she doesn't look away. Other men appear from the door behind her. Rill keeps talking, but she ignores him. I can see that things are not going well. Why should they give Rill money? Why not just take Anissa for themselves? I can't hear any of what they say over the rising murmurings of the crowd.

I step in between Anissa and the woman, blocking her view, and I point to Rill. At the sight of me she hesitates. She nods to one of her men and he produces a pouch, briefly checks the contents, and drops it on the counter by Rill. I expect Anissa's voice to ring out and threaten them, now that they've seen me, but there's too much confusion, too much noise. Anissa and I are holding hands tightly, and I check for exits.

The door is too far. There are too many outside, now beginning to spill inside. One of the men behind the counter reaches across to grab for Anissa and barely misses as she jumps back. Rill snatches the pouch from the counter and turns as if to run. Everything is falling apart. But I can't panic.

I send my awareness inward, following the sense of that cold sliver as a guide. I pull back into myself seeking that formless space, intentionally this time. I speed the signals along my nerves so that time seems to slow. Everyone around me slows. I send my awareness outward. I map the location of every adult unknown to me in a defined radius around our location. Their coordinates appear to me, and I place a mental red mark over their signal. I enter the beam command and activate it. Around me, faster than even my enhanced nervous system can detect, white light that produces no heat appears in a blinding column around each target.

As I return myself to normal operation, I see Rill and our eyes connect. For the first time we truly see each other. The moment passes. He drops to his knees, hiding his face.

Then I am fully back to myself. I notice noise again, the roaring of the beam, screaming, sounds of panic. The ash of my targets floats through the air as we're enveloped in sudden darkness. I feel Anissa clutch at my arm with both hands.

Then it's unnaturally quiet. Anissa is choking back a few high-pitched sobs. Rill stands and looks around with terror in his eyes. We are alone in the room with the dark, smoking piles on the floor. I feel flakes of ash settle on my hair.

"Shit! Shit!" Rill sees me and recoils, stumbling backward across the dirty floor.

"I told you I was dangerous, Rill."

He runs, and I check to see that the pouch is clutched in his fist. I want him to have it.

Finally, I can turn to Anissa-my-Daughter and take her in my arms, cradling her close. For her comfort and for mine. I find a door behind the counter and stumble toward it. Inside there are a few chairs and I sit Anissa down in one. I hate to do it, but I ask her to calm down. I tell her I need her. Because the beam can't protect us indefinitely. I estimate it will need eighteen minutes to fully recharge and, even at capacity, it has a limit of thirty-two simultaneous targets. We have to get away from this town and reach Tribes-Under-the-Dome. And I need Anissa to tell me how to do it.

Part Two

"What is Dictum 3?" Anissa asks me days later, without preamble.

"You understood that man."

"Yes."

I say, "Dictum 3: to assign no preference among humans."

"So, you're remembering," she says.

"Some."

"Does that rule mean...you're not supposed to take my side?"

"Yes."

We are quiet. The heat from the floor of the truck rises up around us like a smothering blanket. Anissa drinks and passes me the canteen.

"Even if you're Momma?"

"I do not have any guidance in the case of personal relations," I say. "Or I cannot remember it."

"Are there more rules?"

"There are five Interaction Imperatives: to preserve the physical and biological environment, to preserve human life, to assign no preference among humans, to pass no moral judgment on the activities of human individuals or societies, to take no part in the organization or politics of human social structures."

Saying the words brings to my mind images of white corridors, scoured clean but worn and somehow dingy all the same. A smooth door with a placard beside it. Bright, cold lights.

I want to see more but my head pounds with pain and I let the visions go.

Anissa is still mulling over my words.

"Well, I think you try hard to do all those things. Sometimes I thought you were acting strange but now I see why."

The thought of all those terminated targets haunts me. A precious resource, destroyed. But Anissa's words are like a balm. I reach out and stroke her smooth cheek. There is nothing I wouldn't do to keep her safe. I would violate every last dictum, no matter how much it pains me.

"Anissa-my-Daughter," I whisper. The sound is lost in the noise of the truck we ride in, but she slides nearer to me on our bench, and I wrap my arm around her shoulder.

Anissa sleeps with her head in my lap. I am afraid to lay down because the vibration of the truck aggravates my injury, so I doze on and off with my back against the inside of the truck. It is little more than half full. Crates of trade goods are tethered against one side, but lax leather straps slap against the metal of the large, square container on the other. It is unpleasant to ponder whether those straps have ever bound human cargo, whether this truck and its drivers have ever transported a girl from Tribes-under-the-Dome far, far from her home.

The Intha driving the truck haven't needed to check the container behind them, so we've been safe. They were clearly in a hurry to leave the depot, before the disturbance they heard could delay them, and we've been driving nonstop every day. They are busy manning the contraption that gives it power which is nestled between the cab up front and our cargo space behind, and which apparently must be tended frequently. In the front of the cargo space, we can feel its heat radiating through the walls, so we keep back toward the doors.

To escape detection during our trip we have only to keep quiet, ride along, and sneak out at dusk and dawn to stretch our legs. Then we can feel the relative cool of the night on our faces, relieve ourselves, and bury the evidence of any food we've consumed. Then we resign ourselves to another day in the truck and climb back in. It's easier to sleep when the truck is not moving, at night.

Our fear of being found out has faded. We need the Intha to find our destination, but out here alone on the road they pose no threat to us. But I push that thought away. Finally, we have enough to eat, enough to drink, protection from the sun, time to sleep. It's hot, we're dirty, Anissa's skin is still tender with burns, and my head wound remains untreated, but we are better situated than we have been.

I lose track of how many days we travel, and although I could easily access that information by turning my focus inward to the flat dark inside my head, I do not. The trip will be over when it is over.

And finally, it is.

The truck slows and turns, and we hear the grinding of the metal-rimmed wooden wheels on rock. We jostle side to side and then roll to a stop. The engine runs down and is quiet but for the hissing of escaping steam. Yet we can still see light through the seams of the container.

"Is the truck breaking down?" Anissa asks.

"I don't think so," I say. "We've gone off road. We may be near our destination."

"Are they going to check back here?" Anissa asks, sitting upright.

We wait quietly but hear almost nothing.

I steal to the gate at the back of the truck and lift the latch. I inch the gate open, listening for any sound from the drivers. It's past noon and the white-hot sun is still glaring down. I see no one around and the road stretches out behind us, bare and dusty. I sneak around to the right of the truck and stop, stunned. Half-hidden behind low hills, a dome rises above the arid landscape. It's built of something almost colorless and networked over with the faint lines of intersecting supports. Its arching back disappears into the hazy air as it stretches away into the distance. The dome is so large I cannot see the entire breadth of it, yet somehow, it's remarkably invisible. It simply fades into the baked clay and pale chalk of its surroundings.

My eye catches on something darker showing through the hills at its base. A settlement, buildings of some sort. Without thinking, I turn my focus inward and send my vision telescoping into the distance. Details jump into view as the spot comes rushing toward me. Crude buildings shaded with metal roofs and tattered tarps lifting in the breeze. I could sharpen the focus even more, but I push it all away.

I continue around the truck quietly. The great, bright contraption that powers the thing is shuttered away, dark and quiet, and the drivers nap in the shade to either side of it. I can feel the heat coming off it even from here, and I wonder how they can bear to be so close to it. Better to be shaded, I suppose, so long as they don't cook. I see the side of the closest Intha man's face, and it is thickly encrusted with the horny skin patches of the Intha, some of the worst I've seen. What a face for a girl of Tribes-under-the-Dome to first see as she loses her home and her family forever. What a terrifying journey.

A short ways down the road I see a gate and a building off to one side. It all appears deserted. The drivers must be waiting to approach it at the proper time of day.

I go quickly back to Anissa. She is crouched by the exit, but I motion her to get back.

"Stay out of the sun," I tell her. "We are still too far to walk. There's a checkpoint but it's not open yet."

"Where are we?"

"I don't know. I saw a great dome, and a settlement beside it."

"We're home!" cries Anissa, forgetting to keep her voice low.

"Why is there a town outside of it?" I ask.

"It's a trade spot! There's a market there. You know, so Tribes-under-the-Dome and Intha can sell stuff to each other."

"Can we simply walk back under the dome?" I ask her.

"No, they control who comes and goes. I think there's a gateway. I'm not sure what it's like if you're trying to get in from outside."

"Who controls it?"

"The border crew."

I wait for her to explain it to me.

"You don't know about them? The border crews live outside the dome. They're there to keep us safe. If they see me, they'll grab me back right away! As soon as they see I'm

Riches." She adds darkly, "And they'll punish any Intha trying to keep me."

"We've seen enough of that," I say.

We snooze the rest of the day away and wake when the drivers start the truck again in the late afternoon. The truck tilts and growls and bumps over unseen obstacles, and then the ride smooths out.

"We're back on the road," I tell Anissa.

We wait in uneasy silence until the truck stops again, and the sound of our engine joins the noises of others still running.

I ease the gate open and peer out. There's nothing behind us but sunset-lit road. I step out onto the rocky ground and peer around the side of the container. Our truck is in line behind two other vehicles, and up ahead is the gate, which now seems to be operating.

I turn back to the truck and lift the gate. Anissa is there, eager to get out, but I block her way.

"Wait..." I tell her.

But her eyes alight on something beyond me.

"The crews!" Anissa cries, jumping to the ground.

I try to urge her back inside, but she is leaping and waving her arms. I send my vision across the dirt expanse and see, in the twilight, men riding in a small truck. The driver sees Anissa and points, and the others stand. I catch Anissa's arm before she can take off across the ground.

"Anissa, stop. Stay here. I don't want you to run off."

I look to the Intha drivers of our truck, a man and a woman, and they are just seeing us. Without hesitation they leap from the truck on the other side and run.

Anissa's face is alight, and she's bouncing up and down on her toes and straining at my grip, watching the border crew truck approach. "They're coming!"

"Then let's wait for them," I say.

"Home!" She looks beyond me toward the dome. "Home! We're almost safe!"

The border crew, if that's who they are, arrive quickly. I cannot contain Anissa, she runs out toward them as they spill from their smaller truck. Two immediately streak off after the Intha man and woman. I can tell the border crew men are more like Anissa, long-limbed and lean, and they lope across the dusty ground and grab the thick, short Intha by their necks and wrestle them to the ground.

One of the other border crew men runs up to Anissa, and she leaps into his arms as he sweeps her off the ground, and they laugh with joy. I think she must know him.

"Awha, and who are you, sissy?" he asks.

"I'm named Anissa," she says breathlessly. "Stolen from Sas Tabo long back. I'm Riches. I want to go home!"

"Peace-in-the-Sky?" I hear a respectful voice at my elbow. The remaining border crew man ducks his head to me. "Are you traveling with them?" I pause a moment to fully understand him. His accent is different than Anissa's.

"She's with me!" says Anissa. "We hid on this truck to get back here."

The two border crew men return with the Intha, shoving them against the truck and holding them at bay using some weapon with mounted barbed bolts.

"These?" One man gestures to the Intha he's pointing his weapon at.

"Girl traders," Anissa spits out bitterly.

The border crew men nod and turn back to the Intha with a purpose, motioning with their weapons for the Intha to walk toward the checkpoint. They keep their weapons closely trained on the backs of their necks.

I watch them go and feel the weight of knowledge that we brought this on them. Did these two Intha ever traffic in people? What will happen to them, because we chose to stow away in their cargo?

A border crew man is already helping Anissa into the small truck. The man at my elbow tries to usher me along, thwarted by the fact that he cannot touch me.

"What will happen to the truck drivers?" I ask.

"Any Intha caught in company of a Tribes-under-the-Dome girl are in trouble, Peace-in-the-Sky. Big trouble." He shakes his head to shame the Intha, not to sympathize with them.

"They did not choose our company," I tell him, as I walk toward the truck where the others impatiently await me. "They did not know we were on their truck."

The man shrugs and makes some vague response, which is drowned out by Anissa urging me into the vehicle of the border crew. She sits up front with the driver and leans over the seat to hurry me along. The other man climbs in back with me and watches me shyly from the corner of his eye.

Our little truck starts up noisily with the four of us onboard, coughing black smoke, and we start off toward the dome. There can be no conversation over the clamor of its smelly engine, so we watch the road ahead. Anissa is radiant. The man beside her glances at her happily.

* * *

The border crew settlement nestles against the outside of the dome. The dome itself is like a shadowy hill, half-glimpsed in the dark, but there are lamps posted at intervals along the streets of the town. We are hustled through those streets, protected from curious onlookers, and led toward the tallest building, a big square mud-and-concrete edifice with windows of irregular size and shape scattered across its face. It looks very different from the other buildings around, which are constructed of discarded parts and natural elements. The people we pass look most like those of Tribes-under-the-Dome, but many have features and skin that recall the Intha. There are places, it seems, where the two groups mix more freely than I had first thought they might.

We are led through a wide doorway in the large building, and inside it is dark and crowded. There's a wide courtyard in the center, open overhead to the ceiling several stories up. Surrounding the courtyard, I dimly perceive a maze of small rooms and narrow corridors.

As soon as we are noticed, people begin to crowd around us. I reach for the beam switch, holding it with my mind, preventing it from being set off should I be jostled. The man with me is doing his best to hold people back. All around us are dark curious faces, everyone is talking at once, Anissa is talking loudly and happily, and nothing is being communicated.

A booming voice rings out, though, and the crowd starts to quiet and pull back. A big, broad-shouldered man with a colorful drape across his shoulders is making a path through the throng.

"Move back, move back, crew! Let me in! Make way for the boss! Let me see what you've dragged in!" His voice is loud and commanding, but perfectly amiable.

His face lights on Anissa and he peppers her with questions without waiting for an answer.

"Awha, look at this beautiful child! Are you Riches, sissy? Are you hurt? How did you come here? What are the...Shit!" His eyes light on me. "Shit, what is this? Peace-in-the-Sky? Step back, men, step back! Show some respect, or we'll all be fried."

I am suddenly the center of attention. Anissa comes to my side, and I put my arm around her. The big man looks stunned, but it doesn't take long for him to start talking again.

"Peace-in-the-Sky. Welcome! Always welcome. You honor us. Welcome back."

I open my mouth to speak but he breaks in. "Are you injured? Shit! What's happened?"

"I'm alright at present."

"Know that here we keep the Preserve for Tribes-under-the-Dome. Always. The sacrosanct, the plenitude, the prospect. How can we serve you?"

"Just see to my daughter, please. Let her get cleaned up, let her eat and drink, if you can spare it."

"For you? For you we have everything!" He gestures expansively with his arms. Everyone around us seems to echo his hospitality with their smiling faces. I am struck by how expressive they are, how mobile their faces are compared to the grim Intha.

He waves us along with him deeper into the building and the crowd makes a space for us as we go.

"Peace-in-the-Sky, your visit is very welcome, especially just now. You know our need, I guess. You know." He gives me a broad smile.

"I am taking Anissa-my-Daughter home," I tell him. "We are passing through on our way under the dome. We have not come to stay."

He turns his smile on Anissa. "Anissa, is it, sissy? Do you know me? I am Orco, boss of this crew."

"Where are we?" Anissa asks.

"Border crew headquarters at Dipol trade spot. How did you get to be out?"

"I was stolen!" Anissa says. "Inthas took me. I was out there for weeks and weeks. I went so far! Momma found me and brought me back." She smiles at me.

The man, Orco, nods slowly.

"Not taken from Dipol, of course," he says.

"No, Sas Tabo," Anissa says.

Orco makes a sound of disgust. "It is not safe there. Not safe! Here, we don't let girls into the trade spot."

He looks at me as if for approval. But I say nothing.

"Men only, or old women who've clearly taken the cure. It's just too dangerous otherwise. You should be home with your people." He nods to Anissa. We come to a staircase fastened to the inside of the building that winds its way up to higher floors.

He lowers his voice as we begin to climb. "Did they hurt you, sissy?"

Anissa looks down. "No. Not that kind of stuff, anyway."

I think of how they were treating her when I first saw her in the cage, and I hope that's the worst of what she experienced. It shames me that this stranger kindly asks her about it, and that I never thought to.

Orco brightens up. "Not many are so lucky. I will personally get a guide for you to take you back to your Riches. It will be the happiest moment when they see you again! How I wish I could be there!"

Anissa is so excited she is bouncing again and the stairs creak under her slight weight.

"And you, Peace-in-the-Sky. Are you going under the dome, too?"

"Where my daughter goes, I go," I say, though I am preoccupied with examining the struts supporting the stairs.

We come to the top floor. It's nicer up here, with painted walls and doors on the rooms which are arranged around the periphery of the building. The center of the floor is open all the way to the courtyard of the first floor, where there are many busy people around.

"Here is a room for you," Orco tells us, pushing open a door. "For very special guests. My own room is just two doors down. I'll send someone up with some water so you can take a bath. Then maybe some food. You don't want to sleep the night away, do you? Are you so tired?"

"No," I tell him. "We've had hours to rest while riding in the truck."

"Then take some time. I will send for you around midnight, and you can come see our compound. We're not Tribes-under-the-Dome, of course, but everyone here is border crew and it's very safe. These rooms up here are particularly safe, sissy, though if you want to explore you should have a guide. And don't leave the building."

"I won't," Anissa promises.

"Peace-in-the-Sky, you go where you want." He smiles. "Of course. You don't need protection. And we'll talk business later."

He leaves us and we make ourselves comfortable in the room. It's the nicest place we've been so far. There is a bed and a short table and chair. A man brings us two buckets of warm water, a piece of soap, two worn drying cloths, and a pot of something clear and slimy.

"Aloe!" says Anissa happily. "From Tribes-under-the-Dome."

We take off our clothes and Anissa hands my shirt back to me. I put aside the dusty shade cloth Rill gave us that I'd wrapped around my chest.

"Orco speaks as though he knows me," I say to Anissa.

I wash her carefully, not wanting to get soap in any sun blisters which may have broken.

"Oh"—she looks like she is thinking—"he recognizes a Peace-in-the-Sky, like anyone would."

"And they call you sister?"

"They're just being friendly. I'm not really their sister anymore because they're not Tribes-under-the-Dome anymore, not out here. But I don't mind."

I wash Anissa's hair as best I can, then pat her carefully dry and daub her with aloe from the pot. She sighs with relief and stretches her arms and back.

"Why is everyone here a man?" I ask, scrubbing Anissa's sheath and the small undergarment she had on under her Intha pants.

"They're second or third sons of Tribes-under-the-Dome," she says. "You know."

"Anissa, I do not." I hang her clothes out to dry.

"They come out here because it's hard for them to marry under the dome. But out here they might find a half-Intha wife. And there's more space."

In the second bucket I quickly wash myself, though I don't dare get water near my head injury. I rinse the shirt that I had lent to Anissa, wring it out, flap it nearly dry, and put it back on.

"They need more space because it's crowded under the dome," I guess. Any bounded population must expand until it fills the space.

"Tribes-under-the-Dome can't shelter every baby born and grown. They just won't fit," Anissa says. "That's why a woman can only make one girl. And once she does, she has to get the cure. But she can make sons first, as many as come to her. But if it's a lot they come out here, because there's not enough room."

I told Orco that we were not tired, but as soon as Anissa is clean, she slips under the blanket on the bed. At first, she talks excitedly about a pet she hopes is waiting at home for her, a parakeet which is called Hyacinth. I hold her hand until her words come slower and slower, then she is fast asleep. Later, when there's a soft tap on the door, I slip out alone.

The man outside gives a start when he sees me.

"Peace-in-the-Sky!" he says.

"Yes."

"Well, that's what Boss told me, but I've never seen one."

The man is young, not a child but still smooth-faced. "I'm Nandi. I'll guide you back to Riches after you've rested up. But Boss sent me to see if you wanted to come down."

"Anissa-my-Daughter is sleeping," I tell him, "but I would like to see Orco again."

"I can take you." Nandi seems to wear a perpetual half smile, like he's anticipating something amusing.

I follow him down the staircase and he keeps glancing back at me.

"I thought you'd be taller. You're short as an Intha."

"I hope you've been told that you cannot touch me," I tell him.

"Oh yes, loud and clear. I'm the respectful type, anyway."

"It's not out of respect. It's for your safety."

"Oh, I know. The pillars-of-flame. Coming down from the stars." He gives me a wondering look as though he'd like to see it.

"Anissa believes it erupts from the ground," I say.

"Boss says it comes from above," Nandi says. "He knows about things."

I nod. That is why I want to see him.

* * *

Orco is talking to other people, directing loudly something being arranged on the first floor of the crew's building, but when Nandi leads me up, he excuses himself.

"Come with me," Orco says, arching his arm like he would wrap it around my shoulder, but not quite letting it land. "I don't like to have you out in the press, you know." He gives me a knowing look. "Too dangerous."

"You don't like things that are dangerous," I say. He's said those same words before.

"No. I keep it safe here. That's my job." He smiles. He's led us to a corridor with less traffic. There are three rickety chairs in one of the turns, and he sits expansively in one. I perch on another.

"Aren't I dangerous?" I ask.

"Yes, yes," he nods. "But your advice? Worth everything."

"Orco, I do not remember you."

"Awha, no? Well, I don't expect such a thing. You must meet many, many people." He motions to a passing group to continue by.

"My injury has clouded my memory." I pause for a moment, but I want to trust him. I've seen his kindness to Anissa. "I have felt very lost here, since I regained my senses. I know almost nothing about this place."

His dark eyes are warm. "How were you hurt?"

"I don't know."

"Whoever did it fried for it, I'm sure. I thought it would be impossible to do that to you! I suppose maybe if they ran up behind you and hit you with a single blow? But who would dare? Who would dare?" He threw his arms up like it was incomprehensible.

"Also," he added, his voice quiet, "it looks very bad. Very bad. Will you survive it?"

"I have so far," I say.

"Well, I hope you continue to thrive, Peace-in-the-Sky!" He gives me a wide grin.

"Thank you."

"And you have a real interest in this Riches girl. She must be special. She must be part of some larger plan, for you to take an interest?" He gives me a private smile.

"She's my daughter," I say.

And now he gives me the same non-committal look and polite nod I've seen him give me several times since we've arrived.

"You doubt me."

"What you say, I believe," he says, holding up his hands.

I look him in the eye steadily. His smile doesn't fade, but the moment is tense. He stands up.

"Please come with me," he says.

Just down the hall there is a door that he pushes open, and waves me inside. I step through the narrow doorway and see a person standing at the back of the small room. When I move, the other person moves also.

It is my reflection.

What surprises me most is that she does not look surprised. Her face is a peaceful blank mask. She is short and her skin is dark. Her hair is white. Not the curled, wispy white of an old woman's hair, but short and straight and thick and unnaturally bright. And the eyes. Violet, oddly reflective.

I watch myself reach for my arm and feel it. It is flesh, warm and alive. I take a deep breath and feel air come and go from my lungs. I make myself aware of my heartbeat. I blink my eyes and curl my toes. I turn my head and get a glimpse of the wound in my head. But I shy from examining it too closely. What's done is done, and I'm certain there's nothing anyone here can do to aid me. But I do not know how I know that.

I feel confusion and distrust and unhappiness and none of it plays across my face.

I step back out of the doorway.

Orco is there looking at me.

I know why he showed me myself. I look different from everyone else I've seen.

"You've seen me before," I say.

"Yes, though you looked different then. Devan, the man who was boss before me, showed you to me when you visited us long ago. I've heard other stories, too, and the descriptions are always different."

"Then how do you know it's me?"

"That hair," he points. "From miles away I'd know that colorless hair. And close up, well, who else has shiny purple eyes? No one. Now you're walking around looking a little like

Riches with that dark skin, but I saw it brown like the Intha and heard of it looking pale as chalk."

"What makes you think I'm the same person as those others, then? Maybe there are many of us." I feel as though there are many of us. Or, at least, there were.

"I don't know. But only you come down here."

I pause for a moment.

"Come down here? Down?"

He shakes his head. "You're the one who knows everything. Now you're asking me questions. But you never explained it to me."

I just look at him.

"I have so many things to talk with you about, Peace-in-the-Sky. Just let me get some things ready. Make yourself at home here, please. Anything you need just ask for it. I'll send for Nandi, and he'll show you anything you'd like."

"No," I say. "I'll go back and sit with Anissa-my-Daughter until she wakes."

"Then I'll have Nandi bring you some food. Get some rest. Maybe you can start to heal? If there's a way I can help, I will. Nothing would please me more." He sends me away with a broad smile and a wave. "I will see you soon."

* * *

I start back alone, fighting the aching in my head as I try to remember. I make it to the base of the stairs before Nandi catches up to me.

"Need anything? Let me walk you back," he says.

"You said you've never seen Peace-in-the-Sky," I say, "but I've been here before."

"One time, but that was before I left Tribes-under-the-Dome. Before I was born, even. Not many people see Peace-in-the-Sky twice in their lives. Most people don't even see you once!"

He follows me up the stairs, and at the top I see Anissa peeking around our door. She smiles when she sees me, and I feel some relief from the confusion of before. Her happiness clarifies my purpose for me, time and time again. I examine her features closely as I grow near, comparing them to what I saw in the mirror. But it's hard to compare a youthful, smiling face to a grown face that is forever calm and still.

Since Anissa is already awake, Nandi takes us to the hall where everyone eats. It's crowded and loud and hot, but the food smells good and we pass many smiling, curious faces. Anissa basks in the attention, pulling herself up tall with a raised chin. She is young and strong and beautiful, and she knows it, and I am happy in her wake, admiring her as much as those in the hall. I remember what Orco said about it being dangerous to have me in a large crowd, so I steer Anissa to a spot at the end of one of the long tables, close to a wall. Nandi sits down between us and the rest of those at the table. He seems proud of his role as escort and protector.

Plates are brought soon, the same food for everyone in the hall.

Anissa looks at hers with a little sigh of disappointment.

"No avocados? Mangos?" she asks Nandi.

He laughs. "We don't eat like that out here, sissy. Food from there almost never escapes. There's barely enough in there for Tribes-under-the-Dome. Why do you think me and all my brothers are out here in the first place?"

As we eat the cactus spears, wilted, bitter greens, and strips of cured meat, Anissa asks Nandi, "What tribe are you from?"

"Sante," he says. "Most at Dipol are. Some from Pepper. Almost no one from Riches or other Tribes-under-the-Dome. They go to Sas Tabo or Chimiminga trade spots."

I listen to the names gratefully. Hearing them stirs the muddy swirl of my memory.

We finish and send our plates back to the kitchen. Anissa wants to walk around and see things, so Nandi takes us on a tour. The crew's job is to defend the dome's borders and the trade spot, so there's rooms with maps, rooms with stored weapons, rooms with goods confiscated from the Intha, now being re-purposed. There are sleeping rooms and washing rooms and two kitchens and a laundry. Everything you would expect in a building meant to house many people.

Nandi shows us a large room with benches lined up in front of a raised table.

"We keep the Preserve just as we were taught," he says to me with a smile.

I understand him to mean that many people gather here to practice a religion.

"The sacrosanct, the plenitude, the prospect," Nandi murmurs as we leave. Archaic words with no real meaning in this dialect.

Next, we see a large bay where trucks are stored and repaired.

"You don't use the same heating device the Intha power their trucks with," I remark.

"No, we're not steam powered. We use fuel-burning engines. It's tricky making it but we can drive our trucks when the sun is down. Very useful." Nandi smiles. "You taught us, they say."

"I don't see the truck we came in," I say.

"No, we can't keep it. Too valuable to the Intha. We'll trade it back to them."

"You give it back?" Anissa asks angrily.

"Have to, sissy. Those engines of theirs are so important to them, they would get violent if we kept them. But we can ask such a high price, and because they used it to steal girls, they can only grumble, really."

"They'll just use it to steal more girls!" Anissa says. She is almost shouting. I put my hand at her back to calm her.

"They use those trucks for all kinds of things," Nandi says. "And they can't actually steal many girls. We make them almost impossible to get."

"Nandi is not the one who decides policy," I tell Anissa. "Talk to Orco if you are unhappy with it."

"Because you won't!" she says to me. "You won't take sides."

"Anissa-my-Daughter..."

"I want to go home!" she says, suddenly wilting. "I want to go home, Momma. When can we go?"

"Let's go back to our room," I say. I nod to Nandi, and he starts off down another corridor. Anissa follows along with her head drooping.

Back in our room I settle her on the bed, and she curls up in a ball. I pat her hair until she begins to relax.

"I will talk to Orco," I tell her.

"About the truck?"

"About going home. I can discover when we leave and how we can best prepare. Once we know when we're going the waiting won't seem so bad."

Anissa nods miserably.

I open the door to find Nandi.

"Is there something she can have to do? Something to look at? A way to pass the time?"

He disappears and returns quickly with some dice, a sort of peg game, and some small, whittled figures with scraps for clothing.

I take the things to Anissa and try to interest her in them. Then as soon as I can, I slip back out to Nandi.

"I want to see Orco," I say. I follow where he leads.

* * *

"Peace-in-the-Sky!" Orco booms when he sees me. "Very fortunate you come when you do! I was going to send to see if you were free."

"Are you ready to send us home?" I ask.

"Surely you would rest some more? Your girl is not ready to travel just yet? And I have to arrange it, you know. Get the permission chips. Come with me, come with me. We can talk."

He waves Nandi away and leads me down a crowded corridor on the ground floor. To my surprise we approach an exit, and there's a car waiting there. I step out into the night, which is well-lit from the lamps now burning brightly. The car takes us through the narrow passageways of the settlement, which are busy with people, and out toward the silvery edge of the dome itself.

I watch with wonder as we draw nearer. It's beautiful. An innovation far beyond anything I've seen in my travels, and yet it feels ancient. It stretches up and out and away from us, nearly blotting out the sky. It doesn't obscure the horizon; it is the horizon.

Orco is not as impressed as I am. He steps out of the car just a few strides from the wall and looks at it with disgust. The driver of our car cuts the engine, and Orco gestures to the cloudy material that forms the sides.

"Now, dearest Peace-in-the-Sky. Here's what we face. What can we do? The rat problem inside grows and grows, and soon we will have safety problems as well. Already the crews talk about organizing patrols to watch these areas during the day. The day! Because the Intha could be out in their solar trucks at some spot we cannot even see from the trade spots, working their way inside."

I look more critically at the structure of the dome. The surface of it is so abraded that I cannot resolve anything inside, I only get a vague impression of dark shapes.

"It's cracked," I say.

"Yes, it's cracked!" He waits for a moment. "But how can we repair it?"

"You might patch it or block it somehow. I don't think that you can repair it," I say.

"No, not a patch!" He shakes his head. "The Intha will just rip that away. But you can teach us how to really fix it. To make it new once more. You built it, after all."

I look at him. Although I feel surprised, I know now that he cannot see it on my face.

"I did not build this."

"You did! Peace-in-the-Sky did. And you always have answers for our problems. This one? This is a big problem."

I look at the dome silently.

Orco says, "I thought perhaps if we heated it somehow, and got a lot of sand in the melted parts to seal it up? Is that how it's made, with melted sand? Like lightning strikes in the desert."

"No, it's not glass. It's a metal-fiber-reinforced polymer."

"Awha, you see! You do know," he says. "This crack is small. I can show you some of the bad ones if you will travel."

"There's no need," I say. "Orco, I cannot repair this. Anissa and I need to get back under the dome. I need to take her home."

"Let me send her home, then. But we need you out here, Peace-in-the-Sky. Otherwise, how can we keep Tribes-under-the-Dome safe?"

I say, "I will not be separated from my daughter. And I hope that the people inside will remain safe despite the cracks. The dome overhead still protects them from the sun's rays."

Orco's expression grows dark.

"I'm not talking about exposure. I'm talking about maintaining the Preserve! That is the problem. Wasn't it you who taught us the Preserve is 'the sacrosanct, the plenitude, the prospect'?"

I recognize the words from Nandi's benediction. And without considering how it's possible I search the terms. Sacrosanct: not to be trespassed upon. Plenitude: full or complete. Prospect: expectations for the future.

I'm aware of Orco watching me. His expression shifts from glowering to worried.

"Peace-in-the-Sky, you must be broken yourself," he says. His eyes scan to my open wound.

"I don't recall teaching you those terms," I say.

"Awha, I can see that you remember nothing," he says. "The damage is as bad as you said. I just couldn't believe you." He taps his finger against his lip and frowns. "But how can I fix you?"

"You can help us," I say, "by sending Anissa-my-Daughter and me back home. She doesn't want to wait."

"She?" he says, and lifts an eyebrow. "Does she command Peace-in-the-Sky?"

"I want to take her home," I say.

He laughs. "Then I will work on it. Faster, just for you."

"Thank you," I say, though his tone carries a hint of teasing and I'm not sure if he is serious. "I'm sorry that I cannot help you with your problem."

"Awha, but I will ask again," he says, ushering me back to the car. "When you start to remember."

I don't want to be caught up in these problems, I want to continue my journey with Anissa. But the engine of the car starts and conversation is no longer possible.

* * *

I return to Anissa and Nandi accompanies us to dinner. Orco joins us for a while, too, and adds to our interest so much that we can hardly eat for people crowding around to try and talk with us. When he leaves, we finish our dinner, then sit. Everyone lingers over dinner, and Nandi chats with friends. He introduces us with a hint of pride, calling Anissa 'sissy.' Many of those who are introduced to me nod and murmur the Preserve benediction and smile. Some reach out as if to take my hand, but catch themselves and just smile and nod again. Then gradually the crowds begin to thin.

The sky is graying, dawn is coming. I walk Anissa back to our room, supporting her on my arm. She is pleasantly sleepy. We are just walking through our door when I hear someone behind us. It is Nandi.

"Boss wants you, Peace-in-the-Sky," he says with his customary smile.

"Now? We were just speaking with him. Anissa-my-Daughter, wait for me. Lay down. I'll be back soon."

She waves drowsily and sits on the edge of the bed. I follow Nandi down the hall.

"What does he want?" I ask.

Nandi shrugs. "Didn't say."

Instead of walking down the stairs, though, we cross to another room on this floor. Inside is a wooden ladder leading up through the ceiling. I hesitate, but Nandi waves me up.

"Boss is up there," he says cheerily. "Go on, if it holds him, it'll hold you."

The flat roof of the building is covered with a thick layer of grit and sand. There's a breeze. It's cooler than I expected. Above me the sky stretches endlessly in all directions, dark and speckled with pinpoints of light. In the East glow bands of pink and gold, streaked with gray-blue clouds.

I almost don't notice Orco, though he is the only thing up here besides myself.

A big gleaming smile shows on his dark face. Looking over his shoulder, he holds out his hand to me and I join him on the edge of the roof. I can tell he means for me to stand closer, but I keep a space between us.

"I like you like this," he says. "Small and dark. It suits your only mood."

"My personality was the same before, then?"

He laughs. "Awha, yes it was."

"Why are you up here?"

"Looking at the sky. Pretty isn't it?"

"Beautiful," I say.

"I want to show you something that can be seen this time of day, this certain time of year. Do you know what I'm talking about?" His normally booming voice is quieter, though still as rich and warm as ever.

"No."

"How strange. Last time we were up here, you showed me." He steps closer and puts his arm around me.

I arm the switch.

But he doesn't touch me, his sweeping arm directs my attention upward. My eyes scan the sky, but I see nothing.

"That little twinkle, you see it?" He points, his hand close to my cheek. "A little silver spark..."

I do see it. A flash of silver close to the horizon. Not a planet. Not a star. Something reflecting the rising sun. Too far away for even my aided sight to resolve.

"What is that?" I ask, not expecting an answer.

"A station in low orbit," Orco says. "Your words. I can't understand such a thing."

I glimpse the white corridors again, flooded with bright colorless light. Doors that slide open and air-lock behind you, numerals incorporated into the walls to tell you what deck you're on because they are all the same...

"Are you alright?" Orco asks.

I bring myself back to the moment and turn to look at him. I am uncomfortably aware of his muscular bulk compared to my own small build. We are standing closer than I remember.

"Does that stir up some memories, Peace-in-the-Sky?"

"Some," I say. I wish he wasn't talking so I could focus solely on what is running through my head.

"You'll remember. More and more. I can help you. And then together we can solve all our problems..."

I am ignoring him, my mind racing, until I feel his thick fingertips stroke the back of my shoulder.

I jump away from him. "Are you mad?" I ask angrily. "Consider not only yourself, but those on the floors below you!"

"Awha, you weren't so cold before! The last time we stood on this roof."

I am stunned.

He continues. "You say that Anissa is your daughter. If that really is true, then who is her father? Have you thought of that?"

He holds his hand out to me. But I don't take one step in his direction. I send my thoughts racing, looking for some evidence...

"Peace-in-the-Sky," he says quietly.

"Stop interrupting me," I say. "I need time to think. Thank you for showing me the station." I nod to the horizon. The sky is brighter now, and the silver flash is no longer visible. "Good night."

Orco does not follow me. As I descend the ladder, I remember Anissa is waiting for me. I nearly collide with Nandi as I leave the room with the ladder in it.

"Whoa!" Nandi holds up his hands, smiling. "Did Boss make a wrong move?"

"Why did you wait?" I ask curtly. "My room is just down the hall."

Nandi laughs and falls in behind me, stepping quickly to keep up. But before I reach my door I slow and turn to face him.

"How old are you, Nandi?"

He shrugs. "Twenty, maybe?"

"Thank you. Goodnight."

I slip into my room. The light outside is brightening but in here, it is dark and still. Anissa is asleep on the bed, her clothes still on. I shift her toward the wall and slide in beside her.

"Momma," she murmurs, sliding her thin arm across me.

I wrap my arms around her and relax into this welcome touch. If I had ever felt so close to someone else, wouldn't I remember it? The way I do with Anissa?

"How old are you, Anissa-my-Daughter?" I whisper.

"Ten," she says.

And, according to Nandi, whom I believe, I haven't visited here once in his twenty-year life. I thought so.

* * *

I sleep as deeply as I always do. It's Anissa who wakes me as she shifts position in bed and digs her elbow into my arm. She is asleep again after a moment, but I lie awake. I can feel that night is coming on. The heat of the day is fading. If we are to go under the dome, we must switch our nights and days again. I am determined that we'll leave during the next daylight cycle. I had better warn Nandi so he can prepare.

Nandi arrives and we three go to breakfast. It is not so crowded as the other meals, and thankfully Orco does not appear. I encourage our group to eat quickly, and when we get back to our room, I send Anissa inside and stand in the hall talking with Nandi.

"Where can I take you today, Peace-in-the-Sky?" he asks. "Boss will send for you later, maybe, but we can go wherever you want until then."

"I've seen enough. It's time to go back under the dome. We leave as the sun rises, Nandi. You should get some extra sleep today if you can."

Nandi's smile wavers and his eyes slide from mine. It's only a moment, but I recognize instantly what it means.

"You've been told not to lead us away," I say.

He holds up his hands. "Oh no, I will! But, awha, Boss says when."

"Orco does not intend for us to leave," I say. But as I say it, I realize it's only me that Orco wants to keep. I could send Nandi to take Anissa home and he might do it.

"Nandi, we are leaving. Anissa-my-Daughter is homesick, and we have spent enough time here. You must make a choice whether to trust me and be our guide, or to serve your boss."

He looks surprised.

I say, "Remember who I am."

Nandi looks at me intently, and I feel as though he's searching for something in my face. Which I know to be utterly blank.

I hold out my hand.

He looks down at it, then back up at me with a question in his eyes.

I extend my hand farther.

He takes a deep breath, and reaches out slowly to take it. I shake his hand. He laughs nervously and glances upward.

I drop his hand. "If I had called the pillars-of-flame, you wouldn't have time to look for it," I say. "Be prepared to go at dawn. What can we do to help you prepare?"

"Awha," he runs a hand over his short hair. "We'll take a car. I can get a key. I'll take some food for myself. I can't take anything from Tribes-under-the-Dome. You can do anything you like, I expect." He smiles at me. "That's it. What else do we need? There's water everywhere in there. Skito balm! I'll get some."

I can tell by the way he's speaking that he's nervous. But I hope that he won't tell Orco what we're planning.

"If you think of anything else that we can help with, come find me, or tell Anissa and she will relay it to me," I say.

He nods. Then he smiles a big smile. "I'd better go. Gather stuff slowly, throughout the night."

"Get some sleep, too," I tell him.

"I will, I will." He waves to me as he turns away down the corridor.

I return to Anissa and play the dice game with her. She enjoys it and I watch her smile and laugh with satisfaction.

"We're going, aren't we?" she asks.

"Yes. I've talked to Nandi. But we are leaving without Orco's permission so do not talk with anyone about it."

"What? Why would he want to keep us?"

"He wants my help," I say.

"Well, you can stay and help him," Anissa says easily.

My hand stops in the act of throwing the dice.

"Because it won't take long and you'd come along right away, afterward, right?" she adds.

I throw the dice.

"No, it is not a problem that is easy to fix," I say. "And I don't want to send you alone with Nandi into a place that I don't know. Or don't remember."

Anissa says, "I'd rather have you with me, anyway."

* * *

When Nandi comes to get us for lunch, he tells me that Orco wants to see me afterward. As we walk down the halls he admits—and I can tell he's been instructed not to tell me— that Orco has a trip planned for me. A small group is to go out in a truck and they're taking some supplies so it will probably last the remainder of the night.

After lunch I tell him to escort Anissa back to our room and to stay with her. Watch over her. Then I ask him how to find Orco. He seems anxious letting me go on my own, but I tell him I can find my way, or ask anyone along the way.

When he and Anissa are out of sight, I follow his directions for half the way, then turn and walk out of the crew's building using a different exit. There are many that see me, but everyone only smiles or waves.

It's nice to be out on the streets. There's a breeze and people of all kinds to watch. Here they live better than the other places we've been. They're wearing bright clothes and eating street food with their hands and laughing or arguing.

I see a group of dirty, rough-looking Intha men walking down the middle of one street. They're looking around them defiantly, and the crowd parts for them a little. The tall border crew men look down at them with some hostility, but there's no fights. And half-Intha women and children are everywhere.

I want to see the trade spot itself. I ask a couple I see walking together. But they don't answer me, they just stare.

"What are you?" the man asks.

The half-Intha woman looks from me up at her man with wide eyes.

"A godshard," she hisses to him.

"Awha, that's true?" He looks at me. "Peace-in-the-Sky?"

"Yes," I say.

They both stare at me a moment more and another man walks up to us.

"Peace-in-the-Sky?" he asks.

"Yes. I'm looking for the trade spot."

"I'll take you!" A little boy who's been listening to us runs up.

"Don't touch her!" the woman warns him.

"I know, I know," the little boy says. "Come on, godshard. Follow me, follow me."

So, I do.

"You have a scripp for me?" he asks, as we walk briskly along.

"What is that?" I ask.

"A scripp, a scripp! So I can buy in the market." He bounces impatiently.

"No. I don't have anything."

"Don't matter, don't matter. I tell my friends: godshard following me around the market!"

It's a pleasure to follow his quick steps through the crowd. He glances back at me every so often, smiling to show crooked teeth.

"This is close enough," I say when I can clearly see the dome's edge and some high gates obscured by a crowd. "I'll find my way. Thank you for your help. Go find your mother, now."

"Mam's busy," he says. "I go and tell Moggi! He won't believe me. Now he got to let me play in the third!"

The gates to the market are heavily guarded, and there's a long line waiting to get in. No one gets in easily, no matter what they look like. No carts are allowed through, it seems, so everyone waiting has a heavy pack on his or her back, piled high with wares. Two Intha directly ahead of me are carrying racks with pots and pans and wooden spoons lashed to them.

It's hot in a crowd, even at night, and everyone waiting looks tired and frustrated. I walk to the front of the line where four guards are searching merchants. Two other guards stand by the entrance, holding long wooden poles with sharp metal tips. Each one has a bolt-throwing weapon hanging from a wide belt.

The market behind them is walled off with big sheets of repurposed plastic and metal. There is no way to see inside without entering. The market is attached to the side of the dome and there must be an entry into the dome inside, but I cannot see it, and I cannot see an easy way to get through that way. I was hoping I could take Anissa and simply talk my way through, but it doesn't seem likely. There's nothing to do but return to the border crew. I hope by now that Orco has left on his trip without me.

I take an indirect route back and simply watch the people around me. Many of them stare back, with curiosity or fear or interest in their eyes.

The building of the border crew is dark inside after the lantern-lit streets. It takes me a few turns to orient myself and find the way to our room. Nandi stands outside, still guarding Anissa after my instructions hours ago. I am pleased with him.

"Are you ready for the morning Nandi?" I ask, as I step past him and open the door.

The room is empty.

I round on him and cut off his answer. "Where is Anissa-my-Daughter?"

"Awha, she's with Orco..."

I stride down the hall and Nandi hurries to catch up.

"She's fine!" he says.

"She's a hostage," I say, not looking at him.

At the bottom of the stairs, I pause. He stops, too, and I say, "Take me to them!"

He starts off at a lurch and I'm close behind him. We wind through corridors until we come to the vehicle storage room, the bay door opened onto the small hours of the night. There's a small crowd there. Orco is balancing his bulk on a chair and Anissa sits beside him on the ground. Behind him stand several men loosely holding long pikes. There're other men, young and old, gathered around, too.

Orco is telling a story, his arms fly out in animation of his subject, and everyone is watching him and smiling and nodding along. Anissa looks happy and unharmed. I slow.

I walk between two of the larger trucks and emerge into the group across from Orco in his chair. Nandi is close behind me. But I feel more his anxiousness than his support.

Orco stops talking when he sees me and smiles, waving me over. I stay where I am. Anissa stands up to come to me, but Orco wraps his hand around her arm.

"Let her go, Orco," I say.

He releases her and wraps his arm around her shoulders, instead. A gentler hold.

"Come over and let's talk," he says warmly. "Goan, pull up a chair for her."

"We're leaving," I say. "Nandi, get the truck ready."

Nandi shifts from foot to foot.

"Why won't you speak with me, Peace-in-the-Sky?"

"I have nothing to say to you. Thank you for your hospitality. We're rested and now it's time for us to leave."

His wide smile looks strained. "You are not yourself," he says. "Let me send Anissa here back to her family. Nandi will take her. Nandi, get the truck ready. Go on."

After a shuffling pause and a glance at me, Nandi heads for a truck.

"You cannot keep me here against my will," I tell Orco.

"Why won't you come over and talk with me?" he asks. He stands up from his chair.

Anissa looks up at him with worried eyes.

"Let me go," she says.

"Tell Momma to come and have a little talk. I have to shout just to have a simple talk."

"Momma..." Anissa's voice is worried.

I walk half the distance. The men holding pikes circle around to my sides. They still seem relaxed and their hold on their weapons is loose. I see no one carrying a projectile weapon. With the exception of Anissa and Nandi, I have everyone in the room targeted. I see them simultaneously as people in the room with me and as dark spots on a map with red hashes over them.

"Orco," I say.

"Will you fry us all?" he asks, his tone light.

"No. I will take Anissa and go."

"Come get her, then." He drops his arm from around her shoulders and she stumbles to me.

I take a few steps to catch her, but Orco moves quickly and catches my arm in a tight grip just as one of his men shifts forward and sweeps Anissa away. He pulls her back among the trucks, but waits there, watching Orco and me.

I look at Orco's fist tight around my upper arm. No one has ever touched me like that before. It's painful and intrusive.

"You see?" Orco says. "Just as I thought. You cannot call the pillars-of-flame." He tilts his head and taps his finger against it. "You're too damaged." He smiles.

I retreat inside myself and speed the impulses along my nerves. Everything seems to slow, and I reach out, trying to target the vehicles around us. But I cannot. I can't target inanimate things. One of the trucks near us has some grain spilled in the bed of it. I can smell it. And gnawing those grains, oblivious to the people around them, are a handful of rats.

Blinding light fills the room and men scream high and fearful. Pikes clatter to the ground and men fall to their knees, their arms above their heads.

Orco bellows and jerks me off my feet. I bite down and taste blood, so strong is the effort of blocking the switch that would terminate him.

Dust settles. The truck beside us smokes with a metallic stink. The rats are now a scattering of ash across a truck bed.

My vision returns to normal, and I see all around us men are falling back from us. The man who held Anissa has released her, and she crouches near a truck, watching me anxiously.

Orco lifts me to my feet.

"You cannot hit me, I am too close," he pants.

"False. Only my mercy stands between you and oblivion, Orco."

He is breathing fast and his eyes are struggling to adjust to the dim light. His gaze darts around the room but I can tell he's not able to make sense of what he sees.

"What can you possibly gain from antagonizing me?" I ask.

"We need your help," he says, and his voice has a note of desperation in it I have not heard yet.

"I will not help you," I say.

He pushes my arm away and I move out of his reach.

"You forsake us, Peace-in-the-Sky," he says hoarsely. "You charge us with defending the Tribes-under-the-Dome for all time, and now you abandon us."

"You cannot know my plans or my priorities, Orco." I put my arm around Anissa as she comes to me. "I am leaving now."

"When will you return?" he calls to my back, his voice breaking.

I find the truck Nandi is in. His eyes are wide, and his hands grip the wheel tightly. Anissa climbs in and I fit in beside her. We are squeezed in a row on the bench, and I slam the door behind me.

I reach over Anissa and put my hand on Nandi's arm.

"Nandi? Ready?"

He nods without looking at me and starts the truck, and we drive out into the dawn.

Part Three

The early sun makes us all squint. The light is warm though the windows. Hot, even. Soon it will be painful. But for now, the truck's canopy shields us.

"I don't have any permissions," Nandi says above the sound of the engine. "I'm not sure if we'll get Entry."

"They will let me in," I say.

Nandi gives me a quick glance. "I wasn't any kind of help to you back there."

"Not to worry," I say. I feel weary. No one was killed, I did not violate Dictum 2. I upheld all the Interaction Imperatives. And yet, this is not the way I wish to interact with human societies. It is not the right way to do things.

"Momma can take care of herself," Anissa says. "And me. And you, too, Nandi."

Nandi smiles at her. I turn from both of them and watch the landscape roll by. We are skirting the dome, bumping down a rocky path that leads to the entry point. Nandi says there is no Entry for outsiders at the trade spot. There is only one place where they allow people to apply for admission.

"It's getting hot," Anissa says. "How far, Nandi?"

"Not far. Dipol is the closest post to the Entry. We'll be there before we start to cook."

* * *

I expect a long line, but there's no one visible. We see only a weathered, worn shack with an open porch and a tacked-on veranda to the side, with a dusty truck parked under half of it. We pull in beside it. There are two men on the porch who stand up as they realize our truck is stopping. They jump off the edge of the porch and rush out into position. Both are wearing protective plates on their chests, and they plant their feet and aim bolt-throwing weapons at us.

"Hold!" one shouts.

Both Nandi and Anissa freeze a few paces from the truck, but I keep walking. The two men, who are tall as Tribes-under-the-Dome but also thickly muscular, train their weapons at my chest. I walk up to them and look them in the eyes.

"Peace? Peace-in-the-Sky?" one says.

I reach up and push the end of that one's weapon away from me. He jumps back from my hand. The other keeps his weapon trained on me but steps back uncertainly. I reach behind me for Anissa who comes running up and slips her warm hand in mine. Nandi follows her and we all walk past the two men and up the stairs into the shack.

There's an old woman there standing protectively in front of something concealed by the wide legs of her pants.

"I warn you!" she says loudly before we can speak. "Anyone wanting Entry needs permission chips from the bosses of all five border crews. I won't open the gate for anyone else. No exceptions. I don't care who you are."

"She's Peace-in-the-Sky," says Anissa. "And I'm Riches."

I look out the back door of the shack and see a steel double door set into the side of the dome. There's an electronic control lock sealing it.

"Where's the remote key panel?" I ask the woman.

She frowns. "All three of us have to enter our numbers. Kill any one of us and you'll never get in. You have to get permission chips, or we won't help you."

"I am not going to kill anyone," I say. "But you overreach your authority. Peace-in-the-Sky has permission to enter at any time."

I step around her and see a black metal key panel box on the floor, covered with dust. The men from outside are standing in the doorway. I kneel by the box and the old woman steps away from me reluctantly.

"You need our numbers," she warns me. "You can't guess. If you push too many wrong numbers, it locks for days."

I rub grime from the keypad and key in my code. The display flashes "OVERRIDE" in red and then "ENTRY" in green. There's the sound of a bolt slamming open from the door out back.

The woman looks at me, unsure.

"Sorry to cause you alarm," I say. "Thank you for your work here. It must be a lonely post."

The woman stammers, "Awha, it is. The men switch out every month but I'm always here."

I wave Anissa and Nandi toward the door.

"You're from Tribes-under-the-Dome," I say.

"Only someone who's lived in there understands how important it is to keep it safe."

I see that Nandi and Anissa are waiting by the steel door, their eyes squinted against the brightening light.

"You must miss it," I say.

A sudden flash of pain crosses her face, but she doesn't answer.

"I am sorry," I say. I nod to her, then leave to join Nandi and Anissa.

* * *

Nandi hands out bags with supplies for each of us, then I slide the latch on the control lock. Nandi helps me to pull one of the heavy doors open. Humid fragrant air washes over us and lush leaves unfurl themselves out the door. Anissa cannot contain herself and pushes eagerly through the verdant screen, disappearing immediately. Nandi gives me a nod and then follows. I see only green but I duck my head and push through. Cool leaves brush my face, branches scratch at my legs.

I turn to close the door behind me but the woman from the shack is there, carefully tucking in the greenery and swinging the door shut. There's a resounding clang, then the sound of the bolt shooting closed.

I am hemmed in all around but not concerned. I breathe the air deeply and feel the moisture against my skin as I start to cool after being in the harsh sunlight. I hear Anissa's laughter ahead and push through the brush. There's a path under my feet and I follow it to a shady clearing.

Anissa and Nandi are there, broad smiles on their faces.

"Momma, Momma, Momma!" Anissa leaps at me and throws her arms around me. "You did it! You brought me home. Thank you, thank you, thank you!"

I feel a surge of sharp love for her. I rest my hands on either side of her happy upturned face and press my forehead against hers, eyes closed.

I pull back and look into her eyes "You thank me? Of course I did this for you, Anissa-my-Daughter. What else could I do?"

Nandi is smiling at us, too.

"And thank you, Nandi, for your help," I say.

"Awha, I have not helped you. But I will!" He takes a paper from his bag and unfolds it. I see that it is a hand drawn map. He traces his finger along it.

"We have four days, I think, until we make it to Riches county. Anissa, do you live in Riches capital? Or in a camp?"

"Just outside the capital," Anissa says, looking at the map. She points to an area hesitantly. "Around here."

"Is that map accurate?" I ask Nandi.

He shrugs. "It'll give us an idea. We can ask along the way, too. We'll pass some smaller camps of my Sante tribe."

While we've been standing talking, black long-legged flying insects have been slowly gathering. Anissa slaps at her ankle.

"Skitos," Nandi says, opening his bag. "That's something I haven't missed."

He and Anissa take a pot of some oily paste and smear it on their wrists and ankles and necks.

"Skito balm. Keeps them away. Mostly." Nandi offers the pot to me.

"It's gross!" Anissa says. "You have to eat bananas. If you eat the bananas here, they don't bite so much, and you won't need this stuff." She makes a face at the oily smears on her skin.

I decline the balm. The insects haven't bitten me yet.

I look around us. I can't see further than a few feet into the growth. In comparison to the landscape we just left, this is close and crowded and almost claustrophobic. But I find that I like it. The light is dim, even now that it is full daylight. The dome shades everything, of course, and the canopy of leaves overhead, straining ever upward toward the light, catches much of it. It is shady and cool where we stand.

"Everyone ready?" Nandi asks.

Anissa is bouncing on her toes, eager to set off.

There is a single, narrow path visible under the press of leaves, and Nandi leads us to it. I reach out to push branches away.

"Awha..." Nandi reaches for me tentatively. "Please, treat every tree, every leaf with care. Everything in here belongs to someone and is carefully tended. To harm someone's plants is a terrible crime."

So, we push our way carefully through, slipping by boughs when we can and bending them carefully when necessary. The canopy is high above us, shrubs fill in the understory, and vines wind through it all or creep along the ground. Some plants bear large, brilliant blooms, or tiny green fruits, or long brown pods, or heavy seed heads. Although the foliage is rich and verdant and chaotic, it is clear that the trees are planted in rows and that species are evenly interspersed. The effect is one of a lushly flourishing farm, rather than that of wilderness.

"This is all planted. Everything is food?" I ask.

Anissa sings out, "Cashew nuts and macadamia! Plantains! Coconuts and cacao! Guava and bananas! Yams and taro! Cinnamon and ginger! Turmeric!"

She goes on and I listen to her voice and the quiet chirps of birds and the sound of distant running water. I see some large blue and black butterflies. Life is everywhere, thick and intertwined and woven together at every level.

"I'm so hungry," Anissa says, interrupting her list. "I want to eat right away."

"You know we can't eat from the trees," Nandi tells her. He offers her a strip of dried meat, but she waves it away.

To me he says, "Many people live under the dome and it cannot be expanded to accommodate more, so every scrap of available land is busy growing food to feed them all. And every year people must leave to keep the balance in here. It looks like a bounty, but it is only barely enough."

Anissa is not interested in my education on the matter. "I want tangan stew," she interrupts. "I can't wait! My auntie makes it with black pepper. I like it spicy!"

She turns back to flash me a smile. "You'll like it, too, Momma!"

"If I've had it before, I don't remember it," I say.

I should ask her about where we're going and what my place there is, but I don't. I stop reaching for memories, inwardly turning from the swirl now stirring in my mind. I want to enjoy this trip and the shock of beauty all around us. I don't want to grapple with beam switches, access codes, white corridors, a station in low orbit. Soon I will be home, and whether I can remember it or not now seems unimportant.

I watch the scenery, inhale the scents, breathe the thick air. Always with an eye to Anissa's bobbing head visible through the leaves ahead of me. Anissa-my-Daughter. It is pure joy to watch her bloom in a place where she can be safe, where she doesn't need to be so savvy and shrewd. Here she is simply a happy child.

* * *

It's late in the day when we reach a tidy red clay-walled hut roofed with fronds. There's a clear space around it carpeted in moss. A naked little boy is jumping up and down, singing a song to a bright bird perched on the edge of the roof. Occasionally the bird answers back in trills and warbles, watching the boy with tilted head.

When I stop walking, I feel a wave of nausea and heat wash over me, and it takes me by surprise. It's a moment before my vision clears fully. I swallow several times, stand up straighter and take deep breaths. I stand at the edge of the clearing while Nandi and Anissa approach closer.

Nandi calls out to the hut with a phrase I can't translate, and a woman leans out of the shadowed doorway. They speak for just a moment, and she comes out into the yard and scoops up her child. She is wearing a cloth sheath with a strap over one shoulder. It is dyed in complicated geometric swirls with rich yellows and a deep rust. The woman and the boy are alone.

She and Nandi smile and laugh and gesture, both at ease. I wonder if he knows her, but I remember making that mistake before when Anissa greeted members of the border crew.

Nandi waves a hand in my direction, and the woman stares at me in awe. I incline my head, but she only watches me with a hint of fear in her eyes. When Nandi introduces Anissa, she grins broadly at her and lets her boy down, and he comes running over to Anissa. She squats down and makes faces at him, and he laughs and pulls at her hair.

"She says we can camp here," Nandi says, coming over to where I wait. "She'll feed Anissa, and I told her I have food for myself, but she wonders if you need to eat." He adds quietly, "Every morsel of food here is so important."

"I will eat only what is left that she can spare," I say.

We walk over to the woman and Nandi relays this in their dialect. It is similar to the crew's and to Anissa's dialect, and yet still subtly different.

Then we sit, and it's a relief to rest my legs and my throbbing head. Perhaps I should have been drinking more as we walked. I drink now from a clay bowl the woman gave us and feel some relief.

Nandi sits with me, and we watch Anissa and the boy play.

I wave a fat buzzing insect away from my head and Nandi looks at me, concerned.

"Look in your bag," he tells me.

There is a pot of skito balm, some strips of dried meat, and a colorful swath of cloth.

"You can cover your head," Nandi says. "Tie it like this." He holds his arms up and mimics wrapping it around.

I wrap it loosely and then tuck the ends in carefully.

"That will keep the bugs from getting to it," Nandi says. "Tie it tighter if you have to. You don't want them getting in there and eating away at it." He shudders.

* * *

Later two men come home, one I take to be the woman's husband and the other must be an older relative. Nandi embraces the men like they are brothers, and they talk and laugh loudly. When they see me, their expressions become more guarded, and they ask Nandi quiet questions.

I listen to the men talking as closely as I can, waiting for the intricacies of their dialect to become clear to me. By the time the woman comes out of the hut carrying a bowl on either hip, I understand them well.

Anissa and the boy rush over and chorus "thank you, Momma," as she sets down the food. The adults watch the children eat greedily with patient smiles, then they begin to eat.

Nandi asks them about every person he once knew and gets from them all the news they have, and now their conversation turns to what prices may be had in the market for various wares. The woman hands me one of the bowls with some food left in the bottom. It's sweet and dense, a root cooked to tenderness in some highly seasoned sauce. The taste is complex, far from the simple foods we had outside the dome. If Anissa was accustomed to this, she must have found our other food bland.

After the meal the older man pulls two mangoes from his bag and cuts slices for us all.

"For this occasion," he says, nodding at me solemnly. "Welcome, welcome, Peace-in-the-Sky."

"Thank you," I say.

The light fades and the family goes inside their hut to sleep, while we travelers stretch ourselves out on the mossy lawn. Nandi swats skitos. The air is thick with them. Anissa smears more balm on her ankles and wrists and curls up against me, resting her head on my arm.

* * *

She wakes me early in the morning. Birds are calling all around us. I lay on my back looking up at the pattern of leaves above us. They are many shades of green, brown, and burgundy, all interleaved in a peaceful patchwork bright with the morning sunlight behind it all.

For breakfast there is a warm drink Anissa is excited about, and she gives me a sip of hers. It has a rich, bittersweet taste and it's thick enough to eat with a spoon.

"Atole," she whispers with an excited smile. "It's made with cacao."

I hand her small cup back to her and she drinks it slowly, eyes half-closed.

Nandi embraces everyone as we prepare to set out, and Anissa hugs the little boy, and we get underway. It is a long day of walking, but the pace is easy. Anissa and I have been accustomed to walking, it is Nandi who calls a stop.

"My feet!" He sits down to rub them with a laugh. "I ride in the truck too much in my new life."

We all sit.

"Is it nice being back, Nandi?" I ask. "Or is it hard?"

He laughs. "It is both. I didn't want to leave the first time, and when I have to leave here again, it will be hard again."

"I am sorry I brought you here," I say.

"No! I'm grateful to visit! I may never have had the chance again."

"You would have been separated from your family forever?" I ask.

"Oh, they may come to visit sometimes, at the trade spot. But the crew is supposed to be my family, now. That's what we must do, to keep the Preserve. The sacrosanct, the plenitude, the prospect."

He waits for me to say something, but I don't know what he expects.

* * *

We find a group of clay huts late in the afternoon and decide to cut our day short. They are Nandi's tribe again, the Sante, and they know him. They plan a gathering, and some people walk over from other camps, so that by evening there's a large group and lots of food. Always just enough for everyone to eat well, but not more. Anissa eats heartily and I'm grateful for their generosity to her. It's always a pleasure to see her nourished. Nandi embraces each newcomer and sheds tears, and they tell stories and answer his eager questions.

I sit away from the crowd. As it grows late, Anissa brings me a little food she wants me to try and sits with me. I eat, and she leans her head on my arm. When I finish, I wrap my arm around her.

"You are missing home," I say.

She wipes tears away.

"I'm happy for Nandi," she says.

I feel proud that she can put aside what she has wanted for so long to see how nice this is for him.

"I am, too," I say. "It would be good if he could see his parents again."

"But we can't travel to the Sante capital," Anissa says, looking at me. "It's too far out of the way."

"We will go home first, Anissa. Then Nandi may have some time to visit his home before returning to the crew."

"He's not supposed to do that," she says. "Once you leave Tribes-under-the-Dome, you don't return."

"Don't you want me to change things to make it easier for Nandi?" I ask her.

"No. Well, yes, Nandi is nice. I like his smile. I wish he was my brother," Anissa says thoughtfully. "But it's so important to keep Tribes-under-the-Dome in and the Intha out.

Otherwise..." Her face twists sadly. "Otherwise, the Intha will take everything."

Her words settle on me heavily. "Ask Nandi to come to me," I tell her.

She looks at me with a worried expression. "Did I get him in trouble, Momma?"

"No, no."

She gets up and walks back to the crowd, giving me a backward glance.

A few moments later Nandi joins me. He is flushed with the excitement of the night, cheeks round and reddened, with a broad smile that touches every part of his face.

"Nandi, we are glad you have this gathering tonight. It must be good to see people you know."

His smile fades. "It's making Anissa's heart ache for her family," he says.

"It is. But we will see them soon. Is it possible to reach her Riches tribe tomorrow?" It is not only Anissa's desire that drives me, but fear over my deteriorating injury. I wish to have her somewhere safe before I am no longer able to travel.

Nandi pulls out his map.

"A long walk," he says, "especially since we stopped early today."

"Maybe if you had something to cover your feet."

"They could make me something from layers of plantain leaves. But even the leaves are so valuable. They break down to make the rich dirt needed to grow everything. I don't dare ask."

"I will ask them," I say.

Nandi looks uncomfortable. "You could speak to Veras. She's the elder mother here."

"Send her to me so that I can thank her," I say. "We leave early tomorrow, Nandi. With lots of ground to cover before dark. But enjoy yourself tonight."

"I will," he says.

When Veras comes I ask her to sit with me. She squats near me. There is no fear on her face, but she is wary. For the first time I speak their dialect.

"Thank you, Veras, for taking care of us and for welcoming back Nandi with such a happy gathering."

Her wariness fades and she smiles. "He is kin! My cousin's husband's nephew. Not our blood, but our family, all the same. And thank you, Peace-in-the-Sky, for honoring us with your visit. I have never seen you, but my childhood was full of stories of all the things you did for Sante and all Tribes-under-the-Dome."

"Maybe you will repay me with a small favor. We have far to go, and we must move quickly. Nandi is our guide, but his feet grow weary. Do you have anything for him?"

Veras looks surprised. "Does he need sandals?"

"If there're some you can spare," I say. "And some food for his journey."

"Alright," she says. She seems confused but not angry. "We diligently conserve our crops. For our future, the one you have promised us, we do keep the Preserve. The sacrosanct, the plenitude, the prospect."

"I am not testing you," I say. "I am sure that you do. I'm asking you to bend the rules because of the necessity of my journey. And I don't visit often."

She nods. "It is true."

"Thank you," I tell her.

* * *

We wake very early. I set the pace this time. By now I am more practiced at slipping past the foliage without damaging it, so I push us to go quickly. Anissa trots excitedly behind me, and Nandi keeps up with us and does not complain.

My head aches. My scalp and face are burning with an internal heat. I loosen my headwrap, but it doesn't help. I drink deeply each time we stop. I don't want to turn inward because of the effort it takes, but I'm forced to so I can divert more energy to physical function. I must keep walking.

A thick fog passes us, and moisture beads up on our skin and drips from the leaves all around us. Little puddles form in the cups of dried leaves on the forest floor, and rivulets run among the roots, finding streams to join. When we hear sounds of human habitation, we conclude that a settlement is nearby, but we can see nothing, so we push on through the fog.

By the time it lifts Anissa has begun to recognize the area. She chooses our paths, though Nandi still consults his map. Day has faded to afternoon, and we push ahead faster and faster. A few times I reach out to tree trunks to steady myself. I fight vertigo.

Finally, Anissa gives a happy cry. I look up and try to focus, as my vision has narrowed to a small field.

* * *

The homes of the Riches tribe are clay like the others we have seen, but they are less squat, with more windows and wider doorways. The roofs are fashioned from halved bamboo shafts arranged neatly in multiple layers that collect water and guide it to tubs under the eaves. In front are narrow beds of flowering plants that attract showy butterflies and buzzing bees. Behind are neat gardens, delineated with string, that grow bunches of small red fruits and herb bushes of many kinds. There are narrow paths all around the houses and throughout the settlement worn deep into the dirt. The forest crop crowds all around, divided into parcels marked with brightly colored string that winds its way through the understory, looped loosely over branches to keep it up out of the dirt.

We pass mostly women and children, who stare openly. Little boys wear un-dyed skirts of brown cloth, but the women wear an intense bright red that sets them off from the greenery around them.

Despite our long, hard march Anissa is bouncing with excitement. She speeds down the path ahead of us, leading the way. Nandi stops to exchange some words with onlookers, and they gasp and clap in excitement. Some run ahead, maybe to bring news of our arrival. Before long, we attract a crowd that follows along with us. I know their language already. It is Anissa's and I have been speaking it since I first woke in that swinging cage among the Intha.

Many in the crowd reach out to Anissa, patting her head, squeezing her hand, and she has smiles for them all, but she presses forward. Our path takes a turn, and the way opens up to another small group of huts. Hustling down the path to meet us are a group of women of all ages, and children around them in a cloud.

In the lead is a woman who has both hands pressed over her mouth.

Anissa screams and sprints forward.

She collides with the woman, and they wrap their arms tightly around each other. The woman sobs painfully and Anissa cries on her shoulder. The other women surround them and some of them cry as well. Others shout joyfully and the children bounce and jump and pull at their mothers.

I stop.

The crowd behind us surges forward and around me, and joins the celebrating group, and I see only the backs of those on the margins.

After a few minutes, I feel Nandi at my elbow. He must have stayed behind with me.

"Peace-in-the-Sky?" he asks carefully.

I don't answer.

"Are you upset? You must have known..."

I hold up my hand to stop him talking.

He hovers nervously.

We stand that way for a long time.

And then the celebrating crowd is thinning. Anissa's story has been told and heard. Joyful songs and little dances that arose spontaneously are over. People are walking back to their homes, wiping their eyes of tears, carrying their children. Some of them pause to stare at the unusual sight of a Peace-in-the-Sky, if they even recognize me for what I am with my hair nearly covered. But none approach me.

I see the woman again, and she has her arm tight around Anissa. She looks at me, and Anissa glances in my direction but her eyes slide from mine guiltily. Their faces are pressed closely so that I cannot hear their conversation at this distance. The woman pushes Anissa firmly into the arms of a nearby relative, who pulls the protesting Anissa away to what must be their home.

The woman approaches me. Her eyes dance back and forth between me and Nandi.

I wait motionless as she walks. I see her simultaneously as a red hash on a map and as herself. I see her thick, dark hair, where mine is colorless. I see she has breasts to nurse a baby. As I do not.

She stops at a distance from me, pauses for just a moment, then gets down on her knees and spreads her arms out in front of her, pressing her face into the ground. The dispersing crowd pauses and some groups watch us. I can see their confusion.

"Peace-in-the-Sky!" the woman says at last, raising her head. "Godshard!"

Anyone watching is now silent.

"Let her speak," Nandi says quietly. "Let her come closer."

I don't say anything, but after a moment Nandi calls to the woman, "Come speak to her."

The woman gets up and halves the distance between us before kneeling again.

She looks up at me with tears and dirt all over her cheeks. I see the arch of her eyebrows, the rounded chin, the shape of her bottom lip. All familiar to me.

"Peace-in-the-Sky, you returned to me that which I love most. She whom I cannot replace. Anissa is my heart and my joy and my life. No favor I can do for you will ever equal this favor."

She waits, but I say nothing. I am frozen in place.

"Anissa tells me that you...traveled together." The woman looks at Nandi nervously, then back to me. "She may have said things that...don't ring true. Understand, ever since she was little that one was so very, very clever. She could tell a story so smoothly. Maybe I should have raised her differently, but it was so delightful to see her cleverness. And now I hear that even when she was so far from us and so hopeless, somehow, she found her bold words. And it has saved her."

She pauses again for me to respond. I am utterly, unblinkingly still.

"Please forgive her anything she's done. She's only a child. And she had no one to help her." A few tears run down the woman's face. "Anything that's mine I give you, anything I can do for you, I will do it. Come stay in my home, it's yours as much as mine. Let's celebrate together, all three?"

When the moments stretch out and I still don't answer, she and Nandi shift anxiously, exchange glances, look to me again.

"Please. Come whenever you'd like. Thank you, thank you."

She presses her face to the ground again, then gets up and backs away, smiling through her tears. She turns and goes back to her hut where relatives run to embrace her. She sends one last look over her shoulder before she's drawn inside and there's the sound of excited shouting and happy crying. Before long the smell of cooking fires is everywhere, and there are pots banging and people talking and laughing in every hut.

Nandi still stands just out of my field of view to the right.

"Peace-in-the-Sky? Are you alright?"

I turn and leave the path, walk to the edge of the forest, and sit with my back to a wide tree there. Nandi sits beside me.

"Are you broken?" he asks quietly. "Can you speak?"

"I can speak," I say. My throat is dry.

"I'm sorry you found out like this. I thought you knew. I thought you surely must know."

I don't answer him. Because I did know. I knew all was not as it seemed. But I had held onto hope that there was so much I did not understand, that perhaps when all was made clear I would still find Anissa-my-Daughter in my arms.

We sit until it begins to get dark. My ears ring with the pain in my head. People sometimes pass us on the path and smile or nod before continuing. Many of them are going to visit Anissa's hut.

"Can I help you somehow?" Nandi asks. "What can I do?"

"There is nothing," I say.

"Can I put my arm around you?"

"No."

He waits longer and I say nothing. Skitos gather one by one and circle us lazily.

"Awha, Peace-in-the-Sky, how can I serve you? You scare me."

I turn to look at him.

He gives a little exhale of relief. "What comforts you? We could slide together." There's a little laugh in his voice as he says it.

I feel a surge of irritation in all the emptiness I am drowning in.

"Are you offering sexual intercourse?" I ask.

Nandi laughs warmly, only a little abashed.

"This shell is androgyne. It's not equipped for that," I say.

The smile on his face slides away. "You're wearing a shell?"

"This is a shell," I say.

"It's not your body?"

"No."

"But...where is your body, then?"

"Dead," I say. "Long dead."

Nandi lapses into confused silence.

After a moment he says, "I got you to talk again."

"Nandi, go. Join their celebration. Go enjoy yourself."

"No, I'm sticking by you." He leans against the tree I lean on, his arm brushes against mine.

He smears his ankles with skito balm, then pulls some food from his pack. Offers me some, but begins to eat when I shake my head.

As it grows dark an old man walks cautiously over to us.

"Come stay with us?" he asks. "My old wife invites you. We have a sleeping mat for you, even. Our two younger sons left not long ago for the border crew in Sas Tabo."

"Thank you," Nandi tells him.

He stands and offers me his hand, but I can stand without help.

The inside of the hut is cool and black. I augment my sight with infrared as Nandi and I find the sleeping mat they have laid out for us in the main room. There's another room behind it, and the old couple disappear into there for the night.

We lay down on a mat woven from grasses and worn thin and soft with use. Nandi puts his arms around me from behind and pulls me close. I am numb. I am here, but I don't feel present.

"Nandi, I am going to sleep now," I tell him. "You must wake me in the morning. I can't wake myself."

"Alright," he says.

* * *

It's not him that wakes me, though, it's the old woman. She comes into the room and starts to quietly prepare food. Nandi is asleep behind me. For a moment I mistake his arms, his warmth, his quiet breath for Anissa's presence. I swallow and it feels like I'm trying to swallow cold scraps of metal. The side of my face is burning hot.

I ease away from Nandi and stand up.

The old woman steals glances at me but won't look me in the eye. I walk to the wall of the hut where there is an old mirror hung. It's cloudy and some spots are flaked away. I unwind the cloth from my head and turn so that I can see my wound. It's crusted over and mostly dry now, my white hair caked into the mess.

I reach up and try to scrape some of the gore away with my fingernail. Alarms go off inside my head, but I silence them. Then there's only the pain to deal with. I pick away dried blood and fluid and underneath find angry red flesh, inflamed and rotting. Outwardly the wound is healing over, but within it is festering. This wet climate is accelerating things.

Then I search deeper. I get my nail under the edge of a piece of cracked bone, a fragment of skull that is held in place only by dried fluids. I pry up the sticky edge.

The alarms, heard only inwardly by me, blare so deafeningly I can hear nothing else. Red warning pulses obscure my vision.

But I enhance my sight and, during the brief periods of clear vision I have, I inspect the pink matter under the skull fragment. I enhance my sight again and again. Through the red flashes, despite the poor light in the hut and the clouded mirror, I glimpse sparkling filaments running through the brain tissue. I wretch violently, though I have nothing in my stomach.

I take my hand away and let the piece of skull move wetly back into place. The alarms are dampened, and my vision slowly clears. The pain is still there. It will take longer to subside.

I take deep even breaths. I gently wind the cloth around my head again. If only I had looked when Orco showed me his mirror, maybe I would have been prepared for yesterday. If I had truly thought critically about myself...but then I was always thinking about Anissa. Thinking about getting her home. I had put aside every other line of inquiry to be dealt with after Anissa was safe.

I walk to the door of the hut and look out into the morning. Mist and the smoke from cooking fires mingle to obscure the other huts and the pathway and even the encroaching forest, which appears as a hazy, even green. I look to my left. Down the path that way lies Anissa's hut. I cannot make it out clearly.

I watch that way for a long time.

"Peace-in-the-Sky?" Nandi asks quietly.

I turn away from the door. The old woman has set out some food on a bench, and everyone is gathering to squat around it.

"Come eat a little," Nandi says.

I go and sit with them, but I don't eat. They eat and talk quietly and send me glances from the side of their eyes. The old woman is curious. The old man is cautious. And Nandi is concerned.

When they are done the old man clears away the clay bowls.

I walk to the door again. The mist is clearing. Men of all ages with bags and tools over their shoulders are dispersing into the surrounding forest, following footpaths that are visible only as they part the leaves. Some carry young children on their shoulders.

"We can go and visit later this morning," Nandi says. He's come to stand just behind me.

"Visit?"

"Go to see Anissa, and her family."

I feel like I've been struck. It's a moment before I can reply.

"No."

"No?" Nandi asks. "You want to give them a day or so, first?"

"No."

"What are you saying?"

"We set out this morning, Nandi. I need a clear view to the sky. Find us the fastest way out from under the dome."

"What?" Nandi turns to look at me.

"This shell is dying."

"Awha! What will happen?"

"I need to return to the station. If this shell dies with me in it, I also die."

"What about Anissa? You should at least say good-bye to her."

The smell of Anissa's hair suddenly returns to me. I almost reach out to touch her. But she isn't there.

"No. I need to leave," I say.

"Just leave? But you can make time for this one thing."

I turn away from him.

"Peace-in-the-Sky? I don't understand you. You called her your daughter and you believed it, right? You really believed it? And now you want to just leave her?"

Anissa, huddled under my arm with her eyes squeezed shut. Anissa running ahead of me and laughing. Anissa curled up warm beside me at night. Anissa's voice calling me "momma."

"Peace-in-the-Sky?" Nandi prods.

"The quickest way out from under the dome. I need an unobstructed view of the sky."

Confusion in his voice, Nandi says, "At the height of the dome are air cleaners that vent to the sky. If you're desperate you could go there. Climb the ladder. There're locks but I bet you can open them."

"You'll guide me?"

He laughs in surprise. "You're really going to do it? Yes, alright. I'll guide you. I do what you say, don't I? You're Peace-in-the-Sky."

I turn my head and for a moment we look at each other.

"I'm sorry," he says. "I can't understand you. You're a god, really, aren't you? Though they tell us over and over again that you are not. And your face is like a mask. But I will help you."

"My face *is* a mask," I tell him. "And thank you."

It takes Nandi only a few moments to prepare. He studies his map, gathers our bags and drinks, borrows a strigil to scrape away the stale skito balm. He thanks the old couple but tells them nothing about our plans, and we leave.

It is full daylight, and warm and humid. Women are emerging from their huts to carry water and tend the gardens. Children play in the open spaces, racing each other down the narrow paths.

But we turn between two huts and the forest swallows us. Happy sounds from the settlement fade behind us. I strain to hear Anissa's voice one last time, but I cannot.

Anissa. The soft feel of her skin. Her small hand with long, narrow fingers clasped in mine. Her tiny pink fingernails against her dark skin. I stop walking.

Nandi stops, too. "Are you alright?"

After a moment of silence I say, "I am not well."

Nandi says, "Let me carry your bag."

It is almost empty anyway, and he folds it up and tucks it in his.

I start walking again and Nandi walks behind me, letting me set the pace. Every step is an effort. Leaves brush my face. We pass near someone working in the forest, though not close enough to see. We hear the rustling of dry leaves and the chipping sound of a tool against wood. We walk on and the sounds fade. Chip, chip, chip.

Anissa, Anissa, Anissa. I will never see her again. It would be nearly impossible to return in the time frame of her life span.

I stumble on a rock and fall to one knee.

"Peace!" Nandi jumps forward, reaches out to me, hesitates, then takes my arm and helps me to my feet.

He peers at me anxiously. "You look ashen in the face," he says.

I will never see her grown to a woman. I will never see her children.

"Peace, can you walk?"

"I can."

I set my foot on the path. It is only wide enough for one foot at a time.

Nandi follows close behind me.

Noon approaches and our pace has slowed to a halting walk. The heat in my face is like a fire.

"Peace-in-the-Sky, what is wrong?" Nandi asks when we stop to drink. "Are you dying? Is your heart breaking?"

"I don't know myself," I say, and my voice sounds whispery to me. I drink more. "Perhaps it is both."

I want to lie down, but I'm afraid to lose consciousness.

"But if you get back," Nandi says worriedly, "you can be fixed, right?"

"My consciousness will be transferred to another shell," I say. I lean my elbow on a moss-covered rock. I'm too tired to search for words that will be more meaningful for him. And I'm still myself processing all the memories that are leaking back—disjointed, disordered, disquieting.

"You get...another body? And you'll be okay, right? You've done it before?"

"Hundreds of times."

"And you'll still remember things?"

Anissa. Coming to shelter under my arm from the torment of the Intha. Feeling her start to feel safe.

"Yes." I start to slide away from the rock.

Nandi leans forward and offers his hand.

"I will carry you there," he says. "But will you be able to make the climb? It's a long, long ladder."

"I don't know," I say. "But Nandi, you cannot carry me through this underbrush. The path is too narrow."

"Parents carry their children, don't they? My own father carried me on his shoulder so that I could help him work our crops."

"You yourself are tired and worn," I say.

"For you, I will make a mighty effort," Nandi says, his smile broad.

I like him. Very much. I like all of them. The crowded Tribes-under-the-Dome, the pushy border crews, the Intha violent in their desperation for survival. I cannot help it. It is part of my design.

"I will shut down all but the most essential functions," I tell him. "I may appear dead. When we arrive at the ladder you must wake me."

"Awha, how?" he asks. "I'm afraid to be rough with you. I'm afraid to even carry you when you're not awake to know it's just me. You can still call the pillars-of-flame."

"Perhaps," I say. "Try making a loud noise close to my ear, or pulling back my eyelid."

"It scares me when you talk about things uncertainly," he says. "If you don't know, who does?"

I drink again and again. I am so thirsty.

"Ready?" Nandi asks.

"Yes," I say. He takes my arm and bends down to pull me across his shoulders. My head swims as he stands, and I start shutting down while I can still control myself. The gentle rocking of Nandi's plodding gait lulls me and then, all at once, everything is gone.

* * *

A pulsing blue light in my vision. Then Nandi's face above mine. He looks hot and weary.

Then there is sound, too.

Running water. A bird calling.

"Are you back with me?" Nandi asks.

I sit up.

"Yes," I say.

This shell still lives. I am somewhat rested. Behind Nandi I see a stainless-steel ladder glinting among the leaves.

Nandi sits beside me. "It took me a while to find it. A narrow ladder in all this." He gestures around to the greenery. "I had to set you down and climb a tree to see above the canopy and spot it. Climb a tree! I clambered over someone else's tree."

"Thank you," I say. "I know it's taboo for you."

"Because Peace-in-the-Sky says it is," he says. "So, I thought, for you I could do it."

"Thank you. But I only said that resources must be carefully conserved. It was Tribes-under-the-Dome who carved the forest into pieces for the exclusive use of each family."

We walk to a nearby stream and drink. I am still thirsty, but it is not the desperate ache it was before. I splash water on my face.

"Are you still thinking of climbing?" Nandi asks.

"Yes. Though I need fuel for the effort." I reach out into the bushes and break off the tender ends of branches, and chew them.

Nandi watches me with wide eyes. "What will the man think when he comes and sees his foliage like this?"

"When I have gone up," I say, "I want you to leave. Go see your family. Ask your mother to feed you. Stay for a while and visit."

"I would never ask Mam to break with the Preserve," Nandi says.

I tear up handfuls of some low-growing legume and eat it, leaves, stems, roots and all.

"You are hers; she will feed you. I would instruct you to remain with your Sante tribe for the rest of your life, but I don't think there's a place for you there anymore."

"Awha! Why are you doing this for me?" Nandi asks.

"I want to repay you," I say. "Or, more truthfully, I want a better life for you." I want a better life for all of them, though I am in no shape to aid them. There are many, many injustices in their world, and it pains me that so many are upheld by traditions established by Peace-in-the-Sky.

Nandi just watches me silently while I eat a handful of hard, dark berries.

"Those aren't for eating," he says.

"It doesn't matter," I say.

We go to stand by the ladder.

"Will I see you again?" he asks me as I look up.

The ladder extends far, far up until it disappears into the thickness of the air.

"No," I say. "Given the damage to this shell, and the difficulty of coordinating any trip, it's unlikely that I could return in your lifetime. Even assuming that my trip is approved, which is even less likely."

Anissa. I see her peaceful, sleeping face. There's a pounding ache in my chest.

"What will I tell Boss?" Nandi asks. A question directed more to himself, but I answer anyway.

"Tell him that I was impressed by his need and moved by his plight. Tell him I am thankful for his gift of your guidance under the dome. Tell him I will return in the time of his successor to repair the dome."

"Is that true?"

"No. Or, at least, I doubt that it will be."

Nandi sighs and looks sad. I wait for him to ask me what his people should do. I wait for him to ask for guidance and direction and hope. I wait for him to ask for prophecy.

But he doesn't. It's not in Nandi's nature to grapple with the larger concerns. He sees only the people around him and his relationships with those he cares about. And I do not fool myself that any hasty parting instructions could cause meaningful change. There is too much to be done here, and I find myself too broken to be useful. Just as Rill said.

"Is there anything else I can do for you before I go?" I ask.

He meets my eyes and his smile returns.

"I'll miss you," he says. "I wanted to figure you out, but I guess I won't."

"No."

"It's too much to think I might be the man who slides together with a god." He smiles his reluctant smile. "But can I have a kiss? I'd remember it the rest of my life."

I feel a familiar stab of irritation, this time tempered with forbearance.

"If you wish."

He hesitates for a moment, steps closer, and touches his lips softly to mine. Then leans back and looks into my eyes.

He laughs nervously. "I guess I'll never see you smile, either."

"If it makes any difference," I say, "I do smile. But the nerve impulses are blocked from changing the muscles in my face."

He laughs. "Awha, that I really do not understand."

"Good-bye, Nandi," I say. "Thank you."

"Peace-in-the-Sky," he says solemnly.

I look up. And I start to climb.

* * *

By the time I rise above the canopy, I am exhausted. Nausea, chills, a burning ache in my head and neck. I am not as recovered as I hoped. I climb a while more and pause to look down. The treetops look like a verdant, rolling field. The heat from the sun above, even filtered through the dome, is growing. The air is becoming thick with the smoke being gathered into the filters high above me. I hyperventilate to saturate my blood with oxygen in case respiration becomes difficult.

Then I selectively choose all non-essential processes to shut down. I stop biologically necessary functions knowing it will kill this shell. I am now dying. I have several hours. And in those hours, I need to make this climb, reach the top, activate my beacon, and return to the station. And if the shell dies? This hole in my heart where Anissa once lived will cease to cause me such pain.

I close my eyes and imagine I rest my cheek against Anissa's smooth cheek. I breathe in the smell that is her and only her. And I climb.

To my brother Wyatt. Your unbridled excitement for the first carried me through the second.

Station in the Sky

Part One

I open my eyes.

White, overwhelming light. Metallic glints. Sounds of alternate humming and hissing.

I open my mouth and try to speak, but I just babble. My mouth is loose and slippery.

I raise an arm, but it flops across the thin mattress uselessly. It's like trying to use a numbed limb. And it's not only my arm, it's my legs and my face and my mouth and every muscle in my body.

I say my body. But it's not my body. At least not yet.

I close my eyes and lay still and slip in and out of consciousness. For weeks. For months.

* * *

I open my eyes.

The light is not so blinding. I can make out shapes and light and dark and I can move my head and watch the world move with it.

I hear sound. A voice, probably, though I cannot understand it. A darker shape looms into my vision, and I see eyes. I cannot tear my gaze away from eyes.

That's how it works when neurons are making connections in a new shell. The new body functions and behaves like an infant, capable only of autonomic movements, instinctual responses. You have to learn how to use it. And, like an infant, it'll be a year before I can count on being able to use my body with some measure of control as I wait for nerves to make connections. Unlike an infant, I will spend that time fully conscious, impatient, irritable. Or perhaps that's the experience of infants, as well. I can't remember being an infant. No one can. But I can remember growing into new shells, over and over.

I do not like growing into a new shell.

* * *

When I can sit propped up and hold a spoon, I begin watching playbacks while I practice feeding myself. History. It's things I have known for centuries but of course there are always gaps in your memories.

An arm glides out with a whir to accept my empty bowl. It's streaked with slurry from a previous meal when I fumbled the bowl while handing it over. I see my own flesh arm, now apparently a sallow brown. It's no longer the deep, rich color of *her* skin...

A program runs daily to teach me speech. I listen to a recording through tinny speakers, and I'm meant to formulate responses. I wish I could say nothing at all. I've never considered simply neglecting to learn to speak. I could also fail to learn to eat. All our meaningful nourishment on board is semi-liquid. I could drink it and never bother chewing the wafers. I could fail to learn to walk. I could lie here inert, if I wished. I could die. I do consider it.

* * *

It's at least a year before I can leave Reform and shuffle through the scarred white corridors. I know every accidental gouge in the smooth plastic, every scuff on the metal floors. It's how I navigate. Otherwise, every hall is the same. Beside my door there's a small screen with a playback on eternal loop. I pause to watch it with a mechanical resignation.

A baby screams, wrapped tightly in a swaddle. A skinny child sits on a park bench reading a book while other children play in the background. A young woman with glasses sits at a round table with others, all consulting texts and comparing notes.

In the last clip, a pinched-looking woman with hair pulled tightly back is leaning over a large folio. All around, filed neatly in the stacks and only just visible in the gloom, are endless rows of books. The woman's lips are drawn thin across a narrow face. There are no other people in the clip.

Alone. In a library. Late at night.

The plaque over the playback reads *Donna Whitacre*. I enter my cell.

* * *

It's weeks before Andrej comes to see me. I know em not because of eir appearance or voice, which have changed many times as ey changes shells, but by eir mannerisms and patterns of speech. There are only about thirty of us left, so we know each other's habits. Well.

"You didn't make a report," ey says.

"Hello, Andrej," I say, matching eir toneless inflection. "It is good to see you. I appreciate your visit."

Ey doesn't change expression. "Your report is delayed."

"I'm not ready to report," I say. My freshly reactivated datalink has been buzzing in my head with reminder notifications, but I have centuries of practice ignoring it.

"Med says your shell was badly damaged when you were retrieved from the surface. Even if your memories of the time you spent on Survey are not fully intact, any fragments would still be useful for our records. Particularly any information regarding how you were injured."

I *was* injured. I nearly died, though that's not why I activated my beacon for an emergency pickup. I left because I was done. Because Anissa no longer needed me.

"I know all of this as well as you," I tell em. Eir job was once my job, until we switched.

"And yet you haven't made a report."

"And yet," I agree.

Ey waits for a moment for me to add anything, then abruptly turns and leaves.

* * *

I seek out Jayd myself.

I stand outside eir door watching eir playback.

A fat-cheeked sleeping baby. A child with one bloodied knee playing soccer in the street with bigger boys. A scowling teenager slouching in a hard chair outside an office door. A young person hurling a brick into a rioting crowd, then running while choking smoke swirls all around.

The plaque reads *Jayd Collins-Brown.*

Ey doesn't turn when I enter. Ey is painting. All the walls of eir cell are painted, from floor to ceiling and all across the ceiling, in one endless, ever-evolving mural.

Ey says, "Donna."

"Jayd."

I sit on eir cot and watch em paint. "Pointillism?"

"One of the few styles I haven't mastered."

Ey dabs away at the walls, which have been transformed into pastel days on riverbanks with pale people in strange costumes in the shade of unfamiliar vegetation.

"You were hurt on Survey?" ey asks when ey takes a break, standing back and flexing eir hand.

"Badly."

"How's your memory?"

"Full of holes," I say.

"But worse than usual?" Ey finally turns to face me.

"Hard to know."

"Andrej wants your report." Jayd picks up a paintbrush and wipes it carefully.

"Andrej has an unhealthy fixation on reports."

Jayd says, "We all have unhealthy fixations," and gestures at eir walls. "That's all we have left."

Silence. Not companionable silence. Grim silence.

"Did you enjoy your unhealthy fixation this trip?" ey asks.

"What's that?"

"People."

I look away. There's only one person I'm thinking of, whom I'm always thinking of. Anissa. Anissa who was, in the end, not my daughter at all.

By the time I recover myself, I see Jayd has gone back to painting. Ey picks up the conversation again.

"While you were gone, the Council discussed sending drones to the surface instead of a surveyor."

"Did they?" It's unwelcome news.

"I didn't think you would like that."

"Of course not. Drones cannot interact meaningfully with people. They are only for automated tasks..."

But I'm not really thinking about drones. I'm thinking about how the Council was planning to replace me, as if someone thought I wouldn't be coming back.

"I was unable to report my injury to them from the surface," I say. "Why would they feel alternate survey plans were needed? As far as they knew I was whole and functional."

Jayd gives me a mild look. "Surely you recall other times when the Council has considered if your work on Survey is truly necessary."

I feel my suspicions scatter. I remember nothing about how I was injured, and only parts of what happened afterward on my survey. On the surface I operated with the vague notion my injury had been maliciously inflicted, though my muddled mind could produce no evidence for the conviction. Not then, and certainly not now.

I admit, "Yes, you're correct. They are always trying to cancel surveys."

"Always? We've had that discussion surrounding your past four surveys. The hundreds before that we did not."

"Every time that matters for the present," I say.

Jayd says, "I'd forgotten how surveys change you, Donna. It ruins your sense of time. You return behaving like a transient human, not an immortal stationer."

"We're not immortal," I say, reaching up to touch the side of my head where a neat hole had been knocked into the side of my skull.

We stop talking. Ey paints. I watch.

"Have you had your Condition rotation this cycle?" I ask after a while. "Let's go together."

"I have been skipping those," ey says. "I'm working."

"Ah. How long since you last exercised?" I ask.

Ey says nothing.

"Jayd?"

"Maybe...five years."

I notice eir body. It's hard to remember to notice bodies. But eirs is spindly and brittle looking.

"Jayd. You're going to ruin that shell."

"What does it matter?"

I don't remind em there are a finite number of shells. Instead, I say, "Training a new shell to paint always sets you back years in your work."

Ey pauses and puts down eir brush.

We go together.

* * *

The shell I've been given isn't a surveyor model. It's not built for Earth's gravity, but for Station's. It's comparatively easy to control, but has no real power to it. It's not equipped with all the tech, the weaponry, the sensory capabilities. It feels sluggish and blunted compared to Peace-in-the-Sky. I miss that shell.

I work this one as hard as I can. Jayd works eirs carefully. Then we rinse our shells off and put fresh robes on them. It's always hard to start thinking of a new shell as your own. It doesn't look or feel like the one you occupied before. Only parts I can't see or feel are the same—brain matter, neural tissue, artificial glands meant to stimulate nerve growth, reinforce memory, and interact with Station data links. Those are the only things I carry with me from shell to shell. That's why looking at the backs of my own hands is sometimes a strange experience.

Jayd and I exit Condition and part ways at a juncture of corridors. Ey is going to Fabrication to get more paints, and I'm going to Records. I've already ceased to pay attention to the body I use to propel myself through the corridors. It's best, I find, if you don't think about your body at all.

A useful habit on Station, but perhaps one of the reasons I found it so hard to remember who I was after I was injured on Survey. If I'd really looked at myself carefully, perhaps I would have seen enough to shake loose the memory that I wasn't entirely human. Not like humans on the surface. I would have known then I couldn't possibly be Anissa's mother.

But that alternate path fills me with misery. To have never believed myself Anissa's mother? The thought causes distress almost equal to the pain of losing her, the pain of returning her to her own true mother and seeing that, after all I'd brought her through, she did not need me at all.

* * *

My heavy heart does not prevent me from navigating the corridors to the Records room. Without once recalling the path there, my feet simply find it. If my playback is to be believed, I was always comfortable in places like Records. It's the closest thing we have to a library on board. But even as a Records clerk I spent very little time here. No one spends much time in Records, not even Andrej.

The room has a stale feeling to it, though the cleaning system still accesses the floors. There are four private booths, two on each side of the hall, for viewing playbacks in various forms. The main console for clerks is in the center and requires a Records-privilege datalink to activate. I find it helpful to see everything laid out before me, even if that same datalink allows me to access most of this information in my head with just a thought.

My Records-privilege also allows me access to more in-depth parts of Records. I can see everything needed to ensure Records is working properly and structured usefully.

With a Med-privilege one could view patient Records or peruse medical textbooks and training videos. With my Survey-privilege I have access to an enormous body of Earth history, climate data, human behavioral studies, and the like.

And any stationer could come to Records and study Station history or view general information about our daily existence. Once they might have read expansions on the personal narratives playing on the screens outside our cells. It was unfortunately a close analysis of these that first led some stationers to doubt the accuracy of the playbacks. It caused our second mass die-off—twelve stationers, who couldn't reconcile their hazy memories of themselves on Earth with the playbacks designed to keep us from forgetting ourselves, decided they could not live with the ambiguity.

Living with ambiguity, or ignoring it, is an important skill on Station. The remaining stationers ignore their playbacks as easily as I ignore my new shell. And the offending data that caused so much distress is now Rchived, a process which makes it unsearchable and inaccessible to most stationers.

The most important information in Records is reports on the changing atmospheric conditions on Earth, radiation levels across the surface, tracking of the magnetic poles as they continue to stabilize, and the integrity of the dome and its inhabitants. That is our mission, after all. Our purpose. To preserve the human race for a time when the Earth is habitable again and humans are able to live sustainably on the surface.

I didn't come to Records to review our Mission Imperatives, however. I came to refresh my memory on all that led up to my most recent survey.

I pull up reports from Med and Reform during the year I was growing into my surveyor shell and re-familiarize myself with that incarnation of Peace-in-the-Sky. I go back to the year before when the shell was chosen and re-animated and made ready. I study the Council meeting that authorized the survey. My objective, apparently, had been to travel into the region of highly irradiated territory the Intha call "Salvage" to scout for usable materials. I see myself, two shell-changes back, arguing for the survey, and watch playback showing other stationers trying to impose their personal agendas on the mission. Nothing unusual there. Everyone has a personal project—or fixation, as Jayd has named it—they want satisfied.

And I review the Council meeting that happened while I was away. Commissioner Lisa Guadalupe presides, and everyone on Station is present for the meetings. I watch as the heads of different divisions—Med and Fabrication and Maint and Flight—discuss whether or not sending drones to the surface would satisfy their aims. No one mentions me or the fact I am not present until the very end, when Guadalupe briefly points out my upcoming report may be of use.

There is one stationer, then, who is on record fully expecting my return. Perhaps ey has some insight into why my existence and expertise on surface matters was not considered important.

* * *

I review records for days but there is not much else that strikes me as relevant. So much data, so much noise, so little clarity. I leave Records reminded of much information I had forgotten, but with no obvious support for my conviction I was hurt purposefully.

I pass my hall mate's cell on the way back to mine, and ey must hear me because eir door slides open.

"Donna? I'm surprised to see you around so soon."

"Hello, Raina," I say. "Sufficient time has elapsed for me to change shells." I'm not surprised ey has lost track of time. We all do.

"Well, come in." Ey steps back to make room for me to join em in eir cell.

"You did my extraction?" I ask.

Ey gestures for me to sit on the bed and takes the chair so ey can see emself in the small mirror on the wall. As stationers we long ago lost any interest in physical appearance, and though our shells are perfectly capable of expression and body language, we have had little use for it. Shells designed for the surface must be prevented from reacting so we can remain fully impartial among humans. As Peace-in-the-Sky, I couldn't smile. And on Station, I don't bother.

But Raina makes a particular study of the expressions of the face. Eir eyes cut to the mirror, and ey makes a concerned face.

"Yes, I answered your beacon. I'm not surprised you don't remember. I have never seen a shell destroyed like that. I didn't even want to touch it. What happened to you?"

"I don't know."

"You don't remember anything?"

"I remember many things," I say. "But I don't remember my injury."

"Too bad," Raina says. "It seems like it would make a good story. Was there a struggle? Could it be turned into an epic?" Ey glances to the mirror and tries for "hopeful."

"I'm sorry I don't remember more," I say. I get up to leave. It's very distracting talking to em when ey is trying to emote.

"No, sit," ey says with a placating wave of eir hand. "Don't go. Tell me what you do remember. Who did you meet?"

"The Intha in the drylands, the Tribes-under-the-Dome..."

"The Intha are still there? We never thought their population would grow."

"They persist. I would not say they thrive," I say.

"What a desperate people they must be."

I nod and sit again. The Intha are a desperate people. And they do terrible, desperate things.

"Did you learn any unique stories among them? Something that might interest me?"

"I met one, yes. I could tell you his history. I don't know that it would inspire you."

"Tell me." Ey leans forward to start a recording. "What was eir name?"

"Rill," I say. "Most likely short for O'Rill or Ov'Rill. Many of the Intha have names like that."

"Well? What did you learn about em?"

"He lives with his wife in a shack. They have a garden, a flock of fowl and creatures they call camels for riding distances. They are very isolated."

"Why does ey live so far from other Intha?" Raina asks.

"I don't know. But it's not uncommon. Some Intha gather in small settlements or even towns, but many live on family homesteads. Perhaps to avoid competition for resources."

Raina waves this away. "What is eir passion?" Eir eyes cut to the mirror, and ey expresses intensity.

"I don't know. He does have a child with his Intha wife."

"Is that unusual?" Raina asks.

"I'm not informed about Intha fecundity. Certainly, mortality rate is high."

"Ey lives in fear of the day ey loses eir only child?" Raina asks, looks to the mirror: pity.

"My impression is that he is frustrated sinking so many resources into a child that most likely will not live or may very well be sterile."

Raina's hopeful expression goes flat. "What about the wife? What does ey feel?"

"She."

"What?"

"She. A woman. You remember how it is on Earth. They have conventions regarding gender and use distinct pronouns." Even though I find dispensing with the gender binary to be a positive thing stationers have chosen, still it feels wrong to refer to the woman in a way she might not like.

There's a moment of silence as Raina regards me. I don't know if ey remembers gendered pronouns.

"How does the wife feel about the child?" ey asks finally.

"I did not speak to her."

Raina stands up now. I do the same. Ey walks to the door and it slides open. "If you think of anything more inspiring, or with a little more pathos, come tell it to me."

I nod and leave. I stand outside the closed door and watch the playback under the plaque reading *Raina Chua*.

A toddler in a crib surrounded by plush animals. A little girl perched high in a tree, eating an apple. A teen paragliding with snow-capped mountains in the background. A woman in flight gear climbing into the cockpit of a jet.

I know I won't be telling em anything. If ey wants to discover something about misery let em go to Earth emself. I let heartache for Anissa wash over me as I walk back to my own cell.

* * *

I go through the slow, circuitous process of making a formal request to meet with another stationer, waiting for a reply, and accepting the date I am given weeks away. On Earth I often felt like events were happening too quickly, that I hadn't time to fully grasp the consequences of an action before I was forced to make a choice. On Station there is no such problem. One may take weeks to make a decision about the smallest detail. Months to research a problem. Years to complete a project. I struggle to readjust my internal clock to my previous pace of life.

And, eventually, it is time for my appointment with Guadalupe.

As a commissioner, ey has better quarters than other stationers—a short hall all eir own, decorated with a mural in the Proto-Cubist style: a villa in the hills above a placid blue sea, a hazy mountain range across the waters. Jayd painted it long ago, the only change ey has ever made to Station that remains. It's a very restful work.

Beside the door there's a name plaque, *Commissioner Lisa Guadalupe*, and a playback, just as we all have.

A bald baby in an elaborate dress is posed for a formal portrait. A girl walks just behind eir father into a richly appointed meeting room, each as serious as the other. A young woman in a tailored suit speaks at a podium in front of a crowd brandishing signs. A woman sits behind a large, polished desk in a spacious office with marble floors, two flags limp on their poles behind em.

Ey was born to this. At least that's what we are led to believe. I don't remember how we were chosen for our roles here on Station.

As I stand watching, I hear eir voice from inside, "Hello, welcome."

But the door hasn't opened yet.

"Please, come in. Welcome. Will you take some tea?"

I listen as ey cycles through an entire one-sided conversation. When ey starts again from the beginning, I knock. The door slides open.

"Surveyor Whitacre," the commissioner says, and I can hear the smile in eir voice though it thankfully doesn't touch eir face. "Welcome back from your survey."

Eir cell has two rooms, a larger antechamber with a table and chairs, and private living quarters behind. The table, white and scuffed like everything else on Station, is set with two delicate cups sitting in two small plates and a teapot, which steams.

Ey offers me eir hand, which I take awkwardly, then ey gestures me toward a seat.

A visit to Guadalupe always involves some tedious, long-extinct ceremony. I sit at the table, and ey sits as well and pours me some tea in a practiced, precise way.

"Chamomile is all we have left. And after so long in storage it is mostly tasteless." Ey lifts the cup to eir lips. "Dr. Singh may grow some for us again, and then we could enjoy it as it's meant to be enjoyed."

The liquid in the cup is entirely clear. I don't bother to try it.

Ey sets eir cup down in its little dish. "And what are they drinking on Earth these days?"

The question catches me off guard. "Water?" I can't remember being offered something with any social significance. "Under the dome I had something served hot. It was called atole."

In my memory I see Anissa's face above the cup, inhaling the steam, then offering me a taste.

The commissioner is marking something in eir log. "I will have to research it."

Guadalupe has been an ally. When I propose a surface survey ey listens with an open mind. Although ey doesn't vote and eir role on Station is intended to be one of neutral arbiter, eir approval can certainly sway the others.

"You may have heard my shell was damaged," I say.

"I was waiting for your report," ey says smoothly.

"Yes. I haven't made one yet."

"I had noticed that," ey says. "We usually ask our surveyors to make a report before leaving Reform."

No one but me has been to the surface in recent memory. Andrej hasn't asked for a surface survey in a very long time, and the others who were once trained for the position are gone. But, as Jayd reminded me, I'm thinking on shorter time scales than the other stationers. What seems to me irrelevant history is, to Guadalupe, the established protocol.

"I am sorry to make an exception," I say. "Many of my memories were lost. As you may have heard, my shell sustained a head injury."

"Damage to the head? That is serious. How did it come about? I thought surveyor shells had protections against violence."

"They do," I agree. "An aggression-triggered adrenaline spike may activate a response beam from Station which targets an attacker. But it only fixes on the signature of a living creature. I may have fallen, or been hit with a falling rock, for instance." I'm not certain how much of this Guadalupe recalls from previous survey efforts. "And also, any damage that happened to my shell before reaching the surface would not trigger the beam."

I am hoping my last suggestion will draw some meaningful response from em, but it does not.

Ey only says, "You have no memory of how you were hurt?"

"No. I have a few vague memories of preparing for launch, but then I remember nothing until I regained consciousness on the surface after the injury."

"Do you recall what it was you wished to communicate to me before you launched, then? I didn't respond to your query before you were dispatched to the surface."

My memory offers no clues. "I contacted you before I launched, and we never followed up?"

"Yes. It's not established protocol, for a surveyor to contact me directly so near to launch. Any alterations to Survey objectives should be brought before Council. I cannot respond to personal messages."

I know that perfectly well. So I wonder what it was I had to say to Guadalupe.

While I'm thinking, ey says, "All of this should go into your report, Surveyor Whitacre."

I nod. But I don't want to write a report until I can be certain what it should say.

I try a different approach. "I see Council discussed drone surveys during my absence. Was there some concern for me while I was gone?"

"Concern?" Guadalupe looks up from eir tea. "No. We did not have knowledge of your injury at that time, we did not know how dangerous surveys had become."

I try not to wince. I don't want Guadalupe to think of surveys as dangerous, or else I may never be allowed to return.

Guadalupe continues, "Some new projects stationers are taking an interest in, I believe. That was the discussion." Ey continues, "Is there anything of note you observed on your survey? Are the people living under the dome still thriving?"

I pull my thoughts from a launch time I cannot accurately recall. "They are. Their population has grown such the dome can no longer contain them, and they spill out into the surrounding lands, intermixing with the Intha." I do not tell em the dome is beginning to deteriorate, and if left untended it will cease to effectively separate the two populations.

Guadalupe sits back in eir chair. "The populations are mixed?"

"In some places at least, yes," I say. "There are Intha in the drylands, and Tribes-under-the-Dome, and a whole population of peoples who live in between that are of mixed descent."

"Unexpected, but the Intha are descended from humans," Guadalupe says.

"They *are* human," I say emphatically. "We have no choice but to accept that, even without the protection provided by the dome, humans survived. On their own."

"I would not have thought the irradiated landscape would support a viable population."

"The Intha struggle," I admit. "But they persist."

This is not the time for me to argue that the artificial segregation of the two populations is causing problems for both, how the Intha would benefit from Tribes-under-the-Dome agricultural expertise, and the Tribes would benefit from Intha technology and innovation. And all would benefit from more genetic diversity. I know if stationers continue to do nothing, eventually this will happen on its own. And stationers are remarkably adept at doing nothing.

Guadalupe taps eir temple. "The Intha problem just will not go away." But ey offers no solutions, and makes no proposal that a solution be found, so the best course of action seems to be my own inaction.

We stand and Guadalupe gathers the tea set. Each piece is treated with such care it is almost upsetting to watch. I begin to hold my breath, afraid ey will drop something. And there will never be anything like that set again. It is from a time so long-gone stationers can't even remember it. At last, all the pieces of the set are back on their shelves and nothing has been dropped.

"Thank you for your visit," Guadalupe says formally. "I hope that you will visit again soon."

Ey offers eir hand and I take it. The movements feel stiff and unfamiliar. No other stationer observes this farcical ritual, but I try to be patient.

Finally I can exit, and I stand outside the closed door, thinking. I am inspecting Jayd's lovely mural when I hear Guadalupe through the door again, endlessly reciting an idealized taking-of-leave exchange.

I walk away.

* * *

It is Jayd who tells me a Council meeting has been called. I've been ignoring notifications in my datalink in favor of some purposeful research on the feasibility of organic memory recall. When the time arrives, we walk together.

"Was there an agenda?" I ask em.

"I didn't read it."

More stationers join us from other corridors, and we quietly fall in line and head for the Council Hall. I nod to others if our gazes cross one another. All those bland faces in a narrow range of washed-out brown, straight hair that never grows, all cut in the same style. Some bodies a shade taller than others, some thin and others more robust, but all with the same androgyne smoothness. All of us wearing the same simple robes, gray with white piping or light blue with gray piping. It's a stifling sameness after the riotous variety and color I remember from Earth.

The white, featureless walls are a sad contrast to the vibrant flora that crowded around us under the dome where Anissa lived...

I miss the people and the places of Earth so much it feels like a hollow place in my chest.

With effort, I draw my attention to the Council Hall as we enter.

It's a large oval room with seating for every original stationer. Fortuitously located in the center of the Station, it didn't have to be sealed off after the radiation leak that killed many stationers in the upper decks. There's little talking as we enter, and Jayd parts from me without a word to sit in the section for Fabrication division stationers. I head for Records division seating.

Commissioner Guadalupe calls us to order with the same words we've heard more times than we can remember, then yields the floor. Raina performs a spoken word piece to open the meeting. I look away so I won't see eir deliberate expressions. I think of my guide Nandi on Earth, so quick with a smile, his every feeling paraded across his bright features.

Instead, I look around at the stationers arrayed in tiered seating throughout the hall.

It's mostly empty. Those of us left are dotted around the Council Hall in our original seats, emphasizing just how many of us are gone.

I sit in a row of vacant seats where all the other Records clerks used to sit. Only Dakota Jinx remains, down at the end of the aisle. Several rows below me Andrej Vann sits beside Timothy Ju, Survey supervisor. Andrej and I switched jobs but not seats. Stretching out to the right of Andrej is a long line of empty seats. All the other surveyors, none of them living. Only Andrej lives, possibly because ey took a different assignment.

When Raina is done, we return our attention to Guadalupe. Ey sits on a raised dais at the end of the oval hall, alone in the five seats there. Once we had a Commission. Now we have Guadalupe. But I'm glad it's em that remains. I think of Jayd's mural outside eir suite, painted when we still had four commissioners left. As though Jayd somehow marked em for survival.

Guadalupe introduces the first speaker. "Dr. Marinne Singh."

All eyes focus on Dr. Singh. Ey sits in the Med division section with the physician's assistant, Shelley McConnelly. Shelley is focused on eir log, taking notes, as if everything said here isn't meticulously documented. Ernesta Muambe is on eir other side, once a clerk, now the acting staff psychologist. Ernesta watches Singh with an open, patiently expectant expression.

Singh begins speaking. "I would like to remind the council of our previous proposal to send unmanned drones to Earth for collecting materials we need on Station. Surveys have proven both dangerous and unreliable."

In that moment, although no one looks in my direction, I feel the weight of all those minds turning their thoughts to me.

Singh continues. "I think it is time to follow through on that proposal. We need more supplies from Earth, and there are plenty of usable materials lying untouched there. We should utilize that resource. In our last Council meeting, Supervisor Ahmad spoke of the need for more raw materials to supply the Maint division. Supervisor Pursch detailed how Fabrication, now operating under Limited Allotment, is poised to progress to Austerity in the next century. My own project—a modest horticulture operation to revive our seed bank specimens and discover unique new cultivars—is in desperate need of not only building materials but also soil and water."

It's unpleasant to see how far things have progressed in my absence. Ordinarily Council meetings are fruitless and accomplish so little. Years pass with no real movement.

But no one raises any objections as Singh continues. "Supervisor Ahmad's suggestion to dismantle unused sections of Station is a helpful one that will delay our most dire need, but meanwhile I propose we proceed immediately with the plan to ready drones for collection from Earth."

This is an idea I have objected to before, though I've never heard Singh state it so boldly. I feel strongly that our job is to preserve Earth for humans, not to use Earth's resources to support ourselves. We are nearing the end of our usefulness. Human civilization on Earth is just now poised to blossom. However, I do not even consider standing to object. My position here is tenuous. My own injury is clearly considered evidence in support of this new plan.

"I wish to clarify my position." Blake Ahmad from Maint stands calmly. "It is true I spoke about my division's need for more supplies, but it is my opinion that re-purposing unused portions of Station will be sufficient to sustain our operations for quite some time. I simply seek permission to begin the process."

Andrej stands with more energy, and my concern dwindles. If there's anyone who would object more strongly than I, it is the stationer who adheres to the very strictest reading of our Mission Scope statement.

"Mission Imperatives state clearly drones are to be used to harvest biomass from the ocean to support stationer nutritional needs. Only that, and nothing more. Station was conceived to support Earth, not harvest from it. That is outside the scope of our mission and antithetical to our objectives."

Andrej sits down with finality. I think a smile in my mind at eir predictable reaction.

Andrej's official agenda often aligns with my own, though we don't always agree on details. Eir oddities are known and tolerated, considered helpful, even. My own peculiar convictions would not be so well received.

Wenslow Pursch stands and receives a nod from Guadalupe before proceeding. "As Blake has done, I will clarify my position. I fully support the plan to send drones to harvest the unpopulated wastes of the old ruined cities on Earth. We cannot achieve our directives, Andrej, if Station comes apart in orbit. We must be flexible and adapt to the current state of things perhaps not considered by the original architects of Station. Fabrication volunteers to spec out some drones so Council may see what it will entail and whether this body deems it a worthy plan."

Eir eyes travel slowly over all assembled, as if ey's inviting them to agree with em.

No one raises any objections, at least. Ey says with calm confidence, "I will have Sophia take a crew and, in cooperation with Dr. Singh and an appointee from Maint, compose a report of what will be needed."

Sophia Kim, who sits near Jayd, stands, nods curtly, and sits back down.

Guadalupe returns eir attention to the Council Hall. "Very well. Let's put it to vote, please. In a moment I will ask those in favor of Fabrication's investigation to stand. Those who oppose the investigation may remain seated. If the motion passes, we will reconvene in one Earth year to review the findings and determine our next course of action."

Ey turns eir attention to eir log, allowing stationers time to decide.

"Alright," ey says a few moments later. "Let's vote. The burden, as usual, is on the action. If the action does not receive majority, it cannot pass. All those in favor of Fabrication's investigation into the material needs of Fabrication, Maint, and Dr. Singh's horticulture project, please stand."

I'm not surprised everyone in Med stands. There's only three of them, anyway. I *am* surprised all of Fabrication stands. Well, Jayd doesn't stand but no one remembers a time when ey hasn't abstained from every vote. About half of Maint stands, half of Flight. It doesn't even matter whether I stand, as the motion has essentially already passed.

And passed handily. A feat, considering how hard it is to get a majority behind any action. Stationers would usually prefer to privately pursue their own interests. No one ever wants to do anything. That is why it's so frustrating trying to get Council to agree to a survey.

"That was unexpected," I say quietly to Jayd as we file out. I've waited for em just beyond the door.

Ey gives a barely perceptible shrug. Soon we are alone in the corridor leading back to eir cell.

"What's going on in Fabrication?" I ask as we enter eir cell. "I didn't expect them all to stand so unified. Did Wenslow anticipate this vote and persuade you all?"

"No one spoke to me," Jayd says, which is hardly surprising. No one would bother with em.

Ey walks to eir brushes and readies some paints. I sit on eir bed and tilt my head up to look at the ceiling. It hasn't been covered in eir latest Pointillism work, it's still a Batuan style Balinese painting I remember em working on previous to my last survey.

I consider. "Maybe they just want something interesting to do."

"That's Sky Peace talking," Jayd says, only half eir attention on me. "Stationers aren't bored."

I don't correct eir incorrect usage of Earth languages. And I certainly don't argue that if stationers had something more interesting to do, maybe we wouldn't all be hopelessly stuck in our endless behavioral loops.

Instead I ask, "Then why?"

Ey gives the slightest shake of eir head.

"I know you don't care, Jayd. But you know that I do."

"Why should you care?" ey asks. Eir face is inches from the wall, eir hand poised, as ey prepares to paint.

"Because it concerns Earth. You know my fixation."

Jayd sighs. "Now you're hiding behind that term. I wish I hadn't given it to you."

"Andrej is right, Jayd. We're meant to support Earth, not steal their resources to support ourselves. Singh hides eir personal fixation on gardening under the guise of fulfilling some directive to benefit humans."

"The seed vault exists to preserve heirloom crops for humans. That's its purpose," Jayd says.

Ey is right, of course. But I'm no longer convinced Earth needs our heirloom crops. I think about the bounty under the dome, plantains and taro, cacao and ginger. In the drylands the Intha grow dandelions, collards, chilis. All these life-giving crops, already thriving on Earth, already adapted to current conditions, already integrated into the environment. If the groups were to exchange seeds, each would benefit.

"I can't help but feel Singh has another agenda," I say.

"Talk to Singh," Jayd suggests.

"I will talk to Singh. But I thought you'd have some insight into Fabrication's support of eir project. You work there."

Ey is too absorbed in placing a point of paint with eir brush to answer.

"Your nihilism is making this difficult, Jayd," I say.

Ey places the point and straightens up to look at me. "Making what difficult? What is it you're in such a hurry to do?"

"And now you care what I'm doing?"

"You're making *this* difficult." Ey gestures to the spot ey's painting and raises an eyebrow at me.

Which is almost like being shouted at by em.

I get up to leave. "I want to find out how I was injured, Jayd. But I can't focus on that while Station plots to strip Earth of resources. I can't let that continue unaddressed."

"Then go and address it." Ey turns back to eir painting.

I stalk out eir door.

* * *

I request an appointment to see Dr. Singh, who replies with a date in two months' time. If I am to uncover why Singh is so eager to send drones to Earth, and to glean whether Singh eirself ever expected me to come back from Survey, I will have to appear disinterested in the very answers I seek. Importantly, I must also avoid any obvious miscues when talking with a member of Med.

Med expects our Reform process will be imperfect. Some data is lost during transfer of consciousness, and that is why we relearn things after we Reform. However, too many memory lapses, too many irrational thoughts or theories, and a stationer may be diagnosed with an excess of Reform faults. Few things on Station are more guaranteed to strip you of any power or agency. We cannot allow faulty stationers to guide our mission, and there is no known treatment. You cannot recover the data from dead neural tissue.

So it will help my cause to be exceptionally unexceptional when I talk to Singh. When it is time, I pause by the plaque outside eir door—my ritual, to help me prepare myself.

Dr. Marinne Singh.

A fat baby laughing in a bath. A young girl attending a large wedding dressed in colorful wraps. A young woman in black robes at a graduation ceremony of thousands. A grown woman in a white coat with a surgical mask over eir face, stainless tools in eir delicate hands.

Singh opens to my knock and invites me in with wave.

"I'm sorry I could not see you right away, Donna," ey says. "Many stationers have wanted to meet with me about my horticulture project, and I also meet with Sophia's crew researching drones regularly. I'm very busy."

Although eir face is habitually neutral, like all of us, eir diction is a little more personable. Everyone in Med is just a fraction more human than other stationers. There have been times I've found it annoying, and times, after a survey, that it feels comfortingly familiar.

"I look forward to working closely with you on this project," ey continues. "I could use your input, as the only surveyor, on surface conditions and hazards."

"There are many variables to consider," I say neutrally.

"Of course there are. You may want to get a report together on the things we should take into account."

"I did not realize the scope of your horticulture project," I say, hoping ey will be happy to talk about eir fixation, and I might understand better what ey is hoping to achieve.

"Ah, but you do. Or you *did*, Donna. We talked about it extensively before your last survey, and you were so keen to get down to the surface and see what you could do to support the project."

I pause before I react. This is a worrisome miscue, a dangerously large hole in recent memory. I also find it personally unsettling to be told things about myself I don't remember.

To cover my deficiency, I craft the most uninformative response to Singh's statement I possibly can. "I have not seen how it has grown since then."

As we walk down the corridor to Singh's repurposed growing room, I wonder why I was so eager to help Singh before. Because I feel an instinctive distaste for the idea now.

Singh opens a door onto a great long room, which has had interior walls removed. Mismatched tables—obviously borrowed from other applications—are arranged under warm lights. Each has rows of pots, and plants of all shapes, some vibrant looking and others limp or yellowed.

The sight is not surprising to me. I have been here before, and I breathe in deeply like reaching for a pleasant memory.

The air feels fresh. Nothing like the thick, pungent air under the dome, but richer and cleaner than stale Station air.

Singh walks down among the aisles, brushing eir hands gently over the ragged leaves.

"They struggle," ey says. "Old Earth cultivars are not made to survive the current surface conditions of drought, increased solar radiation, and poor soils. But if I can engineer them to be heartier, think what we can achieve. Guadalupe looks forward to sampling heirloom tea varieties."

"The purpose of the seed vault is to preserve crops *for Earth*," I say sternly before I can stop myself, sounding like Andrej. I wonder if ey's seen this place, and what ey would think of it.

"Yes. You know that is my chief concern. That is why I want to make these crops better. To breed new varieties that will spread over the surface and make arid places lush again. Pity we only have crop species in the seed vault. Imagine what might be achieved with samples from all the old Earth biomes. What might I engineer with those utilizing current gene alteration techniques?"

I have a terrible vision of new, unnatural things spreading over Earth's surface, crowding out what thrives there now, interacting in unknown ways and bringing Earth's fragile ecosystems crashing down.

I say, "Surely the best way to fulfill Station's original purpose is to simply transfer the seeds as they are to Earth settlements?"

"Simply? It is not so simple at all, Donna. There is so much to consider. Could the crops survive and what will be their yield? To whom should they be transferred? Is the proper infrastructure in place to support large-scale crop cultivation? Many of these concerns were brought to my attention by *you yourself*, Donna."

I feel eir eyes on me, and I'm conscious of a second glaring miscue.

"The more I see of Earth," I say, "the more confidence I have in the people there to conduct their own affairs. And the less confidence I have that stationers can navigate the political and biological hurdles to successful reintroduction."

"You no longer fear the Intha will seize control of all resources by force? Or the biodome will be unable to accommodate new species?"

I am quiet as I look out over the horticulture room. Those sound exactly like concerns I would raise. They feel familiar and true. Was I previously in favor of Singh's plans to raise new and modified crops on Station and to scavenge the surface for parts to do it? Why then do I feel so deeply opposed to it now?

This whole scheme of Singh's, which Fabrication seems to heartily support, feels inherently wrong to me. I agree with Andrej that it is antithetical to our whole mission here on Station. We are not to remake Earth. We are to simply support it as it grows.

I have been quiet overlong now, and Singh is watching me carefully. "During my survey," I say evenly, "I learned many things. My understanding of Earth, and the social and political systems there, continues to evolve."

"I haven't seen your survey report yet," Singh says.

"I haven't made it."

"You did not achieve the survey objective." It's not phrased as a question.

"I did not travel to Salvage, no. I went under the dome."

"Why?"

"I received my head injury before I could achieve any objectives. While on the surface I was temporarily disoriented."

It's a gross understatement of my symptoms, which included significant memory loss, persistent disequilibrium, difficulty in processing speech, and an impaired surveyor datalink, not to mention continuing tissue decay. Because the trauma of my injury undoubtedly caused many Reform faults, I don't want to discuss the details with the doctor. Although it was em who treated me on my return, so ey most likely already knows.

Singh nods gravely. "It was very serious. Only the regenerative capabilities of a surveyor shell kept you functional." Ey pauses for a moment, watching me. "How were you hurt?"

This is precisely what I wish to discover, but I try not to jump too eagerly into the conversation. "I don't know. I have no memory of that. You're familiar with surveyor shells. How could such a wound have been made?"

"Discrete penetrating trauma to the upper temporal region of the skull." Ey goes still, accessing eir Med-privilege datalink. "Well, perhaps the shuttle was damaged on landing? There was some malfunction?"

The idea immediately takes hold. It seems quite plausible.

But before I can agree, Singh appears to discard that explanation and lands on another. "Are there any projectile weapons on Earth? Anything that would fling a small, dense object?"

I access my own datalink, compare it to my memories from Earth. There were crossbows and pikes, there were rocks to sling and spears to hurl. Certainly it is possible, though most people fear to act violently toward the Peace-in-the-Sky or godshard. They are not aware of the capabilities and shortcomings of a surveyor shell, knowing only the figures of their legends can at times aggressively protect themselves.

I am reluctant to imply the people of Earth may be dangerous, however. "I don't believe I was attacked," I say cautiously.

Singh muses, "The Intha in particular are known to be a rough group, are they not? And it was them you intended to interact with. You know the response beam cannot target a projectile; it only protects your shell from being handled roughly. A design flaw, in my opinion."

With my Survey-privilege I understand why shells cannot be protected from that kind of damage. But I also know my first memories of my last survey are of being held captive by the Intha. I regained consciousness in a cage of their design, with Anissa by my side.

The Intha *are* a rough group. Being excluded from the bounty under the dome has made them covetous and angry. Vilifying them will not solve that problem, however.

"I have no reason to believe such a thing happened," I tell Singh. "Without any intact memories of the incident, I can only speculate."

Singh leads me back out of eir horticulture space and into the corridor. "Yes, speculation seems unnecessary. But we can focus on moving forward with a safer method of planetary exploration. Instead of spending time on a frustratingly fragmented survey report, why don't you prepare the report I suggested on possible surface hazards to drone reconnaissance? I would be happy to accept the latter in place of the former."

I hesitate to agree, and Singh encourages, "It might save you headaches both literal and figurative."

"Fortunately, I have experienced no headaches," I assure em. "Thank you for meeting with me, Dr. Singh, I know you are busy."

* * *

I walk down the corridor, too quickly for a stationer, eager to escape any more scrutiny of my behavior. Back at my cell I sit on my cot and can finally consider what Singh has said.

Ey is certainly taking every opportunity to turn my injury and memory loss to eir advantage, unremarkable for any stationer with single-minded determination to see their private project advanced. Ey concluded, prematurely I think, that I should give up any investigation into how I was hurt, but at least ey was willing to consider the question at all. When I returned from Earth so very damaged, I'm certain it required quite a bit of medical skill to preserve and Reform my neurocircuitry. Singh must have worked quite hard to save me.

But that doesn't mean ey is thinking clearly about my injury. I wonder if ey erroneously dismissed the idea of my pod malfunctioning? I decide to follow up on that angle on my own. Presumably my landing pod is still on the surface. Presumably it sent data about its trip and landing back to Station, or it still has that data onboard.

A Records clerk would need permission from the commissioners to access that data. But someone with a Flight-privilege datalink could see it. So now I need to find someone from Flight willing to put aside their own interests long enough to help me. Raina might help me, but eir attention is always so fractured. Sasha is the clear choice. If I can find a way to start the conversation.

* * *

Sasha actively avoids contact with other stationers. Ey would not respond to a request to meet and may not even answer a buzz at eir door if I showed up in person. A stationer would be patient, so I resolve to wait until we cross paths naturally. Perhaps I linger longer than usual entering and exiting Condition and Nutrition, where ey surely must spend time, but I try not to be unnatural. Finally, I am rewarded as I see Sasha exiting Nutri after a meal.

I give up any intention of collecting a ration from Nutri myself in favor of speaking with em.

"Hello, Sasha."

No answer. Eir eyes pass over my face and away.

"I'd like to speak with you."

Sasha's slow, deliberate gait doesn't falter. Ey makes no objection, so I fall in line, and we proceed down the hall. We pass Flight command center where I know all the pods to be docked. Beyond the doors of the Flight Bay it is dead and empty, as if no one enters unless a Survey launch is imminent.

Sasha's cell is on a corridor just beyond, and I pause outside the door to watch the playback.

The plaque reads *Sasha Galanis.*

A squirming baby lying on a blanket in the grass. A child in a sandbox intent on a sandcastle despite the rowdy children all around. A young person hiking a wilderness trail wearing a large, bulky pack. A cadet in uniform standing expressionlessly in front of a military plane.

"Why do you watch that?" Sasha finally speaks in a strained, whispery voice.

"I don't know," I say. "Do you think they're authentic?"

"No."

I accompany eir through the doorway. The cell inside is completely empty. There is nothing there. It is a featureless white cube.

Sasha walks to the very center and sits cross-legged on the floor. The white in that spot has worn dull.

"Will you speak with me? I know you don't like to," I say.

"It is not a question of 'liking.'"

"I want to know some things about shuttle pods. How they operate. I need someone with a Flight-privilege datalink to give me an opinion."

"The information is available in Records to a stationer with Records-privilege."

"If it was simply a question of going to Records, I would not be here," I say truthfully. "There are others in Flight I could have asked. But I wanted your analytical, clear-thinking response."

For the first time Sasha's eyes focus on me, meeting my gaze.

"Ask then."

"During my last survey I received a serious head injury, and I don't recall how it happened. Is it possible I could have been damaged in the shuttle pod during a rough landing?"

"No."

"Are you sure? What if there was a malfunction?"

"It's not possible."

"Can you access my shuttle pod still on the surface? Is it intact?"

A longer pause. "Yes. No error reports. It is not damaged."

"Maybe some atmospheric turbulence caused me to be thrown about inside the pod without causing any damage to the shuttle itself."

"No. The pods are very safe. Only these conditions may cause damage to the passenger inside: thermonuclear detonation of greater than 80 terajoules, a solar coronal mass ejection with DT equals minus 800 nanoTesla, an antimatter containment failure resulting in…"

I interrupt what is obviously a direct recitation from the manual. "No, not that sort of damage. A discrete, localized injury to the head."

"If you were secured properly that's impossible, Donna." I'm surprised Sasha remembers my name. I take the use of it to mean the conversation is starting to wear. But I have a new idea.

"What if I was not secured properly?"

Sasha considers carefully and speaks slowly. "Failure to secure the shell properly reportedly would result in injuries such as torn axial muscles, crushed bones in the limbs, or oxygen debt in the brain if the mask is not properly fitted."

That doesn't sound like what happened to me. "Your opinion?"

"I think it's unlikely. The shuttle pod will not launch if its sensors indicate the pod restraints are improperly secured, though of course there are limitations to its sensors. It's policy for at least two technicians be on hand during loading to ensure it's done properly."

"Ah. Then I need to know who was present during the loading for my last survey."

"You suspect someone of negligence."

I don't answer right away.

"No. You suspect someone of sabotage."

"There's no evidence of that. No reason to think…"

"Yet you do."

"Do you know who was present?" I ask.

"You could find out in Records or from someone with a Med-privilege datalink."

"Thank you, Sasha." I move toward the door. "I'm glad I talked with you."

"Insight comes from within." Sasha shifts to sit with palms turned up on folded knees, back straight, eyes drifting to half-closed. "Be careful interacting too much with other stationers, particularly those that are faulty. It leads to imbalance."

I leave. It's an ironic closing statement from the stationer most often considered to have excessive Reform faults. After the second mass die-off, it was Sasha who suggested we would be safer not interacting with each other, and the whole of Med disagreed strongly, saying isolation was dangerous. When Sasha went into voluntary solitary confinement, Flight supervisor Ito revoked eir Flight-privilege and Med sent a grounding order. Eir datalink wasn't terminated, thankfully, or I wouldn't have had such an illuminating conversation today.

And a troubling one. Fortunately nothing we said will be repeated to another stationer, or else I risk others thinking I myself must also be faulty. Sasha's conjecture is quite true. I admit to myself I do still believe another stationer deliberately caused me harm. I am becoming more determined to find proof of it. I still don't know why I believe this, but the atmosphere of furtive plans and hidden agendas on board Station is not helping my growing distrust.

Despite Sasha saying that improper restraint was unlikely to cause the kind of injury my shell sustained, I still want to learn everything I can about my launch. If a stationer was to do me harm, that would be the easiest way to do it.

It's time to visit Records again.

* * *

Dr. Singh, eir assistant Shelley, and Koni Odom from Maint were present when I was fitted into the pod. There's no visual in Flight, only audio. I listen to it over and over, but we say almost nothing. I hear the mechanical sounds of being fitted into the pod, and the pod being fitted within the shuttle. Singh and Koni exchange a few words about the harnesses or the latches. Neither Shelley nor Peace-in-the-Sky speak. Guadalupe says I sent a request to em before leaving that was never answered, but of course that would be a silent interaction on the datalink and nothing I could hear.

If someone there tampered with the pod, they did it silently and without the other two noticing, and the shuttle never registered the problem during its flight or landing. And there's no possible way the stationers present could have failed to see me knock myself insensible on the side of the pod while climbing aboard, or some other similar and implausible mishap. It feels like a disappointing dead end. I was foolish to hope for answers from this data.

I do wonder if it's odd someone from Maint is present, so I check other shuttle pod preparations from the past. Singh is usually there, and sometimes Shelley, and often someone from Flight or Survey. But why Koni?

It may be a trivial detail, but it's the only interesting fact I turned up, so I consider speaking directly with Koni. Ey is not isolated as Sasha is, so I will have to approach em carefully as I did Singh. If stationers discover I am investigating what I fear is my own attempted murder, I will quickly find myself in Med with presumed Reform faults. My opinions on any further projects on Earth will count for nothing, my concerns will be dismissed, and I will certainly never be approved for another survey.

It is not a happy thought, and I don't relish approaching Koni. I am not sure what I would ask em. Instead, I become distracted researching Earth projectile weapons and the forces they can generate. Singh's favored suggestion does admittedly seem to be the most likely scenario, no matter how much I may *feel* it to be incorrect.

And while I am spending time in Records, there is so much to learn about the introduction of novel or genetically modified species to new environments. The tremendous potential of it—disease resistant new crop varieties credited with saving great numbers from famine. And the catastrophic consequences when it went awry—gene edited wasps meant to wipe out an invasive population on an island that escaped, causing the global extinction of multiple key pollinator species. The cascading effects can be unpredictable, multi-pronged, and devastating.

It would take me years of study to come to some meaningful understanding of the history here, first having to educate myself within the fields of agriculture and ecology and genetics. But I do not like the implications for Singh's plan to introduce genetically modified plant species on Earth. There are too many variables to consider, and I do not think anyone on Station has any interest in considering them.

* * *

When I get the notification for another Council meeting, I pull myself away from my research and check my datalink for a time stamp. How is it possible so much time has passed already? How long did I spend in Condition exercising this shell? Sitting on Jayd's cot watching em paint? How much time have I spent sitting in this very chair, my eyes scanning words on the screen?

Humans are so busy, so industrious. But stationers lose so much time wandering around inside our own heads, preoccupied with a thousand small, disconnected lines of inquiry and irrelevant tasks which accomplish nothing of importance. I am losing time like a stationer again, and meanwhile years are sliding by on Earth.

* * *

The Council meeting is opened by Darius Jallow, from Maint, who plays a violin sonata. I find it to be rather disjointed; chosen more for its technical difficulty than its beauty to the casual listener. But I enjoy music more than any other cultural or historical piece Guadalupe chooses for opening.

I watch Jayd across the chamber during the recital, see em sitting between two empty seats. Eir eyes are closed while ey listens. And I feel a brief stab of kinship. Like something I would have felt on Earth, when I had forgotten I wasn't supposed to feel those things.

If only I had remembered I wasn't supposed to love Anissa so completely, with every fiber of my heart. I am drowning in loss while Darius plays.

And finally, it's done.

Finally, Guadalupe calls the meeting to order. I attempt to pull myself together and focus.

Sophia from Fabrication is introduced and ey presents the report ey was volunteered for at the last Council meeting. The information displays behind Guadalupe on the large screen. There are lists of material needed by the different divisions, with some speculation on where or how those things might be obtained on Earth, or fabricated from raw materials there. More importantly there are materials lists for the drones themselves, with some highlighted as currently unavailable.

Wenslow Pursch, supervisor of Fabrication, stands. "I took some time to review Sophia's report before the meeting, and I believe we would have to start the operation small, and then scale up as we harvest more parts to make bigger, more efficient drones which can seek and collect more materials."

Blake from Maint stands. "No one from my team was involved with this report. I cannot speak to the feasibility of accomplishing this." I gather ey is not happy with the fast pace of this new project.

My eyes travel down the line of stationers in Maint, looking for Koni Odom, who was present when Peace-in-the-Sky was sent to Earth. And just as my eyes find em, I see em subtly nudge the stationer next to em.

In response, Nauja Holm stands. "I volunteer to review the plans carefully. However, I see nothing listed there now beyond our abilities."

My eyes shoot back down the line to see how Blake, their supervisor, responds to one of eir crew answering for em. Do I just imagine a narrowing of the eyes?

"Excellent," says Guadalupe. Ey seems satisfied with this outcome. "I'll open the floor to any last points anyone may wish to raise, and then we'll put it to a vote."

I am shocked things are coming to a head so fast. Both Andrej and even Timothy Ju, the Survey supervisor who detests speaking in front of others, rise to offer their perspectives. They present facts in strong language but fail to offer any strong opinion, and Guadalupe nods and thanks them for the information, and proceeds to ignore the objections at the heart of their comments. Wenslow asks some questions in a concerned, thoughtful tone, which either Singh or a member of eir own team answers to eir satisfaction. A few others rise and make short speeches without seeming to express any sort of opinion. And this is how stationers usually behave in Council, and why everything takes so long to hash out, but not this meeting. At this meeting there are strong opinions and those look likely to carry the day.

I am flailing, considering raising an objection of my own but not sure what to base it on, when Guadalupe calls on me.

"Surveyor Whitacre, what is the current situation on Earth regarding the dangers of mining the remains of human cities?"

I begin speaking without knowing what I'm going to say.

"The Intha routinely travel into the areas they call Salvage to access resources from the ruined cities. For them it is very dangerous. Radioactive asteroid debris is still present in these areas, and the ruins themselves are structurally unsound, prone to collapse. Despite all this, the Intha derive most of their wealth as a people from these expeditions..."

I'm not certain why I focus on the Intha and their livelihood, as no one on Station cares much for their plight and many wish them gone.

"Yes," Guadalupe interrupts me, "there are certainly dangers to human salvagers, but are there any hazards the terrain offers which may specifically hinder remotely operated vehicles? What did you observe while you were most recently there?"

I am momentarily silent, at a loss, when Dr. Singh comes to my rescue.

"Donna was injured on eir last survey, as many have heard," Singh says. "Ey was not able to complete the assigned survey task. It's best for eir mental health and Reform recovery not to prompt Donna to recall what ey experienced."

I sit, stunned. Singh has not rescued me at all but exposed me. It feels as though ey stopped just short of announcing I am overcome by Reform faults. For a member of Med to say that...for Dr. Singh *eirself* to say that aloud in a Council meeting...

I am only marginally aware of the vote being called, the motion passing, and Fabrication receiving their orders to begin construction of a drone prototype.

We all file out. I carefully avoid eye contact with other stationers.

I'm waiting impatiently for Jayd when I look up and meet Wenslow's gaze, the supervisor of Fabrication. I know em, of course, but we have not spoken often.

"Donna," ey says. "I was sorry to hear about your injury. We rely on your considerable expertise, it's a shame you are still suffering from memory loss."

For a moment longer, we look at each other. Eir expression is open and relaxed. I see Jayd pass us by over Wenslow's shoulder.

I try to make some reply. "The important details are still available in Records, regardless of what I remember. And whatever memory disruption I experienced is in the past."

"But you haven't made a report this time? I looked for it. It would have had so much bearing on our agenda today."

Singh joins us, with Shelley behind em.

"Wenslow, don't press em," Singh interrupts. "What damage is done, is done."

"I am competent to do my job," I tell them, my voice a touch too loud. A few stationers passing by us glance over with their impassive eyes, but I know they've heard.

Wenslow looks at me with the mildest of surprise and waits for me to clarify or expand on my point, but I know better than to continue talking. I'll only make things worse. I feel betrayed and trapped.

I nod at Singh and Wenslow and leave them.

* * *

I go directly to Jayd's room. Finding it empty is another unpleasant shock. Surely ey would understand the import of what just happened to me? Surely ey would understand I need to speak with em right away?

I try to return to my own cell, but I'm caught by Raina in our corridor.

"Did you like Darius' solo?" ey asks in passing.

"Yes." I avert my gaze so I won't have to watch eir expressions.

"I liked it, too. Music definitely evokes something."

Ey pauses.

"Better than words, sometimes." There's a genuine tone in eir voice.

I see eir face is utterly neutral. A sign, I think, ey is truly feeling something. I don't dislike Raina, although ey often annoys me. I think ey does feel. But when ey paints such a garish face on it, it turns false somehow.

"It was kind of Dr. Singh to explain your condition so delicately," Raina continues. "I saw how impaired you were in that broken shell, but I don't think other stationers quite understand the extent of the damage."

"I am no longer in that shell," I say too quickly. "And I am *not* pleased to be considered damaged, and I resent Singh's public implication that I continue to suffer from so many Reform faults."

Raina pauses before responding.

"You *were* damaged, Donna. Badly. You know that."

"It's not a topic for discussion at a Council meeting. And I don't appreciate supervisors approaching me afterward for details. Did you see Wenslow and Singh speaking with me?

Stationers do not loiter in the corridors after a Council meeting like that."

Raina says, "You often wait for Jayd."

It is a jarringly true statement.

"Not to corner em about something said in Council," I retort.

"But why? It's unusual to show such preference. You're not yourself, Donna. And that's natural after a survey. But this time you don't seem to be recovering. Have you considered talking with counselor Ernesta? You know surveyor attrition rate is high."

I have considered seeing Ernesta. But I don't tell Raina that. In fact, I've already said far too much to em. To everyone.

"I'll take it under consideration," I say, and retreat to my cell.

Jayd is not there, as I had briefly hoped. But then, when has ey come to see me? I cannot recall that ey ever has. I forbid myself to entertain the thought Jayd might be avoiding me.

I am too distraught over Singh's public statement to think clearly. Just a casual mention from Singh, couched in terms of protecting me, has exposed me to censure and suspicion.

Despite eir pretense of protecting my mental health, I cannot help but believe Singh wishes to discredit me. Ey saw my distinct lack of support for eir project, and ey must suspect I do not support eir plans to send drones to the surface to gather materials. And despite claiming I supported em in the past, ey definitely still spoke as though ey was trying to persuade me. Maybe I hadn't been in agreement with em as much as ey implied or wished. Since I cannot remember, I cannot say.

I should not have gone to see Singh. I was not as clever and careful, it appears, as I had hoped to be. Just because stationers are self-involved and fixated does not mean they are so obsessed they cannot see what I do.

If I voice my unpopular opinions on the drone project in Council, if Singh will even allow me to, what will Station make of me? Singh and Wenslow, Sasha and Raina already seem to question if I am faulty.

And why should Raina notice or care if I wait for Jayd? What has that to do with anything?

I recognize I am spiraling, and I stop myself. Just as everyone has reminded me, it is natural to come back from Survey thinking, feeling, and experiencing time more like a human does. But now I am Reformed into a stationer shell, living among fellow stationers, and I should be returning to myself. Instead, I am opposing stationers' pet plans for reasons I have not adequately articulated, pursuing an unsubstantiated personal theory, and inviting distrust and censure.

What is keeping me from becoming a stationer again? If it is my love for Anissa...but then, I don't want to lose that. I can't lose that.

Part Two

I keep to myself. I do not make an appointment with Ernesta. I do not query Singh or Wenslow or Guadalupe or Koni or Sasha. I do not visit Jayd.

Instead, I find the echoing, empty places on Station. There are so many deserted corridors and abandoned rooms. It is easy to be alone.

I rediscover the observation lounge and sit in the dusty seats and look down on Earth spinning below us. I dredge from my memory the names of the continents and oceans and seas, the mountain ranges and peninsulas and straits. I pinpoint where the biodome sits, though I cannot resolve it at this distance.

Is Anissa still there? Is she grown now? Time rushes by on Earth for people with short lives. They have so much to do to survive and grow and flourish and make more of themselves before they finally rest forever. Here on Station, we have nothing to do but wait. And it takes forever.

* * *

I still want to know how I was injured, but I have to admit Dr. Singh was probably right. I must have been hit by some projectile on Earth. Perhaps it was an accident. Reluctant as I am to accept that explanation, I have no proof it was otherwise. I fear further attempts at investigation will only contribute to the growing perception that I am faulty.

I try to refocus my thoughts on Council meetings, and on what they plan for Earth. At this distance, Earth appears a huge juggernaut of a planet, filling the viewing screen, inevitable and everlasting. But I know the life clinging to its surface is vulnerable.

The more I come to watch the Earth, the more I want to protect what's there. I want to protect it from us.

At first, I was too overwhelmed by the opposition. Stationers seem so supportive of the project to send drones to Earth, it feels like a momentum I cannot check. Especially as I am in a bad position to speak out.

But I suppose that just means I will need allies. I consider my options. Blake Ahmad, Timothy Ju, and Andrej Vann are those who have most visibly expressed their concern for the project. Blake and Timothy are supervisors and less likely to collaborate with me. Andrej, however, is the obvious choice to approach first. Andrej and I have history.

I remember a century ago em coming to see me, tight-jawed and severe, and proposing ey join Records as a clerk. Ey had valued my opinion then. Ey had wanted to know if I thought such a move would run counter to our Mission Scope. And I had been only too glad to welcome em to Records, and had felt a compelling desire to take eir place as a surveyor. It had been so important to us both not to abuse the power being stationers had granted us. Earth's recovery and human survival were paramount in our thoughts.

It's true Andrej favors a more hands-off approach to our mission, to observe from afar and interfere only in an emergency. And I prefer to go on Survey, observe first-hand human progress, and help directly with smaller-scale problems. But both of those approaches are acceptable within the framework of our Mission Imperatives, so I feel we have common ground.

* * *

I consult my datalink to find Andrej's cell. We were never in the habit of visiting personally. We spoke in subgroups and committees and informal assemblies that have long since been dissolved or forgotten.

Eir playback is not very interesting.

A bright red squalling baby is held carefully between two tiredly fond women. A pale boy rides a bicycle down the middle of a quiet street. A young man sits alone at a darkened bar with a mug of beer in eir hand. A man in a helmet races a car around a track, eir face impassive despite the speed.

I am confident every clip in eir playback shows the same person, as they all look almost perfectly alike. Only the hair changes.

I buzz.

The door opens and Andrej slides through, letting the door close behind em. We stand facing each other in the corridor. This is unexpected enough that I pause, and Andrej speaks first.

"You don't have an appointment," ey says.

"It's not necessary to make an appointment to see a Records clerk," I reply with some confusion.

"What is your business?"

"I wanted to talk to you about the plan to send drones to Earth to harvest materials—"

Andrej cuts in, "I have no wish to participate in that project."

"Neither do I," I say. "But without our input—"

Ey cuts in again, more sharply. "Then why are we discussing the project?"

"Perhaps to thwart it?" I don't want to be so explicit, but ey doesn't leave a lot of room to approach it delicately.

"I will oppose it in Council at every opportunity. You should do the same, as it is in direct conflict with the spirit of the Mission Imperatives."

I say, "We *have* opposed it in Council, but it continues unhindered. I thought if we discussed it beforehand, we might develop our understanding of what's at stake and be better prepared to defend our position."

Ey bristles. "*Our* position? Are you proposing a clandestine alliance? That is both unnatural and inappropriate."

"Andrej, once we were allies. Do you not remember when we switched jobs? How carefully we considered the implications?"

"We have worked together in the past, Donna," ey says, with less umbrage than before. "I will appreciate hearing your voice join with mine in Council to oppose this new project. But you are acting irregularly. You haven't made your survey report though you've been returned from Survey for years. You are silent in Council, but you approach me to conspire on our opinions. This is not behavior I expect from you. I don't wish to continue this conversation."

Andrej steps away from me, eir back to the cell door. But ey doesn't open the door. Ey waits for me to leave. I have em trapped.

So I try again. "What would convince you to work with me?"

Andrej is silent for a moment, either considering or simply balking at the question.

I ask, "Is it making you anxious that there's a blank where my survey report should be? Would you feel better if I filled that space?"

Eir jaw muscles tighten. "I am not accustomed to being asked about 'feelings.' You should speak with the counselor. And obviously I am concerned about incompleteness in Records, Donna. You should be, too. You should do your job and write your report."

I try to suppress any outward signs of impatience. "You want me to see Ernesta and write my report. If I do these things, would you attend an informal committee meeting of stationers concerned about recent changes to mission objectives?"

"I cannot say what I will do. If you had permission to form such a committee, and I received an invitation, I would consider it."

"Thank you for speaking with me," I say. "I consider it a mark of our..." I'm not certain how to characterize our relationship. "...A mark of your professional trust in me that you will hear my concerns. I will be in touch at a later time."

"If you visit again, I expect a notification."

If I had been expecting a reciprocal declaration of trust or regard, it would have been in vain. So I simply nod and leave Andrej standing alone in eir corridor.

* * *

I now have a list of specific tasks to accomplish. I must see Ernesta. Enough people have urged me to that if I do not, it will seem like I am intentionally avoiding it. I cannot put it off any longer.

And I must do something about that report. I try to convince myself filing the report does not mean the matter of my injury is closed. I will include a disclaimer or postscript promising a later addendum. It is not what I wanted, but it will contribute to the impression that I am sound and operating normally.

And I must try to get permission from Guadalupe to form a working committee. If I can recruit to our cause everyone from Survey and Records, which is really only a handful, Blake Ahmad can recruit some from Maint, and Timothy Ju some from Flight, then perhaps our concerns will gain some traction. And others can speak out when I don't dare to.

I'm not certain how Guadalupe will respond, whether ey will welcome differing opinions, or whether ey is sufficiently invested in the new project to find bureaucratic hurdles for me to clear. I don't relish finding out. I realize I have been harboring a notion that Guadalupe is on my side and would help me as much as ey could while still maintaining the appearance of neutrality. I should be careful about such subconscious assumptions.

* * *

I reluctantly send the counselor Ernesta a request for an appointment. It's only a matter of hours before ey replies, with a meeting time only a week away. It is unusually quick for a stationer to respond, and my apprehension about speaking with em marginally increases.

While I wait for my appointment, I work on completing a report, one of the most hastily written and factually vague things I have ever composed. I wince after every painful paragraph, then distract myself with reviewing records which may be pertinent to a committee.

I think it would be helpful to do a thorough re-read of the Mission Imperatives and all their many jargon-heavy subsections. And to find the Surface Dictums surveyors follow, which no one else seems to remember, and understand them in their fullest form. I get lost in tangential lines of inquiry, following every footnote and checking every reference. But I cannot find the record detailing the Surface Dictums. I invoke my fullest Records-privilege access and search everywhere. I go through Survey requirements and directives. Nothing.

I pause to recall the Dictums in my head. I have them memorized, down to the word, seared into my organic memory in case I ever find myself on the surface without a datalink. It's the reason I was able to remember them even when I was injured on the surface. I run search queries on unique phrases, but they don't call up any record.

At first, I fear there is something terribly, terribly wrong with my brain. I truly fear I have invented them, that they were never a part of our instructions for interactions with humans. I ask myself if my head injury could have caused me to hallucinate them.

But no. There was a man on the surface who remembered them. He threw them in my face when I seemed to be disregarding them. And if he knew, then it was because Peace-in-the-Sky, myself or another surveyor long ago, told them to people and their tribe or family passed them down in oral history. There are people on Earth who remember them. So they must exist.

I begin my search again when I am interrupted by the sound of the door sliding open behind me. It floods me with a sudden, breath-stealing fear. I duck my head and whirl around in my seat, heart pounding.

There at the door stands Wenslow Pursch, Supervisor of Fabrication.

"Donna? Did I startle you?"

I take a few surreptitious breaths to steady myself. I have been thrown so off-balance by this Records conundrum.

"Wenslow," I say, keeping my voice as even as I can.

"What are you doing?" ey asks.

I manage to say something non-committal about the Mission Imperatives.

"Ah." Ey nods. "You suspect our new drone project is not in compliance with them."

"Just satisfying my curiosity about some details I'd forgotten," I say, which is my way of trying to remain neutral.

"The Imperatives were written so long ago," Wenslow comments, moving toward one of the other terminals. "Who really remembers them?"

"Well, Andrej..." I resist the impulse to list every name I can think of who may care about them.

Ey nods slowly. "Of course. Andrej feels quite strongly about eir interpretation of our purpose and scope, and such. Naturally you share eir concerns...?" Ey trails off, waiting for me to fill in with my thoughts.

"Naturally I want to view the question from all sides," I say. "And what are you researching?"

Wenslow pauses for a moment, as though reluctant to switch topics. But ey says, "Optics." Ey sits at the terminal but keeps the chair turned toward me.

"A request to Fabrication?" I ask.

"Actually, I'm interested in telescopes. It's a specialty of mine, peering into deep space. We spend so much time focused on what's below us. Sometimes it's nice to stretch our necks and look upward for a change."

I realize I never think about what's outward.

"After the disaster that set this all in motion"—Weslow indicates all of Station—"obviously it's of importance to monitor for another impending strike, no matter how statistically unlikely. Being tied to a single planet, as our species is, is a great danger."

We sit in silence for a few moments as I stare at em uncomprehending.

"What species that you know of, Wenslow, is *not* tied to a single planet?"

"None, of course. All known life is on Earth."

While I am considering how faulty ey must be, ey watches me.

"Have you seen my telescope before, Donna?"

"Not that I recall."

"Why don't you come to my office in Fabrication sometime and see it? Earth is a lovely thing, but the stars are wondrous, too. You may appreciate a different view."

I am astounded by eir poetic language, both beautiful and persuasive. When I don't reply, ey says, "Come if you'd like. It's an open invitation."

Ey turns eir chair and wakes eir terminal. "I'll let you get back to your investigations. But don't feel obligated to spend too much time doing research for Andrej's sake. You're a surveyor now. You can leave the onerous work of a Records clerk behind."

I turn back to my own terminal stiffly and read over the last few paragraphs of my phony report. But it is impossible to concentrate with Wenslow there, so I get up to leave. I pass by em on my way out, and we don't speak.

* * *

I walk through the corridors feeling perplexed, still churning over the question of the lost Dictums. I don't understand why they are so hard to find, but I am certain they're in Records somewhere. I want to ask Andrej about them, but I'm cautious about being unnecessarily alarmist. I will be patient. I will continue my search patiently.

Unfortunately, I am obliged to attend my appointment in Med before my search yields results. I walk to Ernesta's cell after a rotation in Condition, which I hope has prepared me to be calm and reasonable during our session.

I stop just outside and read eir plaque: Dr. Ernesta Muambe.

A happy baby, naked but for a diaper, bounced on a knee. A girl in a bright dress with an over large bookbag heads off to school with laughing friends. A young woman in a short skirt and ruffled blouse standing by a doorway with a welcoming smile on eir face. A grown woman leading a group of children in hospital gowns into a playroom, holding their hands, patting their heads, and encouraging them gently.

Seeing the group of children at the end unexpectedly transports me back to Anissa's village—everywhere happy children crowding around us, laughing and jostling, so excited Anissa has come back home. The children in the playback are quieter and move more carefully. They are sick, I think, and Ernesta's human self is caring for them.

I watch it again. And again.

I never buzz, but the door opens.

Ernesta is there, eir face as bland and mild as any stationer. Is the kindness I see in eir playback there? Maybe around the eyes? I may just be wishing it so.

"Do you take an interest in our playbacks?" ey asks.

"I look at them," I say. "But yours. All those children. It reminds of things I saw on my last survey."

Ey steps out of eir door and looks at the playback eirself.

We watch until the end and ey says, "We don't have memory reaching back that far. I have no recollection of working with young persons."

I watch the playback one more time, and Ernesta stands with me silently while I do.

When it's over, ey says, "Let's go to Med. The psychology room there is a more comfortable place to talk. There are two chairs, at least."

It strikes me as a humorous statement. I don't know any stationer who makes jokes, unless you count Jayd's grim sense of irony.

I wonder why Ernesta didn't ask me to meet em there.

"There's been some talk about you lately," ey says as we walk.

I glance at em from the corner of my eye.

"There are stationers who consider me too faulty," I say flatly.

"Has anyone said that to you directly?"

"No. There's questioning. Concern. Implications."

Ernesta nods. "Perhaps you would prefer more direct methods of communication."

I open my mouth to answer but then I wonder what my answer might tell em.

"Are these official questions?" I ask. "Am I already being evaluated?"

We stop at the entrance to Med. Ernesta looks at me, eir expression soft and easy. "I'm interested in what you think, and how you think. But, Donna, this is not a test. This session is for your benefit, not for Station's. Come in, let's find our room."

I follow em through Med into a small room with two chairs. Not the square, armless ones we have in our cells, but ones molded into a flower-like shape designed to support the arms, the back, even the neck.

Ernesta leans back into eirs, watching me shift in mine.

"These are ergonomic chairs. Dr. Diamandi used to ask patients to relax into them. I don't usually. Stationers are not adept at relaxing. What are you looking for?"

I had glanced at the ceiling, looking for cameras. But I hadn't realized I'd done it until ey pointed it out.

Ey says, "There's audio in here, but the leads to the video feed were destroyed during the radiation leak. And the recording is privileged for Psych Med staff only."

"That's only you," I say.

Ey nods. "That's right. Only me. Of course, I can give permission for Med or Commission to access the recordings, but I have never been asked to. Are you concerned others will hear your conversations?"

I take a moment to compose my reply. "Lately there have been instances where stationers speak about things I expected to be held private."

Ernesta says, "You're thinking about Dr. Singh's statement during Council that you had been injured and were not yet recovered."

"I am."

"I take very seriously the directives of my position to respect the confidences of patients. I can assure you I will not repeat what we say here."

I sit back in my chair again. "I am not certain I can trust Singh to do the same. I don't like—" but I cut myself off before I say something I know will sound petulant and aggrieved.

"You don't like...?" Ernesta prompts. "What is it you don't like?"

I look away, frustrated for bringing up some of the very things I least want to talk about. If I came here to convince Ernesta, and myself, that I'm functioning normally, I'm not going about it the right way.

"Are there stationers you don't like, Donna?" Ernesta asks, taking a different tack.

Names tumble through my mind. But I wouldn't say I don't like them, only that they annoy me, or I don't enjoy speaking with them, or I am suspicious of them.

To Ernesta I say, "I can't think of anyone I specifically dislike."

"A very politic answer. Are there any stationers you specifically like?"

I know what the answer is supposed to be. So I recite history to em.

"Stationers who had favorites or intimate attachments despaired and perished when they found their intimates changed by time, or when they were lost. Passion cannot survive eternity. Disinterested goodwill and cooperative collaboration are safer. We decided that long ago."

"We learned from experience," ey says. "But you haven't answered the question. Do you know the answer, yourself?"

When I don't reply ey says, "I've noticed you waiting for Jayd outside of Council meetings several times."

That's the second time someone has brought this to my attention. "You noticed? Or some stationer mentioned it to you?"

"Do you feel as though stationers are watching you and reporting on your behavior?"

I don't speak.

"Donna, stationers do not keep secrets. What you do is visible to any passing stationer. I have not been discussing your case with anyone. But why do you wait for Jayd?"

"Because ey is—" I catch myself short. I was about to say ey is my friend. But no stationer would say that because we are all meant to be on equally friendly terms.

Ernesta waits a few moments. "Jayd is...?" Ey pauses for me to complete the thought. "Donna, as I said before, this session is for your benefit. You requested it. If you won't answer me honestly, how can we hope to make progress?"

More silence.

"What do you want to talk about, then? Any topic. I'm interested."

"We should talk about how I was injured."

Ernesta shifts forward. "How were you injured?"

"I don't know."

Ey sits back. "Well, what would you like to say about it, then?"

"It concerns me that I don't know how I was injured."

"It is medically appropriate to have no memory of a head injury and the time following. Why do your missing memories from that period concern you?"

I think of how I am sometimes nervous when approached from behind. But how will I sound if I mention that? Instead, I say, "I have never been injured like that on Survey before. And no one knows how it happened. Wouldn't it make sense to learn how it was possible so I can prevent it in the future?"

"That follows logically, yes. But is that why you are concerned?"

I can tell from eir tone ey suspects I have other reasons. I want so badly to say, "I suspect someone on Station of tampering with the pod or my flight somehow, so I would be killed on landing." And I want em to believe me and help figure out how or why it was done. But admitting such a thing will definitely make me seem faulty. I cannot imagine how Ernesta would react if I accuse an unknown stationer of trying to kill me.

Instead, I say, "I consider it part of my job to discover these important details."

"Yes, you take your responsibilities seriously, I can see that. Though you have not written your survey report, which other stationers are keen to have."

"I have begun to write the report. I see it was a mistake to leave it so late."

"Did you have a reason for leaving it undone for so long?"

I contemplate saying I simply forgot, but I'm not sure that's believable. I don't have much experience with deception. "Because I want the report to be complete and accurate, and I do not yet possess all the details."

"And so you were waiting, thinking you would be able to fill in those details somehow?"

Now I've nearly admitted I'm investigating. I cannot stop myself from pursing my lips, afraid to let some other incriminating details slip if I speak again.

Ernesta speaks when I do not. "Have my questions brought to light some behavior you think may be illogical?"

If I don't answer, I incriminate myself. But I can't think of any answer that won't also incriminate me. After a very long quiet pause Ernesta speaks again.

"Donna, I don't want to pressure you. Why don't we discuss it next session? I hope you will come back? I think we have touched on some interesting things, and there's a lot left to explore."

"I suppose I'm an interesting case for you," I say dryly.

"It's not for my benefit, though I do enjoy talking with you. I had questions you could not answer. I think it would do you some good to ponder the answers. Will you think about why it is you wait for Jayd after Council meetings? And why investigating your injury during Survey is so important to you? And then we will meet again in a month?"

We set a time, and I walk back to my cell.

The session unsettles me, and the feeling persists for weeks. I sit in Nutri later mulling it while I chew wafers. Am I suffering from paranoid delusions? Am I unhealthily attached to some stationers and arbitrarily disinterested in others? Am I obsessed with my injury? Although I've told myself I really should not, that already I have shown far too much partiality and everyone on Station can see it, I go to see Jayd.

Ey is on a ladder, working on the ceiling above em. There's only a small patch left of the old mural. Eir pointillist scene is nearly done.

"It's ethereal," I tell em.

"You sound like Raina," ey replies.

"What's on the person's head?"

"It's a hat. People during this time often wore them to prevent their skin from darkening in the sun."

"The sun? But the atmosphere was thick then."

"Even when the atmosphere was thicker, people had to protect themselves during certain times of the day. I don't think cancer was such a problem. They were more concerned about appearance."

"I didn't realize you researched the meaning of the scenes so thoroughly."

"Of course." Ey pauses in eir work to look down at me.

"What will you paint next?" I ask em.

"I will plan that when this one is complete."

"Naturally." I sit down on eir cot. "Jayd?"

"Donna."

"You remember me from before my last survey. Am I so different now?"

Jayd stops painting and comes down from eir step ladder. "My recollection is you have been different since you became a surveyor. But, after this last survey, you seem to have become less adept at hiding it."

"Hiding?" I do feel I am hiding myself, that rings true. I feel as though I am always hiding what I think and feel. If stationers knew even half the heartache I feel over my separation from Anissa...

I can't keep dismay and hurt from showing on my face, and Jayd politely looks away.

"Perhaps that was a poor choice of words," ey apologizes. "What I've observed is you have lost the disinterest in ephemera which is so important for stationers to maintain. We have a long time to wait, Donna. Trying to maintain intensity of feeling, over anything, is impossible on that timescale."

"I am too intense," I say.

"Yes."

We look at each other.

I ask em, "Does it bother you?"

"Me? No. But you're disturbing the other stationers." Jayd starts up the ladder again.

"Do you think I'm faulty?" I ask.

"You know how I feel."

I sit on eir cot.

"You don't care if I am, because it doesn't matter. Because we're all just going to die anyway, and you hope it happens sooner rather than later."

Jayd pauses to look at me. "That is a grim and oversimplified summary of my philosophy."

"Guadalupe once told me ey thought *you* were faulty," I remember.

"Is there any stationer who is not? We all perpetually lose more and more of ourselves as we Reform. As you said, we all just wait to die."

"I don't want to die."

Jayd takes up eir paints. "You will."

"Yes, everything dies. But I'm not ready to die yet."

"What is there left for any of us to do?"

"You still haven't tried the gestural abstraction style," I say, "and I want to go back to Earth."

Jayd pauses, holding eir brush. "What an unusual conversation today. I will not attempt gestural abstraction because it is not founded on technical mastery. I'm surprised you're familiar with it. And why are you so intent on going back to Earth? Does it matter whether we document what happens there? In Council meetings you insist humans are already so capable. There are times I think you are implying Earth would thrive without any further intervention on our part."

"How well you listen to me, Jayd. I do think that. You think it, too, or you wouldn't be so fatalistic about our existence."

"But then why are you needed on Earth?"

"I'm not. I just want to be there. I exist here, on Station. But I want to exist there, on Earth."

Ey looks at me for a long moment, and I try to return eir gaze evenly.

"Possibly you are faulty," ey says.

It doesn't bother me at all to hear Jayd say it.

"Talking to you has been very enlightening," I say. "More so than my session with Ernesta."

"I'm glad you find me useful," ey says, slowly returning to painting.

"I'll come by again later," I tell em as I leave.

"Of course."

As I leave, I feel as though something warm melts over me. Other stationers see me so often with Jayd and find something amiss. Jayd emself has no such qualms.

* * *

I am ashamed of myself as a Records clerk that it takes me so long. But I finally find the Surface Dictums. They have been Rchived. Filed away in long-term, non-updating storage, no longer accessible to anyone without Records-privilege, no longer searchable, no longer streamed over datalinks.

As soon as I get over the shock of the discovery, I submit my disgraceful survey report. I have already seen Ernesta. And now I want to talk to Andrej.

I send em a request as ey specified. It's not an official invitation to a subcommittee, which is what ey will be expecting, so I feel the need to tempt em with a brief explanation. I tell em I have questions about Rchival in Records. Perhaps ey will agree to meet if ey thinks it concerns official Records business.

* * *

Maybe I should be speaking to Guadalupe in the meantime, but I find I can do nothing else but wait impatiently for Andrej to respond. In Nutri one day, I cross paths with Koni Owens. With all my plans and worries, I had forgotten about em, how ey had been present when Peace-in-the-Sky was loaded into the pod transport.

"Donna," ey nods to me.

"Koni," I reply, taking my tray and sitting down at the unoccupied table.

That is sufficient conversation for stationers in Nutri, so we say nothing more.

As I chew my wafers, I think about our previous Council meeting. Maint Supervisor Blake Ahmad saying ey has not yet evaluated the drone specs, and Koni prompting Nauja Holm to say ey thinks it can be done. Just a little nudge.

I only realize I am looking at Koni while I think these things when ey looks up and meets my gaze.

"Ah, excuse me." To cover my awkwardness, I explain, "I was just thinking of Sophia's report on constructing drones to mine Earth's surface."

Koni's eyes take on life in eir otherwise passive face.

"Yes," ey says, getting up and moving eir tray to my table. "You've read it, I presume? I am pleased to be assisting with the prototype."

"Although you're in Maint division, not Fabrication." I observe.

"Robotics is a hobby of mine I have little opportunity to indulge," ey admits. "But for this project, my skills might be quite useful."

"How feasible is it, to program such light craft to operate in such a varied and unpredictable environment?"

"I have complete confidence in the plan," ey says. "I can design a vehicle to be operated remotely until the terrain is mapped, and once we mine more parts I can program and operate a fleet just as easily. Many functions can be automated. It will be efficient and safe. No need to risk our survey shells on the surface."

Like Singh, ey seems to have more far-ranging plans than are being discussed in Council. And ey is using my injury as part of eir justification. "Everyone is very concerned for my safety after my last survey."

"Yes. So unfortunate! We cannot afford to lose more stationers, already we are so diminished."

"I believe what happened to be an outlier event. I hope surveys in the future can be made safer." I hesitate, but I cannot help myself. "You were there, weren't you, when Peace-in-the-Sky was loaded into a pod for the most recent survey?"

"I was."

I wait, watching em, not sure what to ask.

Ey sits patiently.

"Were there any irregularities in the secure harnesses or the ship's onboard safety mechanisms?"

"No. Otherwise we would not have launched. Everything was exactly as expected. Dr. Singh made quite sure of it, as I assume ey does at every launch."

"That's right, it was your first launch, correct? Why were you there?"

"Your memory is as poor as stationers say," ey says regretfully. "We were talking about your survey objective. I was instructing you on how to recognize some of the parts we were most interested in, how to evaluate whether you'd seen a cache well-preserved enough to be worth recovering. I even sent an image capture device with you, so you could relay pictures to me in real time, and I could guide you if necessary. We were very optimistic about the mission."

I get that same uneasy feeling hearing things described I've done, but don't remember. As a stationer it's inevitable, as our memories are imperfect, but this case is beyond that. Until this revelation, I hadn't remembered Koni was so involved. I hadn't even thought of em.

"I cannot remember that conversation," I admit, and ey cannot fail to see it disturbs me.

Ey says, "It must be very unsettling to have been so vulnerable, so endangered, with no memory of the time surrounding it."

I feel a little spark of gratitude. "Yes," I say. "Yes, it is very unsettling."

"Perfectly normal," ey says.

"You are the first stationer I've spoken with who understands," I say.

"They have no experience in the matter," Koni says. "During the radiation leak I was working in Maint. My shell was not destroyed outright, but it was badly damaged. So badly I was immediately Reformed, the only way I could be saved. And I lost much of my memory surrounding the incident, as well as other older memories as well. It was a difficult time for me. I was told what had happened, but I couldn't remember it myself. Very unsettling."

It is such a gratifying story for me to hear. "Thank you for sharing that, Koni."

"A kinship of experience," ey replies. "I'm sure it is difficult for someone normally so shrewd and observant as yourself to be without your faculties."

I pause. Stationers are not in the habit of complimenting each other. Even though ey has spoken matter-of-factly, it makes me uncomfortable.

"I do not believe myself any more capable than other stationers," I reply cautiously.

But Koni is undeterred. "You are remarkably astute, Donna. A fact which makes you a formidable adversary, and one reason why I was shocked to hear you'd been hurt. If it could happen to you in a surveyor shell, then is it really safe to send anyone on Survey? Surely expendable drones are safer."

Ah. Koni circles back around to eir robotics interest. It does not surprise me ey has a fixation which is driving much of eir behavior.

"I appreciate your support of this operation, Donna," ey continues. "We need to access those riches on the surface, all that left over and rusting equipment our forebears abandoned, all going to waste, though we need it so badly. Station needs it, to stay operational, and I need it. I need it to make all the things we could be using."

It irritates me, eir selfish interest in the resources of Earth. Those things are not going to waste, they're being used by humans to build their new civilization.

Ey continues, "If Singh wants machinery to launch agriculture on the surface, if Wenslow wants satellites to explore beyond the solar system, if Survey wants robotic assistance to keep surveyors safe, I am happy to assist. Happy to assist. I just need those parts. Do you understand?"

Never has a stationer given me so much information to digest at once. I am reeling with eir suggestions of what other stationers want. Does Singh have plans to automate crop husbandry? Does Wenslow want to launch craft into space? Does Timothy have survey plans ey hasn't shared with me?

"You have not spoken in Council meetings in support of this project," I point out.

"And *you* have not spoken against it." Koni's eyes meet mine. "For which I am very grateful. I fear the project would be mired in committees for ages if you and Andrej were to set yourselves against it."

I start guiltily, as this is exactly what I am planning to do.

Koni doesn't seem to notice. "But surely our agendas need not collide. I want to send drones to the surface. You want to visit the surface, perhaps more safely. Why shouldn't these things happen simultaneously?"

"You think we could be allies," I observe somewhat coldly.

But Koni's reply is warm and friendly. "I want to assure you since you are supporting my interests, I will take care not to trample yours. You may rely on me."

* * *

The conversation does little to calm my worries. I don't like that Koni seems to assume I will be eir ally, for one. And eir revelations have me worried any committee I form will find itself set against stationers who have made far-reaching plans. Ones they are already highly invested in and have spent considerable resources on. They will not be so easily deterred.

There is little point to sitting in my cell, drumming my fingers, waiting for Andrej to reply. I may as well go to see Wenslow's telescope. I want to know if what Koni says about em is true.

Wenslow's office feels perilously close to the parts of Station that were locked away after the radiation leak. The doorway is open, and through it I see straight across the room to a large window over the back wall, which shows black with faint, fuzzy points of light scattered across it.

I step inside without buzzing. It's a large space, larger than I'm used to in the cramped honeycombed rooms and corridors of Station. But it's mostly empty. There's an oblong metal desk bolted to the floor toward the back which holds some terminals. I realize belatedly the lights are dimmed within.

"Wenslow?"

"Donna. Welcome." Wenslow is to my left, partially hidden behind a bank of monitors.

I walk over to em. "I didn't know Station had any portals looking outward into space."

Wenslow glances at the large window. "It's not an opening. It's only a screen. A display of what my telescope sees."

I approach it and see it is pixelated at close range.

Ey says, "Although I would enjoy looking through a portal, of course I would never be able to see with such resolution."

"What are you looking at?" I ask em.

"A cluster of stars on the edge of the near arm of the Milky Way. They have a complicated gravitational relationship."

I look at the larger among the blurry lights, but it means little to me.

"Allow me to adjust the resolution. Redirect the path. Choose some filters..." As Wenslow speaks, ey interacts with one of the many monitors, and the view on the screen changes.

Now it shows black with bright, glowing points of light, and woven through it are hazy purple and white streaks.

"The Large Magellanic Cloud. You're seeing stars being formed."

I look silently for a time.

"A popular area of study. Fortuitously located. Also quite pretty, as you may observe."

"And you want to send a satellite out to study it?" I ask.

"Send a satellite?" Ey looks out from behind eir bank of monitors. "You must have been talking to Koni. Ey's very excited about the possibilities of what ey can accomplish. But no, I would not send a satellite in that direction. There are much closer targets that may reveal important information. If we were to go looking, which I doubt very much we will."

"Important information?"

"Things of interest to me," ey says dismissively.

"But not to the rest of Station?"

"I cannot speak for other stationers, of course. You've come here today with some very pointed questions, Donna." Ey comes to stand next to me and joins me in looking at the display.

Ey's right. My mask of stationer disinterest is slipping. I say nothing.

"What do you know about how Station was built?" Wenslow asks me.

"Nothing. I can't recall ever studying it."

"No one does. We know our purpose. We don't need to ask who built Station, who wrote our Imperatives, who chose us from among those on the ground and sent us up here."

I turn to look at em, curious.

"Think of it, Donna. The Earth in disaster. The wandering poles and flaring sunspots wreaking havoc on the atmosphere and climate and on Earth technology. The impending asteroid strike and the disastrous attempt of humanity to destroy it, which reduces it to a rain of highly radioactive meteorites pummeling the surface for years. Everything is dying. Whole ecosystems are collapsing around them. They construct the dome and fill it with people whom they hope can survive for generations and generations. They construct Station and place it in orbit, and choose people from among them to be stationers and install them here to look after Earth for the millennia to come."

Ey pauses and turns to meet my gaze.

"I never thought of it in such dramatic terms," I say.

"But it is a dramatic story," ey says. "And we live in its quiet aftermath."

"Did you read this all in Records?"

Ey gives a slight shake of eir head as if the question is irrelevant. "From my perspective, the essential question remaining is: what became of the architects of this great plan to preserve humanity?"

It is the last question I would have thought to ask, but now ey poses it, I think for a moment. "They are the ancestors of the Intha?"

Wenslow looks back to the screen in front of us. "That's your guess? I highly doubt it. The Intha are the pitiful creatures that hid themselves in the dark crevices of the Earth and survived only by the slimmest of chances. If you'd made a study of the matter such as I have, you would come to a different conclusion."

"What conclusion is that?"

Wenslow lifts eir arm slowly to point at the screen. "They left."

* * *

I leave Wenslow's office with an odd, disconnected feeling. Here is a puzzle piece I wasn't looking for. And I have no way of judging whether Wenslow is simply profoundly faulty, or whether ey's discovered something fascinating no one else thought to look for.

I could bury myself in Records for months researching eir ideas, testing eir theories, trying to retrace the path leading em to this wild revelation. But I cannot indulge such distractions now. Earth. Everything centers on Earth, as it must. I have no time to look up to the stars.

I need to counter this plan to send drones to the surface. How much material will we steal from humans to feed Wenslow's irrelevant fancies? How much collateral destruction might Koni cause if ey is permitted to unleash eir army of drones and vehicles and robotic explorers on the surface? How much damage might Singh do to Earth's ecosystems and human economies with an abundance of gene-edited crops?

Stationers are losing their focus and spiraling into myriad deranged pursuits which do nothing to help humans. I don't much care if Wenslow wants to send out probes, or even if ey wants to build a spaceship and leave. I don't mind Koni helping em. And if Singh likes tinkering with crops in eir horticulture room, that is not my concern, let em take eir plants into deep space with Wenslow.

But when their fantasies threaten to spill over onto Earth—that I cannot allow. Humans on the surface have far too much respect for and awe of Peace-in-the-Sky, and stationers barely consider humans. They will not even visit the surface, I'm sure. They will strip the Earth from afar without even noticing the damage they cause.

Guiltily I think of all the harm Peace-in-the-Sky caused inadvertently on Earth with my suggestions and instructions, some ill-considered, others woefully misinterpreted. Perhaps Andrej's more hands-off approach has always been the correct one. Maybe I never should have meddled.

I *need* to remind stationers of our mission's intent and, if at all possible, I *must* convince them our job is done. Our time has passed. Humans survived the apocalypse, and now we need to step aside.

As we were always meant to do.

* * *

We must address the disappearance of the Surface Dictums from Records, as that will hamper any efforts to sway stationers. We need to restore any Rchived records concerning how stationers are meant to interact with humans. When I find Andrej has not responded to my request to meet, I access my datalink and send em another request.

"Andrej. Records search reveals error. Improper Rchive of relevant Records accounts. Please respond. Donna."

I hope it's alarming enough to draw eir timely response, but not dramatic enough for em to dismiss it as the product of a faulty mind.

Then I cannot help myself. I search out Jayd.

* * *

Ey is not painting. Ey is on eir knees at the corner of eir cell, with a strange metal object in eir hand, examining eir completed pointillist work closely.

"What is that?" I blurt with no preamble.

Jayd is not disturbed. "A micrometer. Repurposed from Fabrication. Not ideally suited for this work but Koni modified it at my request."

I don't enjoy discovering more evidence of Koni's usefulness to stationers. "Koni? No one seems to remember ey works in Maint. It's you who work in Fabrication."

"Yes, but Koni is willing to assist stationers with side projects. Donna, I cannot really do this work properly while carrying on a conversation."

"Is it possible for you to take a break?" I ask. "There's something I wish to discuss with you. Well, I wish to discuss it with Andrej, but ey is not available."

"Then wait for Andrej to be available," Jayd says, though ey stands and faces me.

"I need to order my thoughts first," I say. "And you are more patient with me."

Jayd comes to sit by me on the cot, and we both observe eir painting. It has a hazy quality to it.

"It's as if the original artist didn't want you to see the scene too clearly," I say.

"The artists wanted to apply the new science of optics and color theory to painting. It was derided as too mechanical and unfeeling in its day."

"And yet it evokes such warm and dreamy feelings." Only to Jayd would I say such a frivolous thing.

"Donna," Jayd says. There is a hint of rebuke in eir voice, but eir arm grazes mine as ey moves. And though it feels casual, stationers do not touch each other. Such a thing almost never happens accidentally.

Such a little gesture, but I have to close my eyes to keep from being overwhelmed. In my arms I feel the warmth of Anissa, feel the texture of her hair against my cheek, feel her breathing where she is pressed against my chest, feel her thin, strong arms clutching at me.

I push up from the cot and walk across the cell to lean against the opposite wall.

Jayd says nothing.

"About Andrej," I say unsteadily.

"Yes, let's talk about em," says Jayd.

I push thoughts of Anissa away with effort. It was always her I was thinking of. I was thinking of the foods she likes to eat being outcompeted by Singh's super-crops, I was thinking of the Intha losing their Salvage wealth to Wenslow's plundering and descending on her rich home to make up the difference.

"What I need to talk to Andrej about involves other stationers and their plans," I say. "I spoke to Wenslow and ey told me a theory that the architects of Station and the dome did not remain on Earth, but left the planet."

Jayd is silent for a moment.

"Have you heard this theory?" I ask em.

"No, not expressed so succinctly. But reflecting on Wenslow's actions and words over the years, I don't find it surprising."

"Is ey completely faulty?" I ask.

"Hmm. Does ey have any evidence to support this theory?"

"I could comb through Records for years looking for it, I suppose. But have you ever heard Dr. Singh wants to take genetically altered plants to Earth and essentially terraform the surface?"

"I have not, but I suppose that is one logical outcome of eir research," Jayd says. "Is there some connection you're making between these facts?"

"Only that both plans will need considerable resources from Earth to come to fruition. And as Andrej has said, there are provisions in the Mission Imperatives discouraging stationers from doing so."

"Yes, this is the argument we've been having in Council, this is not new—"

I interrupt em, "And the other day I went looking for the precise clauses in Records I would use to counter these plans and could not find them."

Jayd looks directly at me. "What do you mean?"

"I mean that they were no longer searchable. It took me quite a while to unearth them. They'd been Rchived."

"Rchived? Refresh my memory, Records clerk."

"When a record is considered irrelevant, it is placed in the Rchives, a digital graveyard stationers without Records-privilege can no longer access. The process preserves working memory on the datalink. But important things, like Mission Imperatives and Surface Dictums, should not be Rchived. Those are meant to be permanent."

"How many important records have been Rchived?"

"The entirety of the Surface Dictums," I pronounce.

"I have never heard of those." Jayd sounds unimpressed.

"And now, you never will. You cannot possibly access that record. Despite it being a key piece of evidence in any argument against Singh or Wenslow's plans."

Jayd regards me silently for a moment. "You're implying somehow these records were purposefully Rchived by someone supportive of the Council's new surface mining plans? How many stationers have the authority to do something like that?"

This is exactly the question I should have asked myself from the start. I have to think only for a moment, and poke at my datalink for confirmation, before I say, "None. Only the Records supervisor should have the privilege to manually choose individual records to be Rchived."

I almost never see Jayd access eir datalink, but ey does so now. "I must admit I do not know who is currently Records Supervisor..."

"There isn't one. The only two official Records clerks are Andrej and Dakota Jinx. And I suppose I still function in that capacity informally. As far as I know, Andrej was never promoted to have Supervisor Records-privilege."

I consider it. "Of course ey wasn't. Our Mission Imperatives forbid promotions, though Andrej and I once got away with a lateral move. Which is why Ernesta is still formally just a med clerk, and not truly our counselor."

I am rushing through every sentence, my mind flying ahead. But Jayd still speaks with eir same measured calm. "You attach importance to this discovery because you see agency in it. My reaction would be to regard it as some algorithm error. If you wish to convince Andrej, or anyone else, of the urgency you seem to feel, I suggest you discover who logged the Rchive command, or else when it was done, or some other evidence. Otherwise just petition to have it restored."

"I'm not certain who would restore it," I say, thinking aloud.

But Jayd answers, "If someone Rchived it, then there is someone who can reverse the process, I assume."

"Yes, yes." I stand to go. I am nearly out the door before I remember to thank em. "I haven't seen you take such an interest in Station matters in a long time, Jayd. In hundreds of years, maybe."

"It is an unfortunate side effect of my association with you," ey says, picking up the micrometer again and adjusting it carefully. "I cannot avoid getting entangled."

"Such a pity," I say, and it's possible a hint of teasing enters my voice though I try to suppress it. "If you hope to remain aloof you ought to end your association with me."

"I won't," ey says. Ey doesn't smile. But I feel quite certain if we were human again, ey would have.

* * *

I leave em to eir measurements and return to Records. Ey is perfectly right, of course. I need more evidence. With a calmer head this time I make utmost use of Records-privilege to find date stamps and digital signatures, then I capture images of my findings so they are easier to show to others.

I am ruthless in tracking down all records recently Rchived. Some seem unrelated to the current situation, but others are too relevant. An older survey report detailing human utilization of parts from Salvage cities. An historical record discussing the "rights of salvage" in some long-dissolved Republic, which was apparently a complicated set of laws. And even, unbelievably, an actual clause of the Mission Imperatives themselves—a minor paragraph about respecting property rights of humans on the surface.

And although I'm quite certain these Records were chosen intentionally and then manually marked for Rchival, they all have a digital signature which suggests they were routine choices of the Rchival process. It would be more useful to find some personal identifier attached to them, but regardless, the contents of the records Rchived is just too coincidental.

I have assembled what I believe to be a very compelling case.

* * *

Though I am ready to reveal my findings, there's still been no word from Andrej. Disregarding eir preference, I seek em out again in eir cell. Ey does not answer my buzz at the door.

I haven't seen em in all this time, which is not unusual, stationers can go years without seeing each other, but I've been looking for em and still not met em.

It embarrasses me to do so, but I access my datalink and send em a direct message. It's the sort of thing stationers reserve for emergencies. During the radiation leak and subsequent search for survivors, there were many direct channels opened. In any other circumstance it's considered rude, as it holds the channel open for the other party's reply instead of allowing them to respond in their own time. And other stationers can see the active channel, if they choose to do so. It is not private.

Ey does not reply. It does not surprise me, though it frustrates me. Ey's pointedly ignoring me. I have no choice but to go over eir head.

Guadalupe opens eir door to my buzz. I have not made an appointment.

Ey doesn't even greet me. "This is irregular," ey says. I can see teacups set out at eir table behind em, though ey is alone. I am not even made awkward by such evidence of unsound fixation. I am too focused.

"Andrej is unresponsive," I tell em.

"What do you mean?"

"I am trying to contact em, and I cannot. Ey does not wish to speak with me, and I must respect that. But there is a matter of Records security which must be addressed."

"At this very moment? Surveyor Whitacre, your impatience is both unbecoming and unsettling. I'm afraid I must recommend you speak with Dr. Singh..." Ey pauses and eir eyes are looking at something else for a moment.

"You've opened a direct channel to clerk Vann?" The quietness of eir voice is alarming, "Is this an emergency, Whitacre?"

I am on dangerous ground. If I do not make a good case, I will find myself officially declared to have excessive Reform faults, with all of my privileges revoked. I try to find an angle which will persuade Guadalupe.

"A minor one," I say. "Though I fear life is indirectly in danger. I am trying to prevent a panic such as the one which led to the First Eight. I have found what I believe to be mistakes in Records—important Station data is being Rchived in error."

"Come in," ey says.

I step inside.

"It seems to me," ey says, gesturing me into a chair, "you are more likely to cause panic than prevent it. Why would you draw attention to such a thing?"

"If I found it, then others could, too. And aren't you concerned yourself something may be wrong in Records? We ought to investigate this seriously. The information contained there is meant to inform all stationers."

"Records is for Records clerks," Guadalupe says dismissively. "I am not concerned about a few digital errors."

I cannot keep the earnestness from my voice. "Stationers are losing access to information about our Mission Imperatives."

"The Rchival process is automated," Guadalupe says. "No one on Station may interfere with it. And why would they? We all know our duty. We don't need to read it there yearly to remind ourselves. Really, Whitacre, I am willing to let your private delusions go somewhat unchecked"—there's the slightest pause where neither of us acknowledges that we're sitting at a table set for an imaginary meeting—"but when they threaten the well-being of other stationers, I am forced to get involved."

"This is no delusion. Allow Andrej and I to investigate fully and make a report to you. If you were to give one of us the privileges of Records supervisor, we could establish how this happened and perhaps guard against further errors."

Guadalupe says coldly, "That is not possible. Promotions are disallowed. If this is a ploy to gain more authority on your part..."

"I assure you it is not," I insist. "Give it to Andrej. Or to Dakota Jinx. Or allow Timothy to fulfill two supervisor roles, I am not asking for myself. You could even make it temporary. But there are data I cannot access, that *we could not have access to,*" I correct myself quickly.

I'm aware I've listed for promotion those who may be inclined to be my allies, and that my word choice may imply I want research access for personal reasons. I wait anxiously to see how Guadalupe will respond.

Ey answers me with all the authority of eir office. "I will not be coerced into giving your pet projects and your favored theories more weight and authority. I have been lenient with you, even generous. Despite concerns raised about your Reform faults, I have trusted you to participate in our process. I am trusting you now not to raise unnecessary alarm among the stationers. As you said, the First Eight was a serious and dangerous business."

Guadalupe turns eir attention to the channel I've opened to Andrej and reluctantly I do, as well. "You should not have opened this channel. I will ask clerk Vann to close it and to speak with you, but if ey does not share your concerns, I expect you to drop it. Likely ey trusts the Rchival process to proceed unaided as it has done for centuries. Do not go looking for errors and problems, Whitacre. I am trusting you with your Records-privilege. Do not abuse it."

I am chastised, and I make no more arguments. I only nod. Guadalupe rises, walks to the door, and stands by it as I leave.

I stand in the corridor after eir door closes and stare vacantly at Jayd's mural. I failed to make my case convincingly, or Guadalupe is particularly resistant to taking action, and I may have hampered my own future efforts. But I am certain Andrej will take the errors seriously, if only I could talk to em. I hope ey will see the timing of these errors is without doubt suspicious.

* * *

Days pass and my channel to Andrej remains open. Anyone could see it who bothers to look. I am anxious for Guadalupe to tell em to close it. Instead, Guadalupe opens a direct channel to me. I am so astonished I stop in the middle of the corridor on my way back from Nutri.

"Surveyor Whitacre," it says simply.

"Present," I reply.

"I expect you in the Council Hall immediately."

"I am coming now," I say.

No stationer ever wants anything immediately. Ever. And no stationer runs, so I do not now, but I get myself there quickly.

The door opens and I see Guadalupe, Singh, and Wenslow. They stand together shoulder to shoulder and watch me come. As I near, I see Shelley, Singh's assistant, sitting in one of the chairs nearby with head tilted down and a shadow obscuring eir face.

I approach them and stop, waiting for someone to speak.

"Donna, close your channel to Andrej," Singh says.

I don't understand. "I cannot."

"You can. Close it," Singh repeats.

I reach out and it closes. It surprises me but I say nothing, waiting for them to explain.

"What were you and Andrej working on?" Wenslow asks.

I feel a chill of worry. Wenslow has seen me in Records, and surely suspects I was investigating ways to thwart eir plans to mine the surface.

I skirt the issue. "Nothing. I was not able to reach em."

"I see there is a message you sent em earlier," Singh says. "Will you open it for us?"

We are all accessing our datalink now. I can feel them around me in that space. With trepidation I open the message I sent. "Andrej. Records search reveals error. Improper Rchive of relevant Records accounts. Please respond. Donna."

There is silence while they read it.

"Is that sufficient, do you think?" Guadalupe asks.

"Not this message alone, surely," Wenslow says.

They blink out of my data space. More slowly, I follow. I avoid looking at Wenslow while the silent moment stretches too long.

Guadalupe finally speaks. "Whitacre, I fear you have made a terrible error. It seems your rash behavior has caused serious harm on Station."

I wait tensely.

Singh says very carefully, "Andrej Vann has been involved in an isolated die-off event."

It's such a strange statement, even for a stationer, that I have to think about it.

"Andrej? Is dead?"

"Yes," says Wenslow.

"But...suicide?"

Guadalupe says, "Your message must have caused em severe alarm. You know how very important accuracy of Records was to em."

"But? To end eir life? Just because I posed the question?"

"Perhaps your note was just one small piece of the problem. Ey was thoroughly disturbed, I fear," Wenslow says. "There were things found in eir cell which speak of unhealthy habits."

Out of the corner of my eye I see Shelley's head dip another fraction of an inch.

"We have agreed," Guadalupe says, "not to speak of it in depth. What you heard here is meant to be kept private." Eir eyes flick to Wenslow and away again. "Andrej must have had a number of serious Reform faults. Sadly, ey ended eir life. There will be a space ejection burial of the empty shell."

"I do not plan to formally hold you accountable," Guadalupe continues. "I believe your part to be unwitting. But I do hold you to the strictest standards of discretion. Not only in the details of eir death, but particularly in the matter which you and I discussed beforehand. That ends here, Whitacre. That line of inquiry is closed to you. I am revoking your Records-privilege."

And in the wake of something so disastrous as a stationer death, I do not protest. In that moment, what I have uncovered does seem insignificant compared to the tragedy of losing, forever, Andrej.

Guadalupe and Singh turn to each other, discussing details of requisitioning a pod for burial. I step out. The door slides shut behind me, but does not quite close before it opens again.

"Donna." It's Wenslow's voice. The sound sets me on edge. I work to keep my breathing even as I turn. We stand alone in an empty corridor, the wide Council Hall doors behind us.

"I'm sorry about your Records privilege, Donna. But it can't be helped. They need to feel like they have punished you somehow."

I would have thought Wenslow would be very happy to have me prevented from accessing Records. I don't understand why we're having this conversation. Is ey trying to draw me out? I have no idea what is safe to say.

"It is a shame to lose Andrej, of course. But there's no need to blame yourself. I believe it was simply an accident. Yes, ey injured emself in eir cell, but it may have been unintentional. Ey failed to seek Med help when ey should have. I wonder if Andrej even received your message. Ey had been dead for some time."

Wenslow pauses, hoping perhaps I will speak. But I don't dare chance it. I need to think.

"I will rejoin them, now," ey says finally. "I hope I've been able to reassure you."

I walk slowly back to my cell. And I discover, as I walk back, that I liked Andrej. And I miss em.

* * *

I spend a lot of time in my cell turning the problem over and looking at it from different angles. I don't dare go to Records. I am wary of talking to another stationer about it and possibly involving them. I am painfully aware that if Records was tampered with, and it was done by Guadalupe, Singh, or Wenslow, then that person is now aware I have discovered their trespass.

And then, horribly, if I named the timing of the improper Rchivals suspicious, then how am I to view the timing of

Andrej's death? Ey dies right as I am about to reveal to em a Records irregularity that only ey would have taken seriously?

But I can't contemplate that. Whenever I think of eir death, I am overwhelmed with regret. Regardless of what Wenslow said to ease it, I do feel guilt. I cannot help but feel my actions partly responsible.

I miss my rotation at Condition. Possibly I skip meals in Nutri. If I can't steady myself, I will be sent to see Ernesta, or worse, Singh. I must think about this problem with a clear head, but where can I go to find the calm I seek?

I find myself at the door to Sasha's cell. I buzz. It opens.

Sasha sits in the very center of the empty cell, eyes open, looking levelly at me.

I enter and the door closes.

"Andrej is dead," I say. "Suicide. And I fear I played a part..."

"Interaction with the other stationers is poison to the soul. I told you that. For you, and for them, as well."

"There are confounding factors," I insist. "There are other ills not being addressed."

"Donna," Sasha says, almost sharply. "Your frantic presence disturbs the qi of this space. I will guide you to stillness if you can discipline yourself."

With an effort I stop talking and wait. I came here for calm, not to accost Sasha with my fears.

"Sit as I do. Rest your hands on your knees, and let your eyes fall closed."

I do as I am told.

"For a while, just breathe. Feel your breath come and go. Then allow your thoughts to fade. If they resurface let them fade again. Again and again until they no longer plague you..."

Eir hypnotic voice soothes me. Eventually Sasha falls silent, and we just sit quietly. I cannot stop thinking, but I pull back from the most upsetting thoughts when they show themselves. In time my thoughts wander to more pleasant things. And then they return to more volatile thoughts, but this time without ruining my composure. It's natural for stationers to see things dispassionately. I just needed a nudge in the right direction.

I open my eyes. Sasha sits as before, undisturbed, eyes closed.

I look around the cell and wait. Later, I stand up to leave. I go quietly to show my respect to Sasha, a small thank you for the help.

I have time to catch up on my Condition visits. I work hard and take pleasure in the feeling of strength, the ease with which I pull the weights through their grooves. I make sure I am taking regular meals at Nutri.

By the time I get my feet under me again, the Council meeting is upon us. I already know Koni will be discussing the prototype ey was to build and stationers will decide whether it's feasible to proceed with the plan.

And I know Andrej will not be there to speak.

When the time for the Council comes, I wait in my cell silently. Then I wait a little longer to see if anyone searches for me when my absence is noticed.

There's a message almost immediately.

"Whitacre. I expect your attendance. Guadalupe."

I reply, "Guadalupe. Taking time to reflect on Andrej's death. Will attend future Councils. Donna."

"Negative. I expect your attendance. Calling to order now, you have permission to enter late."

I leave my cell and walk quickly through the quiet corridors. But I don't go to Council.

Wenslow's office stands open as before. I pause outside.

Someone is tampering with the Rchival system, I am certain of it. I have been prevented from investigating it and I can't ask for—I won't ever have—Andrej's help. And I can't dismiss the needling feeling there are stationers whose plans benefit from the changes in Records. I'm standing outside the office of one of them right now.

I enter.

There are drawers in the desk with all the terminals. I open each one quietly. Most are empty. One holds some loose mechanical parts whose use I don't know, but at least one seems to have been altered, with an extra piece welded on. More evidence of Koni's helpfulness, perhaps, or maybe Wenslow is also capable of making tools to eir own specifications.

But that's not what I came here for.

I turn my attention to the terminals. One by one I try to get access, but they are all locked and I cannot log in. It's frustrating. Why lock the terminals? Nothing on Station is locked, our privileges dictate what we can access.

My suspicion that Records is being tampered with from these very terminals only grows stronger. But without the Supervisor's Records-privilege that I was hoping for, without even a clerk's Records-privilege, I have no authority. No access.

I stand with my hands gripping the edge of the cold metal desk, mind working.

I'm not a Records clerk anymore. I need to stop thinking like one. I'm only a surveyor, with a Survey-privilege access to Records. What can I do with that?

I query my datalink for information about these terminals, hoping to find out who has locked them. But they are marked as open terminals. So I try to log in again. They are definitely locked.

Is it possible Wenslow has stealthily locked eir terminals and prevented general Station system informatics from seeing it? If so, ey has more privileges than ey should have and is using them to hide things.

But that's all I have time to think about before I really must get to Council. I rush down the corridor, pause outside, and enter quietly. I purposefully keep my eyes down, so I don't exchange glances with anyone, and go directly to my seat.

The talk doesn't pause with my entry. Koni is expounding on some of the particulars of eir prototype while a schematic is projected on the big screen behind Guadalupe. I glance at it through my datalink; several other schematics of potential drone design flick past. I see with chagrin that ey has suggested re-purposing the propulsion units on the shuttles to power the drones down to the surface, then back. Presumably those shuttles would no longer be able to ferry surveyor pods.

"These are fully spec'd out diagrams, and I've determined many of the parts needed are available on Station. To proceed I would need a team from Fabrication to help me determine which models would be most robust given their design parameters. And then we can proceed."

I am in my seat. Several rows ahead and below me I see Timothy, my supervisor, and right next to em an empty seat. There are so many seats in Council that are empty. But Andrej's empty seat is the worst one.

Across the hall Wenslow stands to speak. Ey is offering to put together a team from Fabrication to assist Koni. I give em only minimal attention. I am speculating what ey is hiding on locked terminals. Eir fixation with the architects of Station somewhere exploring space? Eir meddling with Records? Details of eir continued involvement with this Earth-mining project beyond what ey reveals in council, perhaps beyond what has already been authorized?

Might ey be hiding something which would connect em to Andrej's death?

There might be evidence for any and all of that on eir office terminals. But who can I convince to care and act on it?

Anything short of direct evidence Wenslow murdered Andrej and I am certain Guadalupe will not hear me. I have destroyed my credibility with em.

Singh stands to speak. Singh, I think, should care. Ey is our doctor and committed to caring for stationer bodies and preserving their lives. But ey was in Andrej's room and judged the death a suicide. Was ey simply not looking hard enough at the evidence before em, or was ey covering something up?

My thoughts are interrupted when I hear Singh say my name, and suddenly I am attending Council very closely.

Guadalupe replies to Singh. "This does seem an appropriate use of a surveyor's time. Whitacre, I hope you will assist Dr. Singh in this matter."

Guadalupe gives me a level look and I take it I've been given orders for something. I look at Singh but ey is speaking quietly to Shelley and doesn't glance my way.

The Council meeting official video and transcript will be committed to Records approximately twelve minutes after it adjourns, so I will have to wait until then to see exactly what task I have been assigned.

Not long after, the meeting comes to a close. Shanna Perez from Maint and Flight supervisor Bri Ito have raised some excellent questions. Guadalupe directs Blake and Koni to have them answered for the next Council meeting.

The drones have not been given launch permissions yet. I still have time to thwart this plan. Nothing will stall it—and win back my credibility and privileges—better than proving there are bad actors on Station, tampering with Records and...and perhaps someone murdered Andrej.

Perhaps...no, I worry I am becoming delusional. But *perhaps*, dare I speculate *my* injury was deliberate and also made to look like an accident? And is connected to all this?

I am so struck by this possibility that I stand blocking the corridor. I redirect my steps to the observation lounge and peer down at Earth, as though what happened to me there can be seen from this distance. I had put the problem of my own injury aside. But what if all these moving parts are connected? The plans to mine and terraform Earth's surface, the attack that injured me, the tampering with Records, Andrej's supposedly accidental death?

A notification from Singh pops up and interrupts my thoughts. It's simply a meeting time and date, I assume related to what was said in Council.

I quickly consult my datalink to review the video in Council and find Singh has requested my help with eir work on soil samples. I don't precisely follow why, from the proceeding discussion. It seems almost as though this was something Singh and Guadalupe had discussed beforehand

and were simply making their decision public in the Council meeting.

I do not want to waste my time with this new assignment, I want to pursue my own investigations. Then I wonder if this is exactly why Guadalupe has assigned the work to me. To redirect my energies. If there is something to learn from Singh, however, maybe I can turn this time with em to my advantage.

But first, I have to get through my meeting with Ernesta.

* * *

I meet em in Med, and thankfully Singh isn't there. Shelley is sitting at a microscope reading slides. I see purple-and-blue images of ovoids and streaks on the screen.

"What are you working on?" I can't help but ask as I pass.

"Evaluating histopath," Shelley mumbles, too intent on the images to look my way.

Ernesta leads us into the Psych room, and we sit in the strange chairs again.

"Much has happened since we last spoke," Ernesta begins gently.

"You mean Andrej's death?" I don't feel like easing into it.

"Yes. That certainly stands out."

"I've been instructed not to discuss certain things with other stationers. Am I correct in assuming I can disregard those guidelines in here?"

Ernesta leans back and watches me for a moment. "As you know, everything said here is kept in confidence. Only you can decide, though, what you're comfortable talking about."

"It's not a question of my comfort. I'm quite comfortable telling you exactly what's been happening. My question is whether I'm disobeying Guadalupe by doing so."

"That's your decision to make," Ernesta says.

"You mean maybe, I can decide to disobey Guadalupe, and you won't tell em. But of course, deciding not to honor an agreement with our commissioner will not be lost on you."

"It is as though you feel your relations with other stationers are somewhat of a game. And you keep trying to see me as a player in that game. But I am not, Donna. I am here to reflect you back to yourself."

"A game? This is a serious matter."

Ernesta watches me carefully. "I can see Andrej's death is weighing on you."

"Alright, I'll tell you what's happened. And then you'll know why."

Ey settles back and gives me eir full, quiet attention.

"While searching in Records I discovered some records had been erroneously Rchived, and it seemed purposeful. A difficult thing to do, meddle with a fully automated process, yet I could not deny the evidence before my eyes. And so I wished to discuss it with Andrej. But I could not contact Andrej. I tried again and again, and I could not, and then I find out ey's dead. And Guadalupe asks me not to pursue my investigation."

"Does this sequence of events suggest something to you?"

"If a stationer was determined enough to somehow alter Station Records, might that stationer be determined enough to cover up that alteration? Perhaps to cause another's death to prevent its detection?"

"You think Andrej's death is connected to what you researched in Records?"

"I am suspicious."

"And do you recall Andrej's death was a suicide?" ey reminds me.

"Yet I was later told that eir death was caused by some accidental wound ey did not seek treatment for."

"Suicide is self-inflicted death," Ernesta says calmly.

"There are enough unanswered questions, along with the timing of the death, to make me suspect some connection."

"Do you feel Andrej's death has intruded into your everyday thoughts?"

I don't understand how ey is able to remain so supremely unconcerned about what I'm revealing.

"I am not incapacitated. I think about it when I am not engaged with other things." I can at least assure em it's not become a fixation.

"Do you feel you played a role in eir death?"

I answer as carefully as I can. "I was told directly by both Guadalupe and Singh that my message to Andrej was, at the very least, part of what caused eir death. My Records-privilege was revoked, and I was cut off from my work. They clearly both hold me indirectly responsible."

"You, however, hold another stationer responsible."

"I do not absolve myself. I involved Andrej. And though it was unintentional, I regret my mistake."

"Does this regret—?"

I cut em off. "My regret is unimportant in the face of the deliberate silencing of another stationer." It's supremely frustrating interacting with someone who speaks like ey is reading lines from a manual. I cannot seem to get through to em.

Ernesta pauses to think, then changes tactics.

"Let's call it what you fear, then. Murder. You believe a stationer killed Andrej."

It is both liberating and terrifying to hear it spoken aloud. "I cannot know that, but I believe it bears investigation."

"Is there a stationer you believe should be investigated?"

"Whoever altered Records and did not want that to be discovered is the obvious suspect."

"But is there a name?"

"There are several stationers who would like to see this plan proceed without objections, and any of them may have interfered with Records. But I cannot know who without help. I needed Andrej's help."

"In your thoughts, do you feel as though you still need Andrej's help?"

I am so frustrated I cannot stay still in my seat. I shift back and forth uncomfortably. I can tell from Ernesta's tone ey is not interested in the least whether Andrej was murdered or who did it. Ey does not care if I'm right about Station Records being meddled with. None of what I've revealed or confessed has concerned or worried em. Ey is focused only on the rhetoric of our session.

I spend a few heartbeats listening to my breath come and go. It's time to end this maddening interaction before I appear any faultier.

"My conversation with you is making me realize how little evidence there is for this concern of mine," I say at last.

The tension breaks.

"Oh?" Ernesta says.

"Yes. There are unanswered questions, but even those with more information don't share my concern."

"You have a lot of emotions to work through."

"I do." That much is very true.

"I believe you struggle with your dual identity as both stationer and a surveyor, with conflicting customs guiding your behavior."

"It is difficult," I admit.

"I feel entirely justified in telling you that you are not the only surveyor to have struggled with this. Station has lost so many. It is a dangerous thing to wrestle with. But I am encouraged by our talk today."

I take a moment to notice my inhale and I do not point out that Station has lost *all* of its original surveyors. All of them. Andrej was the last. "I still have much to think about," I say neutrally.

"Yes. We will meet again."

Before ey can make a date, I offer one. "Let's meet after the next Council meeting."

"Alright. And you are welcome to make an appointment any time before that if you feel you need one."

"Thank you."

I walk out, counting my breaths.

I remember hiding from the glaring sun, Anissa asleep with her head in my lap, enduring Rill's aggressive questioning. I had only the dimmest idea of what Rill was asking about, the desperate conditions his people struggled with. I stuck to my story. I was helping Anissa. Everything else was secondary and, to me, fundamentally unimportant.

How violent Rill seemed in reaction. Unhinged. Dangerous.

I am sorry, Rill. You were trying to help me see the larger picture, the plight of all the Intha, of everyone you had ever known or cared about, and all I could do was repeat maxims at you. If I ever get the chance to try again for your people, I will do better. And I swear I will do everything in my power to prevent unleashing stationers and their unconsidered plans on the humans of Earth.

* * *

My talk with Ernesta makes me realize just how much proof I am going to need if I'm to shake stationers out of their accustomed mindless behavioral loops. If I need more information, I need to ask the right stationer. And there's one stationer who once surprised me with quite a bit of unexpected information.

I buzz at the door to eir cell. I watch Koni Odom's playback while I stand waiting.

A baby sleeping peacefully on a mat on the floor. A boy swinging at a playground crowded with happy children. A young man in a uniform in line with others all in the same uniform files into a classroom. A man in a neat suit sitting in a gray cubicle behind a computer terminal on an office floor full of others at their own terminals.

Koni's playback is outstanding for being so colorless and uninteresting. But ey never answers eir door so I go to Maint to find em. Maint's workspace is a long bay with individual workstations at wide tables along each wall. Each table is littered with a few stray parts, forgotten projects or broken things never mended. It has an empty, echoing feel, and right now it is entirely uninhabited. I don't see Koni.

I enter anyway and walk down the long hall, just looking at the equipment abandoned here. I can hear my footsteps. There's fine white Station dust on the tables and some of the chairs.

"Are you looking for me?" Someone is standing in a doorway down at the end of the bay. As I near, I see Koni waiting for me.

Ey stands aside so I can enter. This workspace does not look abandoned. There are multiple terminals running, the walls are covered with hooks, each of which holds a tool or gadget, and the tabletops are crowded with electronic pieces and parts.

"This is your office?" I ask.

"It was Blake's workspace. But ey no longer uses it. Ey has an office off the repair bay."

Koni takes the two chairs inside and turns them so they face each other. We sit.

"It's good you've come," ey says. "What can I show you? Would you like to see some detailed models of my drones and vehicles?" I follow eir eyes and see small-scale models covering a table, bristling with antennae, articulated wings, and sensor arrays.

"No," I say. But I look at them for a moment, and Koni waits quietly while I do. Surely this is the work of years, and so much more than the single drone prototype Council asked for. Assembled like this, marching across the table, they look like they are massed for an invasion. It's not a pleasant image.

I turn back to Koni. "I wanted to talk about Andrej."

"You knew em better than I," Koni says. "You and Timothy."

"Do you know how ey died?" I ask.

"No. No one has told me, and I haven't asked. But I know what was in eir cell, of course. It all came back here, to be cataloged and repurposed."

It's an odd thing for em to mention. "What was brought back?"

"A lot of the usual. Cot, bins, a chair. And things I made to spec for em..."

Koni trails off, a deliberate opening for me to ask a question.

"What things did you make to spec for Andrej?" I ask, just as I'm intended to.

"Various scarificators," ey says quietly.

I turn to my datalink for clarification and find diagrams of spring-loaded multi-lancets meant to slice the skin superficially.

"Bloodletting?" I ask, uncomprehending. "For what purpose?" I see that bloodletting was once considered a medical treatment, but I cannot imagine why a stationer would try something like that.

Koni is looking at eir desk, not at me. "You must have noticed things about Andrej? Quite weak, even for a stationer..."

Obviously, Koni wants me to come to my own conclusions.

"Regardless," I push on, "you think Andrej misused this scarificator and bled to death?"

"As I've said, I don't know how ey died."

"If what you suggest is true, then Andrej did die by eir own hand, either intentionally or accidentally." I go stand near the door, but I don't leave. Unwillingly I remember Andrej standing outside eir door, preventing me from entering eir cell or even seeing inside. Hiding something.

Koni asks, "You don't believe it was suicide, then?"

"The timing of eir death..." I'm not sure how much I want to tell Koni. But I can see by the look in eir eyes that ey takes my meaning.

"Suspicious. I believe so, anyway," ey agrees. "Andrej set emself against any and all progress on Station. Ey was outspoken and well-informed."

"Do you think someone would kill em for that?" I ask.

"*Kill* em? Donna. Extraordinary. In all of Station's long, long history no stationer has ever taken the life of another."

"What did you mean by the word 'suspicious,' then?" I ask, annoyed. I feel as though ey's tricked me into revealing my thoughts.

"I mean only the timing was very fortuitous for some."

"Some. Like you?" I say.

"Me? Maybe. But Andrej's opposition most thwarted Dr. Singh and Wenslow. And though ey hasn't revealed eir opinions yet, I suspect Guadalupe has plans that were not best served by Andrej's outspoken dissent."

I say, "I have seen Guadalupe's actions directly. I can no longer consider em a neutral arbiter."

Koni looks at me. "I hold your opinion in this matter very highly," ey says. "If you believe em to be partial, then I will consider em so from this point forward."

I have the uncomfortable feeling of having divulged more than was strictly necessary.

"If you trust my opinions," I say, "then consider my suspicions about Andrej's death."

Koni sits back in eir chair. "As a doctor, Singh is sworn to protect life. Some habits are too deeply ingrained. But Wenslow..." Ey pauses as if considering. "Wenslow."

"'Wenslow, as you yourself revealed to me, has some very unusual theories," I remind em.

"Many stationers have unusual theories. Some are quite passionate about them."

When I spoke with Wenslow, I found em to be reluctant to talk about eir theories. If ey is passionate about them, ey hides it well. But I am now guarded against sharing my thoughts with Koni, so I don't mention it.

"I want to know the truth about Andrej's death," I say. "Ey deserves to have it noted correctly in Records, if nothing else." And I need to know if Andrej was killed in order to unravel the tangle of motives and plots currently aboard Station, but that's another thing Koni doesn't need to know.

"You're asking me to find out?" Koni guesses. There's a keen look in eir eye. Robotics may be eir fixation, but finding out secrets seems to be eir passion.

"I certainly cannot be seen to ask about it," I acknowledge.

"Then allow me to make some discreet inquiries on your behalf," Koni says, with barely disguised relish.

* * *

I keep a wary eye out for Dakota Jinx, the only other remaining Records clerk. I'm not sure whether asking em about Records is advisable, as it may get back to Guadalupe I'm pursuing a Records investigation I was instructed not to. When Dakota arrives in Condition just as I am tying on a clean robe, I'm still weighing the idea. But ey opens the conversation emself.

"Andrej's left," ey says.

"Ah, yes," I reply, not prepared for such a direct statement.

"Will ey ever return, do you think?"

I feel an uncomfortable twist inside. "No. Andrej is dead. Ey will not return."

Dakota disagrees. "You cannot say so with absolutely certainty, though. Nothing is impossible. Every event can be expressed as a probability."

I cannot exactly argue the point, but I don't like the idea of foolish hope. "The probability here is extremely low, though, I am certain."

Dakota says nothing, but I don't think it's sadness or respect.

"You and Andrej were not always in accord, I believe." I recall Dakota once standing in Committee to vote against Andrej, though the motion had already clearly passed. An act seemingly meant only to irritate.

"No," Dakota says rather coldly. "I don't hold with mystics. Andrej was too spiritual. The universe is bound and enumerated by mathematics, not enigmatic ritual."

I try not to look surprised. Andrej was known, even among stationers, to be methodical, punctilious, and pedantic. In comparison, Dakota is nearly fanciful.

"To call Andrej a mystic, surely…" I trail off, uncertain.

"Starvation to induce hallucinations? The universe cannot be known this way. Symbolic logic models reality in an infinite calculus. A wasted, deprived biological vessel cannot engender some factitious acumen."

I am dipping into my datalink to check Dakota's terminology, but I'm not sure it makes sense in the way ey has constructed it. It has the feel of gibberish, and Dakota's unnerving intensity as ey says it smacks of fanaticism.

But I latch onto one detail. "Andrej practiced fasting?"

Dakota regards me with blank, unblinking eyes, and says nothing.

"Unfortunate. And I *do* regret that we've lost Andrej," I say to smooth over the awkwardness.

Perhaps I should question Dakota about Records integrity, I had once hoped to make em an ally in investigating possible Records corruption. But I feel a deep distrust for eir state of mind. I don't think ey would be much help, and I don't want to work with em. How ey avoids suspicion of excessive Reform faults I do not know.

I move past Dakota to leave, but ey advises me, "Remember that infinitesimal chance ey will return."

I don't find comfort in it at all. Perhaps Dakota does.

It makes me sad to think of Andrej starving and bleeding emself, using deprivation to try and reach beyond the meaninglessness of stationer existence. I wish I had known ey suffered, though I'm not sure what I could have done. It's an unpleasant testament that we are often powerless against our fixations, which are not as harmless as we often pretend.

I think back to when I was told about Andrej, with Shelley sitting nearby so clearly stricken by the event, and the distress and seriousness of both the Commissioner and the Doctor. All three were strongly affected; only Wenslow remained calm and reasonable.

I am anxious for some new information from Koni. Because as it stands now, it seems quite likely Andrej may have taken eir fixation too far, with nothing but timing and circumstances to make it sinister.

* * *

The time for my meeting with Singh, as assigned to me in the last Council meeting, arrives while I am still dismayed by my surreal conversation with Dakota, still worrying over the circumstances around Andrej's death. After my unproductive meeting with Singh last time, I'm not sure it's wise to try and pull any more information from em. All that did was expose my distrust of eir project and reveal my memory lapses and miscues.

We meet in eir makeshift Horticulture room and ey has laid out various shallow dishes of soil alongside some instrumentation whose purpose I don't grasp. I am given instructions on how to dose the soil with various solutions, then take samples which Singh will test. The doctor offers no broader explanation, and ey seems to assume I know what we are doing.

We say nothing, and the exercise continues in silence. I cannot understand why I have been asked to do this work, it is not difficult and I'm certain Singh could do it alone or with help from Shelley.

When I have finally carried out all of Singh's directions, we begin to put away the dishes.

"I hope you have gained some appreciation of the process, Donna?" Singh asks with satisfaction.

"I am not clear on why you recruited my help," I tell em, hoping for just a hint.

"So you could see the importance of this project. And the careful work and planning that has gone into it, the hours of testing. I wouldn't want you under the misapprehension that this"—ey gestures to the samples now slotted into the instrument—"is some passing fancy of mine. I have done so much to ensure it is thoroughly researched."

"Your horticulture division? I believe you spend much of your energy here, Singh, I don't require proof of that."

Singh's expression goes a little flatter than usual. "Specifically the soil enrichment project, that so alarmed you before. It so alarmed you that you felt the need to bring it before Guadalupe. But now I hope you will see it is not a 'last-minute addition' as you put it before, and instead an integral part of our plan."

I recall nothing about soil enrichment, and I don't remember arguing with Singh about it. I don't recall watching anything about that in the playbacks of Council meetings leading up to my last survey. This must have been a private conversation.

"If you wish to enrich the soils here for your plants, I don't see why I would object to that..." I venture tentatively.

"Not here. On Earth," Singh says, watching me with eir doctorly look that makes me feel as though I am being professionally evaluated for Reform faults.

"Yes, I remember," I lie. "The soil enrichment you wanted to begin on Earth, correct? What new samples are you testing now?" I point to the vials I've been using to dose the soil samples.

"I still believe my original suite of genetically modified nitrogen-fixing bacteria and mycorrhiza to be robust enough to survive environmental conditions on Earth and outcompete the inferior soil biome there now," Singh says confidently. "I am currently testing which formulations will best spread across our test continent, prepping the soil for the new plant cultivars. You once objected there would be competition among human groups for the crops we introduced. Doesn't it solve the problem if crops grow freely everywhere?"

I am absolutely stunned by the breadth of eir vision, and at a loss for words. If ey is successful, new plant species, bioengineered by Singh from extinct cultivars, will spread across the land with their associated soil bacteria. Will they replace everything adapted to living there now?

"Before you protest again on the basis of the pitiful plant life which survives there now—" Singh starts.

I find my voice, and it comes out hoarse and grave. "Extant ecosystems will collapse."

My suggestion to Jayd that Singh intends to terraform the entire planet no longer seems like an overstatement.

"If done carelessly, that is one possible but extreme and unlikely outcome. That is *why* I'm assuring you"—Singh gestures to the work we've been doing—"that I am not embarking on this project carelessly."

I am not reassured. Ey is going to destroy Earth biomes and remake them...using nothing but crop species? That seems highly inadvisable.

"This should go before Council," I say, before remembering that I no longer have much trust in the Council process.

"It will, Donna, it will," Singh says, in a tone that suggests we have had this discussion before, exactly as we are having it now. "When the time comes. For now, we focus on procuring materials to test our systems. How can I say what is possible if I don't have the resources to properly research? It's hard enough getting that work approved, as you have seen."

I think of a thousand objections such that I cannot choose which one to raise.

"Let us not argue now," Singh says, holding up a hand. "There is plenty of time to consider, plan, regroup, and try again. I only wanted you to see my process. I think it will reassure you, over time, if you watch my work progress. Will you help me with this project? Guadalupe believes it be a good use of your time."

There is nothing to be gained from arguing with Singh now. I leave with as little ceremony as I can manage.

Singh is the expert here. Ey has access to all the Records I reviewed to reach these doomsday predictions. But what ey doesn't have is an appreciation of—no, a *love*—for the Earth as it is, with all the things surviving there. I wind through the corridors to the observation lounge, my new haunt now Records no longer feels like home.

It all comes down to whether I trust Singh. And I find I do not. I do not trust stationers to cherish and protect Earth, even though it is our only mission. Natural selection must choose the organisms best suited to living in the new environments of Earth, not us.

I gaze at the immense blue and white planet below. It is not an empty sandbox for us to play in. It is a living, thriving, complex thing that can grow on its own. I find myself wondering whether Earth ever needed us at all.

* * *

I am still in the observation lounge when Koni finds me.

"Donna. I thought you might be here."

I am pulled abruptly from my quiet communion and turn to see Koni standing by the entrance. An unwelcome sight. I don't like to be found out in my secret spot.

Koni holds up a placating hand. "I'm sorry to bother you here. We can go to my office, if you'd like? I have some information I thought might interest you."

"No, we can talk here. Come in." I say it rather ungraciously, but Koni enters and sits facing me on another of the curved benches around the periphery of the room.

Ey speaks softly as if in reverence for my private space. "It's just as I suspected. The apparatus we discussed is assumed to be the cause of lethal blood loss."

"No one killed Andrej then," I say, not surprised but oddly let down.

"There are some curious circumstances..."

I am growing impatient with eir habit of doling out tidbits. "*Tell me* the curious circumstances."

Koni continues with a more frank delivery. "There was a lot of blood. Shelley, apparently, was very affected by the sight. Ey had to be revived with a mild stimulant."

"My understanding is a scarificator would only make shallow cuts," I say. "What kind of thing did you build for Andrej?"

"I assure you the device I manufactured was safe, producing only superficial slices in the skin which, under normal circumstances, would quickly close with coagulated blood. I consulted medical texts when designing it."

"So what went wrong?" I think out loud.

"It's not clear. For some reason, Andrej continued to bleed until losing consciousness. Ey did not revive enough to call for assistance, and therefore the shell was too electrically silent to allow for Reform into another."

I am already in my datalink, looking for answers. "There are many ways to prolong blood-loss from minor wounds," I discover. "Any number of drugs and compounds and topical treatments have anticoagulant effects. Were there any in eir blood, I wonder?"

"Only Med would know," Koni says. "If they even bothered to pursue that sort of investigation."

"I thought you'd talked with Med."

"I talked with Shelley. But I cannot press too hard, you understand. It's suspicious."

I understand that very well, as I am constantly falling under suspicion myself.

Koni continues. "Given Andrej's dangerous habits, it would seem possible for someone to co-opt the process and make it fatal."

It occurs to me right away it would have been very easy for Koni emself to kill Andrej this way. I only have eir word for it the scarificator was safe. Ey honestly could have concocted this entire story. But if that's the case, then why would ey invent details implicating emself?

Cautiously I ask, "Who do you think would do such a thing?"

"It would have to be someone who knew of Andrej's habits."

"Like yourself?" I venture.

"If I had killed Andrej, I would not help you to investigate," Koni says, with the barest hint of amusement in eir voice. "But are you and I the only ones who knew?"

"Ah. A stationer told me Andrej practiced fasting," I admitted. "And we should consider those in Med. Perhaps Andrej sought counseling from Ernesta, or medical help from Singh. I do not trust Singh to keep information private, ey might have told others. And is there anyone else who knew of this scarificator you made?"

Koni admits it only reluctantly. "...I went over the specs with Wenslow."

The name settles on me like a weight. But before I can say anything Koni adds, "But I don't recall telling em whom I was making it for."

I was already convinced Wenslow was altering the Rchival process. If ey was willing to go to such extremes to protect eir project, might ey also be willing to...kill another stationer? It is *almost* unbelievable. It is almost easier to believe Andrej's death really was just a tragic misadventure for an already weakened, deprived shell.

Frustrated, I break away from the conversation and gaze out at Earth. Koni waits quietly while I ponder.

"So much suspicion but very little proof," I finally say.

"You won't have something definitive to note in Records for Andrej, I fear," Koni agrees.

I had forgotten that's the reason I gave Koni for wanting to investigate Andrej's death. And I'm glad ey reminded me, because I had been about to speculate out loud on Wenslow's involvement in the Rchive failure and now Andrej's death and wonder what else ey may have done.

"Yes," I reply. "Although, I will make a private note of our investigations and suspicions and maybe later, when things aren't so fraught on Station, the record can be corrected."

"Whatever you feel is appropriate," Koni agrees easily. "I hope it gives you some measure of satisfaction you've convinced me, at least. I believe you. The circumstances and timing are indeed very suspicious, and all seem to point to Wenslow.

"It was shrewd thinking on your part to see through this ruse. I would be willing to assist you in fact-finding your perceptive theories any time you may need it."

I nod to feign appreciation that I don't quite feel. And Koni takes eir leave.

* * *

Something about the interaction does not sit right with me. It may be that Koni persists in complimenting me, which is uncomfortable. Or maybe it's just my frustration ey can only bring me hearsay and not factual proof I could act on.

But it might also be that ey pivoted so quickly from seeming to excuse Wenslow to condemning em. I never said I held Wenslow responsible, yet ey assumed I did and agreed with me a little too eagerly. Perhaps it was obvious that's the way my thoughts were trending, true, but ey needed almost no convincing.

No other stationers will believe anything I say that challenges the status quo in the least. They will willfully ignore or refute any suggestion something could be amiss. But Koni needed only my suspicions and no solid evidence to believe a stationer murdered Andrej.

* * *

Station is mired in plots. Once I found us almost dull in our devotion to logical, single-minded service. Now I wonder if any stationer is behaving rationally or transparently at all. There are so many suggestive details and loose ends, but I can't seem to connect any of them. I wish, fervently, I was half as clever as Koni has told me I am.

It's not been many days, as stationers count them, since I've seen Jayd. But it feels like too long to me, and I miss em.

I buzz at eir door and feel palpable relief when it opens.

Ey, thankfully, puts aside paint, brush, caliper, and ladder to listen to me. Eir full attention, only for me, and I am so grateful. It allows me to focus on only the facts that I truly know. Which are pitifully few. But I desperately want eir opinion.

"My first reaction," ey says when I am finished, "is that you are over-fixating on these perceived problems and causing yourself distress—"

I open my mouth to protest, and ey holds up a hand. "But I know that you've been told that too many times already. So I will take your concerns seriously for now."

"Thank you," I say, and I mean it.

"You admit you have no proof and only circumstantial evidence. As I see it, there is no way for you to discover what happened to Andrej. I cannot see a way for you to discover what happened to you. And the only way to know what Guadalupe, Wenslow, or Singh is truly planning is to allow those plans to come to fruition. They will not tell you directly what they intend. I question whether they even have a coherent, well-articulated plan as such."

Unfortunately, I agree with em on all points. "Singh has let slip enough details, though, that I am deeply disturbed. What ey plans— Jayd, we cannot let that come to pass."

"I agree eir plan seems like dangerous overreach."

"Will you stand with me in Council and say so?"

Jayd turns eir eyes back to the painting surrounding us with color. "My voice will not make any difference. And I don't believe yours will, either."

I say, "Singh will pursue eir fixations, eir plan for Earth, with no oversight and only such safeguards as eir own faulty mind can devise, and Guadalupe will bend and contort the rules of Station to enable it. I don't understand why, but that is what is happening. How misguided I was to think Guadalupe would help me—" I cut off, my mind stuttering over details.

"Donna?" Jayd prompts.

I barely hear em.

"I *did* think Guadalupe would hear me," I say slowly. "I contacted Guadalupe, I opened a direct channel to em before my launch. Ey told me I did so, but we never spoke. And Singh told me I called eir soil project a 'last-minute addition' and contacted Guadalupe about it."

I focus on Jayd again. "Those were the same incidents. That's what happened before I launched. Singh told me about eir plan to introduce bioengineered soil bacteria, and I thought it was a concerning development, and I..."

I put my hand to my head, trying to remember, but there's nothing. Only the feeling that I'm right.

"You only open a direct channel when you think something is dangerous and important. I must have been greatly disturbed. But why was it so urgent I tell Guadalupe immediately?"

Jayd, watching me, gives a minute shake of eir head.

"I'm making quite a leap here, but hear me out. I'm guessing Singh was asking me, at that very moment, to take some of eir samples to Earth."

"Why reach that conclusion?"

"Koni also told me ey was going to send a device with me, which ey said I would use to take pictures, but I bet it was a drone. What if they wanted me to distribute Singh's samples over some soil using a drone and see what happened?"

"I find it hard to believe they would attempt something so momentous without getting Council approval first."

But I disagree. "No, they never ask Council. All these plans are proceeding without any oversight, every stationer is doing precisely what they want. Those discussions in Council are just for show, or distraction, or some other purpose I don't understand. Besides, Singh doesn't even believe eir 'tests' are so consequential. Introducing invasive species to a place with no value doesn't matter, and ey can't see why it would be necessary to ask permission."

I can no longer sit. I get up off Jayd's cot and walk to the wall, but there's nowhere else to go.

"Even if that had been their plan, it was thwarted when you were injured and forgot your objectives," Jayd reminds me.

"It is one possible reason why they are pushing so hard for sending drones to mine Salvage on Earth," I say. "Because Singh could quietly send seeds and soil bacteria to be distributed. I don't know why Koni is helping em do all this, though. Ey does not care about Horticulture."

"Not to lend credence to this wild speculation," Jayd says, "but Singh would undoubtedly need Koni's help to modify drones for such a purpose. Koni is the stationer to see if you need something made to spec."

"And Koni loves to be helpful," I agree. "Ey loves to know *every* stationer's secrets."

I hear Jayd repeat the word "love" in a small voice, reminding me that stationers don't use words like that.

I am trying to understand my past self's motivations. "Why would I leave on Survey if I was so concerned about all this? Why did I not postpone and make an appointment with Guadalupe?"

"You *are* fixated on survey trips," Jayd observes. "I can believe you wouldn't want to delay or cancel one. Possibly you gave them a stern lecture on the Mission Imperatives and warned them you'd speak about this when you returned."

I look at em. "Jayd, are you teasing me?"

"'Love' and now 'teasing'? Donna. You have given up all pretense of being a stationer. Do not let anyone else hear you speak like that. In fact, I hope you will not repeat any of the things you have said here. I have let you speculate aloud in hopes you might stumble on an explanation which brings you peace. Another stationer might find your fantasies to be deeply worrying."

Ey is correct. "But you *were* teasing me."

Ey's expression is exceptionally neutral.

"Jayd, I am so very glad to have had your help," I say. "Talking it out has done me immense good, there is no one else who would have assisted me like this. Thank you."

Jayd looks a little stiff at my too-warm declaration. And then ey says something I can tell makes em uncomfortable. "You might consider, if all you're guessing is true, and someone really did allow you to be injured intentionally— which I'm not convinced of yet—and if Andrej was *killed,* as you suggest—which I really struggle to believe. But if all of this *is* really so... Then, Donna, your position right now must be vulnerable."

"That is one data point that does not fit," I agree. "If someone wanted me dead, then why would I be allowed to return, and Reform into a new shell, and walk about Station investigating all these misdeeds? Whoever tried to kill me before, why haven't they tried again? It would have been so easy before I was *this*." I lift an arm and casually flex, and Jayd for the first time notices my shell.

"Uh, I doubt physical strength factors into it," ey says. "And remember stationers so often behave according to their own internal sense of reason, which is not always transparent."

"You mean, of course, they are all completely faulty and unpredictable."

"I do not mean quite that…"

"I regret I have begun to believe it," I say. I do not wish to, but they are making quite a case for it.

Jayd and I both remain quiet for a moment, pondering our own disappointment and uneasiness.

"Previously I implied you were faulty," Jayd says at long last, "but now I begin to suspect you are the only one of us retaining any sense of perspective. Stationers have spent too long in our isolated boxes."

Eir voice has a near undetectable edge of pain to it, and it makes my heart hurt like I am thinking of Anissa.

"Jayd, you have made your little box so beautiful," I say. "It has saved, at the least, a sliver of your humanity."

"Maybe." Ey looks thoughtfully at eir painted walls. "But I think you must trust your own judgment."

I feel a loosening of something inside, something I'd been holding tensed up.

"I will," I say.

* * *

My next plan of action is to question Shelley. Ey was at my launch. Whatever was said there, ey heard. Both Singh and Koni gave me little glimpses of their role, but only Shelley has no particular interest in twisting the facts to eir advantage. I hope to get a straighter answer out of em.

I prefer to just buzz at the door to eir cell, but ey might be more willing to talk if I politely ask to pay a visit beforehand. So I make my request and go about my business, visiting Condition and working myself strenuously as I often do.

My workouts have made me look different from other stationers, and I wonder no one has remarked on it. Stationer shells are insubstantial, but I no longer am. On Earth I would be nothing unusual, though short, but here I feel a physical confidence I do not previously remember having. Stationers don't ordinarily notice their bodies, but one who chances to notice mine would think twice about trying to overpower me.

I think I am only now recognizing my motivation for all this exercise. I pull through another set of reps, then I must go to Nutri and eat. Muscle cannot be built from nothing.

There is no one in Nutri, which suits me as I usually eat about three times what a stationer would eat, and I don't need an audience. Though I doubt anyone would object. The drones harvesting biomass from the oceans for our nutrition have the capacity to feed a Station full of stationers, not our currently reduced numbers.

I sit down with my tray and mindlessly chew the wafers. I am wondering to myself if any stationer ever thought to reprogram the drones to collect less, or perhaps deploy less often, when I have a shock of a thought.

A stationer *could* reprogram the drones which go regularly to Earth. A stationer *could* modify them to carry something down and release it to the surface. And, with all the changes being made to Records, I believe someone could fix it so the drone logs look unaltered. Certainly, Wenslow's terminals were made to look unlocked when they were not.

I don't even return my tray.

I am at Jayd's door as soon as I can get there. I buzz, but ey doesn't answer. I think quickly. Ey wasn't in Condition, I've just left Nutri. The only other place I know that Jayd regularly visits is Fabrication.

To my relief ey is there, and no other stationer is.

Ey is unpleasantly shocked to see me there with such a determined expression. I can tell because though eir face remains passive, ey accidentally drips some paint onto the floor of the Fabrication Bay without noticing.

I step right up close to em. "Jayd, I need you to come with me," I say quietly. There is no other stationer present, but I'm certain there are at the very least audio feeds in here, and I don't want us overheard.

"No—" Jayd starts.

"You told me to trust myself," I insist. "Maybe this is nothing, but I have a terrible theory, and I want to see for myself that it isn't true. Will you come with me?"

"At a later time perhaps," Jayd looks back to eir work and only now sees the paint dripping to the floor. Ey quickly sets the larger container down and screws the lid onto the smaller vessel ey was filling. Some paint smears onto eir hand, and ey stares at it as if ey cannot comprehend how the process has gone so badly.

"Now, Jayd. I have to see now. I will go with or without you, but I would rather have you along. You can tell me how faulty I am if this idea of mine is proved false. I hope that it will be, honestly."

"But where are you going?" ey asks.

I glance meaningfully up at the corners of the massive construction bay. We're in such an insignificant corner of it, I can't imagine that there is recording of this spot. But also I won't chance it.

"I'll tell you in the corridor," I promise.

I want to take eir arm and pull em along, but stationers don't touch each other like that. It would feel to Jayd indistinguishable from assault.

"Come," I urge em instead. "It won't take long. A short walk. Come along..."

I invade eir space and ey steps away, and I herd em into the corridor.

I walk close at eir elbow, speaking quietly and urgently. "It's the food collection drones," I start, but ey pulls away again. I am too close, too intense for em.

It can wait. I say nothing, and we pass quietly through the halls. I navigate to the Flight command center, which is not far from Fabrication, and glance through the glass doors into the darkened launch theater. There are pods lining the far wall, I know, though I cannot make them out.

We are close enough that I feel pulled to them. I want to get in one and leave scheming stationers behind me. But we pass without slowing.

Beyond is the corridor leading to the Flight residence cells, but we don't head that way. We turn an unmarked corner to a disused hall and a strongly reinforced door.

"How can we get in?" The door is vacuum-proof, for when the drones are deployed.

Jayd looks at me. "Why would we enter that room?"

"Who has jurisdiction here? What privilege do we need?" I dip into my datalink and see that we need Supervisor Flight-privilege to open the locked door. That's Bri Ito. I try to think of some way to convince em to open it for me.

Jayd is still waiting for an explanation. "If Singh wants to send drones to Earth to distribute seeds, why wait for the Council to approve, and for Koni to build, the mining drones? Why not simply tag along with the ocean-harvesting drones?"

"They fly over the ocean, Donna. It is not an excellent place to plant seeds."

I note that even after all this disturbance, Jayd's wit is still intact.

"The flight patterns could be changed," I argue.

"Not without a lot of clearance from different privileges. But if you want to inspect the drones, they are stored next door until loaded into the propulsion chamber." Jayd raises a finger and points at another door further down the corridor.

Ey even consents to open it using eir Fabrication-privilege.

Inside I find a small room with exposed machinery for walls, different from the molded white plastic of most Station interiors, and a row of large, roughly cylindrical capsules on a rail feeding through the wall into the next room. They are lined up neatly with no sign of having been disturbed.

Jayd stands quietly by the door while I go down on one knee beside them without quite knowing what I should look for. I settle on the idea of rotating them fully in their slot to view all sides, which makes an unpleasant scraping sound. Jayd winces.

One by one I work my way down the line, finding them all identical and uninteresting. There are only six, and nothing catches my eye until I come to the fifth in line.

Then I gasp. I turn to look over my shoulder at Jayd and slide aside to reveal to em what I see. There's a panel on the side of the capsule which looks roughhewn and badly sealed.

Jayd stands for a long silent moment staring at it expressionlessly.

Then ey comes to kneel delicately beside me. Eir thin hands slide over the roughened panel. Ey compares the capsule to the one beside it. "There's a small hatch here, cut and welded without the precision of the programmable metalwork rig in Fabrication."

"What's in it?" I demand, looking around for something large enough to hit it with.

But Jayd reaches for a maintenance drawer under the rail I hadn't even seen, takes out a short tool with a precisely crooked tip, and neatly releases the panel. It makes a grinding sound as I force it open, as though it's not well-fitted.

Jayd says. "It's empty."

"*Now* it is empty," I say, running my finger along the inside of the dark compartment, feeling for powder or dust. I nick my finger on an uneven seam, but find nothing obvious to the naked eye.

I feel a creeping dread that whatever was in here has already been released on Earth. "They've already done it."

"Perhaps. But this compartment is not shielded from radiation, heat, or cold. Anything in here experienced vacuum, re-entry, and solar emanations." Jayd's calm voice grounds me. "This is not a reliable way to transfer anything living to the surface."

I ask, "Is this part of some routine repair to a damaged drone, then?"

"No." Jayd stands. "That would have been done in Fabrication Bay with more precise tools."

We both stand looking, unsure what to make of it. It's not obvious to me that it's what I specifically fear, but also neither of us can explain it.

Jayd reaches over and traces one tapered finger along another drone, where there is an uneven line etched across the surface.

"What's that?" I ask.

"I've seen it before," Jayd says thoughtfully, "when the torch temperature is improperly calibrated. It makes a more diffuse gouge instead of a neat cut."

"Someone was practicing? Or experimenting to get the technique right?"

While we contemplate, a green light comes on above the rail with an audible click. Somewhere within the walls there is a quiet whir of machinery.

"What's happening?" I demand. "Is a drone being deployed?"

"I don't know," Jayd says.

Small clasps on the rail snick into place around the capsules.

"No," I say. I step up to the first drone in line and grab one of the fins. I rock it in place, nudging it back and forth, then at the right moment put all my weight and strength into yanking it off the rail. I have to jump out of the way to keep my feet from being crushed as it slams to the floor, making a tremendous reverberating crash, and a metallic squeal as it slides to rest against the wall, adding a few dull scrapes to the already scuffed floor.

We both look at the damage with wide eyes. It's such a violent, raw thing for a stationer to have done. I almost cannot believe it happened.

Jayd speaks in a tremulous voice. "Donna, we cannot act unilaterally like this. We must...bring this up in Council or...take it to Guadalupe..."

"Guadalupe will not act. Ey was positively obstructive when I brought the problem in Records before em. No one will listen to us. Koni did not ask for permission before ey tampered with this drone, and I won't ask either."

"You cannot know for sure what's happened here," Jayd pleads.

"Maybe not," I agree. "But I can't wait until someone provides answers."

A red error light comes on in the spot where the drone had been secured, and wheels along the side of the rail spin as if preparing to advance the next drone into place.

I step aggressively forward.

Jayd holds out eir hand. "Wait. Take some time to turn it over in your mind, to do your research. With my help..."

Ey breaks off suddenly when I grab the next drone in line and begin to rock it in place.

"Donna?" eir voice trembles as ey takes another quick step back.

The second drone comes crashing down, narrowly missing my thigh as it catches on the edge of the rail in falling.

I turn and see Jayd's wide eyes.

"I'm going to take every one of these off the line. Then stationers will *have* to examine this process and see what's happening here. It's the only way to force their attention to this matter."

There's a heavy quiet in the room.

Jayd asks, "What... what happened to you on that last survey?"

I look away from em. "I loved. I loved someone."

We are both silent, then even more quietly ey says, "I am jealous."

I turn to see eir face and eir eyes have lost their half-lidded passiveness. When has ey ever looked at me like that? It skewers something inside of me.

"A child," I say. "I had a daughter. It's...hard to explain. But Jayd, you...of everyone on Station...you..." I take a calming breath. "You're special to me."

"Donna," ey leans away from me a little, eir eyes averted. It's so hard for us to witness others feeling something. Ey can't even watch me tell em that I care about em.

The wheels are still winding up. "I must finish this."

Ey looks up warily.

"Stand away," I tell em, and I attack the next drone. When I stop afterward to breathe, I see Jayd standing in the corner, eir eyes squeezed shut and both hands clapped over eir ears. I feel a rush of remorse for how hard this must be. It's too violent for em. And I hadn't thought about the noise of it. I begin to worry we'll be interrupted and prevented from finishing.

I walk over to Jayd and reach out to take eir wrists, but falter. How easy it was to gather Anissa into my arms. And how hard is it to make myself touch a stationer. Even Jayd.

I count a breath or two and, using just my fingertips, gently guide eir hands away from eir ears.

Ey startles at my touch and eir eyes fly open.

"I am sorry," I say. "They may come to stop me soon. You don't have to be here."

We look at each other for a moment.

"I'll go to Blake Ahmad," Jayd finally says. "As supervisor of Maint ey will want to see this, and ey is not supportive of the Earth-mining project."

"That's an excellent idea," I agree. "Ey will be more likely to listen to you. Will you tell em what's been going on, Wenslow's Records meddling and Andrej's death and Singh's plans? Can you talk to em for me?"

"I will," ey says unsteadily. "What will you do?"

"Finish here. And then find Shelley. Once it's discovered what I've done, no one will willingly speak with me again. I need to ask em questions that no one else can answer."

Jayd looks at the drones in disarray over the gouged floor. "I can't shield you from what you've done here. I don't have any influence. It will be bad for you."

"Don't even try to plead my case," I tell em. "It's a lost cause. I will have to wait to be exonerated by Blake's examination of this modified collection drone."

"I will advocate for you however I am able," ey says. Eir wide eyes are looking into mine. For a moment their depths hold me.

I have to look away so I can focus on my task.

"I'm going," Jayd says, standing with eir hand on the door frame.

"Please. Take care," I tell em. Then I turn from em and grab the next drone in line. "Beware of Wenslow. Don't interact with em if you can avoid it. Ey is subtle and dangerous."

Jayd disappears down the corridor. I take a deep breath and begin rocking the next heavy capsule, relieved to finally be taking action.

The last few drones go more slowly. It's an exhausting task. But I keep at it. In my mind I see Jayd's expression as I lowered eir hands from eir ears. It is a deep relief to have em fully on my side. It feels right and good.

* * *

When the last drone topples heavily to the floor, the room is a mess. The rail that held the capsules sheared apart in places, and I gingerly avoid shards of metal as I skirt the fallen drones, my thin Station slippers offering no protection. I check my datalink but there are no alarms or warnings running through the general feed.

That's good because I want to catch Shelley unaware. I avoid Med and hope to find em in eir quarters. Eir plaque reads Sheldon McConnelly.

I try to compose myself and buzz at the door. While I wait, I can't avoid seeing eir playback.

A tiny baby with tubes running to eir nose in an incubator. A freckled boy with no shoes running down an old, cracked sidewalk...

I look away impatiently. Even if it is completely authentic, the stationer is this cell doesn't retain even a shred of that long ago person. If I want to get answers to my questions, I need to connect with the Shelley who is here now.

Ey finally opens the door, and I start as gently as I know how. "Shelley, do you have some time for me? I'd like your opinion on some matters."

"Shall we go to Med?"

"No, no need." I pause, hoping ey will invite me in.

Ey steps back and I enter. There's a chair and I take it, and ey sits on the cot a moment later. Beside the chair is a narrow table pushed against the wall. I scan the things there; a screen for viewing datalink, a tablet for making notes, and behind it all a strange icon of a staff with something twined around it.

I don't want Shelley to feel like I'm in a hurry to interrogate em, so I ask idly about the icon.

Shelley glances at it. "I believe it's something I brought with me when we became stationers. I don't remember its symbolism."

I've already dipped into my datalink and seen that it's called a Rod of Asklepios, that it's of significance to healers and doctors. Stationers are so singularly uninterested in anything outside of their fixations.

"It depicts a snake," I say. "An animal from Earth. I don't know if they still survive. I saw lizards, on my last survey, but I don't recall any snakes."

"Curious," Shelley says, without the least hint of curiosity in eir face or manner.

We are both silent for a long moment, and I give up on an easy conversation.

"I wanted to ask you about...I confess I am still quite upset over Andrej's death."

There's a change in the current of the room.

"I was there when you were instructed not to discuss this, Donna."

I know that Koni has already questioned Shelley about this, but ey was circumspect. I'm now prepared to be a bit more direct in the hopes of getting a better answer.

"You also seemed upset," I tell Shelley. It's a bit of an insult, accusing a stationer of an unbalanced emotional state, but I'm hoping we can agree over the incident being difficult for us.

"Upset? A stationer's death is a serious matter, it affects us all." I can tell ey does take offense, though ey hides it fairly well.

"Death," I repeat. "Not suicide?"

"We cannot know Andrej's intent," Shelley says. "Ey died of a wound. Whether it was self-inflicted or accidental is ultimately not important."

"You were investigating it, though," I guess. "I saw you reading histopathology slides in Med. That was Andrej's tissue, wasn't it?"

Shelley shifts on eir cot. "It is my job to investigate deaths. There have been many on Station, and I have carefully evaluated them all."

"What did you find when you looked at Andrej's wounds?"

Shelley is quiet and still. Ey looks directly at me for a long, tense moment.

"Marinne and Guadalupe gave you very specific instructions not to pry into this matter."

It takes me a moment to remember that Singh's first name is Marinne.

"It would give me satisfaction to know eir death wasn't somehow unusual. I thought you could tell me."

"It's not my place to share Med findings. I defer to my supervisor. As should you."

I can tell this conversation with Shelley is not going well. Ey won't tell me anything. I hope I haven't ruined my chances to get my next questions answered. Those are less fraught, at least.

"Alright, nothing more about Andrej," I say, and hope ey will relax. But if ey does, I can't tell.

I press ahead. "There are things you *can* talk to me about. You know Singh so well. Can you tell me if ey is displeased with me over our conversation before my last launch? We argued, I think, but I cannot remember what we said." I am hoping ey will drop some hints about what was going on at the time, because I can see asking a direct question will get me nowhere.

Predictably, ey says, "I will not discuss matters that don't concern me."

"Are *you* displeased with me for arguing with Singh?" I ask, with a flash of insight. "I do wish I had your goodwill, at least."

"I am a Med clerk. I do not hold particular stationers in poor esteem. I impartially serve all aboard. As you should, Donna."

Ey is twice as infuriating as Andrej. I have no idea how Singh works with em. And it's clear I won't enlist eir help or indeed pry one scrap of information from eir tightly sealed lips.

"Yes, thank you," I say.

* * *

I excuse myself quickly to decide on my next course of action. I wish I had talked with Blake and Timothy earlier instead of waiting for permission to form that committee Andrej wanted. I might have already had them on my side.

If Jayd is going to talk to Blake now, then I can go talk to Timothy. I walk toward eir cell, trying to decide whether to tell em everything or just a few key details.

Ey is not in eir cell. I weigh the consequences of pursuing em about the Station and decide it's worth it. There is no time to act as though I am not desperate. I am desperate.

I walk to Nutri and do not find em. I walk toward Condition. I pass the end of the corridor that leads to the part of Station where Maint is housed. I wonder if Jayd is down there now, speaking with Blake.

A little way further down the corridor I stop. There is something lying tossed messily in a corner of the corridor.

I walk up to it, and I see that it is a shell. And that it is dead.

And that it is Jayd.

Part Three

On Earth, I killed people. I thought a target over their location and called down the beam and instantaneously reduced them to a pile of ash. There were no bodies.

I am not accustomed to looking at bodies. This one, this now-empty shell, is broken and limp and jumbled. It wears a face, the last I saw on Jayd. The last face Jayd will ever have. But I understand it is not Jayd. Eir consciousness inhabited it for a while, but that consciousness is now gone. Forever lost. Ey lived over a thousand years. Ey painted things no one saw. Ey was my closest friend.

I feel frozen. I cannot bend to touch em. I cannot walk away.

Under the head of the shell is a pool of pinkish fluid. I stare at that, to keep from seeing eir face, eir awful vacant expression. I stare at that puddle of pink and wait for my mind to start working. But nothing seems to be working. I am not thinking. I am not feeling.

Cerebrospinal fluid.

I bend and tip eir head just a fraction. There is a hole. Eir skull has been neatly caved in just above the ear. I have seen a wound exactly like that before. In my own head.

My cheeks begin to burn hot. My peripheral vision is crowded out by a red mist. I have never felt anger like this. Never. I don't know what to do with it.

I am running through a corridor. I don't know where I'm going. I slam into a wall as I take a corner too fast, but I right myself and keep running. I pass a stationer and shove em aside.

I skid to a stop outside Wenslow's office, leaning on eir door entryway, panting to regain my breath. Ey's inside, calmly peering at eir scope and making notes on eir terminal.

Eir quiet obliviousness is maddening.

"Wenslow!" I growl.

Ey jerks around at the sound of my voice. "Donna?"

"Murderer," I say under my breath, stalking forward across the floor. I am tightening and flexing my fingers.

"Donna?" eir voice comes out unnaturally high, and ey stands with eir eyes widening. "What's happened?"

"You've killed Jayd," I grate. "That's what's happened."

"Killed?" ey asks, disbelief in eir voice. "Jayd is dead?"

"Ey is. Murdered in the exact fashion you murdered me." I am across the floor, and Wenslow circles away from me to keep the desk between us.

I am taller than em by only half a head, maybe, but my strong arms and broad chest make me seem even larger. I don't chase em around the desk, but I consider going over it to get to em.

"Donna, I did not kill Jayd. I have been here for days. I've discovered a new point of interest...." Ey manages to keep emself from going off on a tangent. "I did not, Donna."

I pause. I have no idea whether to expect honesty from em, or whether ey could lie convincingly. It's not a thing stationers usually do, but then again neither is murder.

"First Andrej, and then Jayd," I say. "Anyone who stands in the way of your plan." I gesture at the visuals on eir telescope. "And before that, me. Me! Before I went on Survey. I would have died if I wasn't inhabiting a surveyor shell. That was a murder, too."

"I did not attempt your life, Donna. And I don't believe that Andrej was murdered. That was an accident. But what's happened with Jayd?"

Doubt is creeping into my mind. It dissolves the fury fueling me, and I feel my shoulders start to shake. I open my mouth to speak but all that escapes is a ragged sob. At first, I do not understand what is happening to my body. I cannot remember ever having wept before. But tears are streaming down my face and obscuring my vision.

Wenslow looks away, hiding me from sight with eir hand. Few situations could be so uncomfortable for a stationer.

"Donna, control yourself," ey says with quiet distaste.

Ey waits for a moment while I squeeze my eyes shut to try and stop the tears, then asks, "How can you be sure it's a murder? Jayd was very fatalistic. Perhaps ey decided not to continue eir life as a stationer."

"False," I choke. "Utterly false. Ey did not cave in eir own head in the middle of a corridor."

"Whom have you alerted?" Wenslow asks. Eir eyes take on that still look telling me ey's accessing eir notifications. Ey's probably searching every stream of information available to see what alerts I may have sent out.

"No one. I found em and I ran here," I say.

"Then we will take the news to Guadalupe and Dr. Singh," ey says.

I frown at the names. I don't trust either of them, or anyone else. I certainly don't trust Wenslow. But there is no one for me to talk to. There is nowhere to go.

"Let them find eir shell," I say grimly. I walk toward the door.

"Donna, they will want to interview you," Wenslow says. "That's two deaths you've been closely involved with."

I turn on my way out of eir door. "Me? You think I am running over Station killing my friends and allies?" I give my head a short, sharp shake. I cannot keep from suspecting em.

"Donna, if you disappear into your cell it will appear very *irregular*. When they see how you've acted here, in my office…" Ey trails off delicately.

But I only shake my head. I am long past caring whether I am judged as faulty. "Are you threatening me? Or bargaining? It's wasted breath."

"I am trying to go about this the proper way," ey says, holding up both hands.

"There is no protocol for dealing with murders on Station," I say. "I may behave howsoever I choose."

I leave, walking quickly. The misery of it is that the person I most want to discuss my situation with is Jayd emself. I swipe tears from my face. I could go back to eir empty shell. Arrange it somehow, show it some reverence. But that won't help em. And it won't help me. And I need help.

Soon I'm trotting down another corridor, working my way back to Flight. I go to the cells where Flight personnel are housed, find a door and buzz. And wait. No one answers. I buzz again. I feel a rising fear. I bang on the door with my fist and shout, "Sasha!"

The door slides open and I'm looking into the impassive face of the hermit.

"You are faulty," Sasha says.

"Yes." I tap a finger in the center of Sasha's chest and ey immediately steps back. I follow and let the door of the cell slide shut behind us.

Without asking, I push the door into the privy closet, draw water into the basin, and splash it over my face, scrubbing away the tears and mucous. It is a gross violation of personal privacy to enter this closet. But Sasha says nothing, betrays no emotion.

When I back out of the closet Sasha is sitting in the center of the room in a familiar pose.

I sit down, too. Collapse onto the floor.

"You are disturbed."

"I am unhinged, Sasha. Jayd is dead." I rub my hands over my face.

"Jayd?"

For a moment I cannot speak.

"You were too close," Sasha says.

Images of Jayd. Eir arm brushing mine. Eir thin wrists under my fingertips. Eir eyes looking up into mine.

Sasha continues. "The closer the connection the more dangerous it is. You were not so upset about Andrej."

"I *was* upset about Andrej," I say angrily. "I am upset about stationers being murdered. This is a horror! What I cannot understand is why *no one else* seems upset."

"There have been no murders. Your injury was a mishap on the surface. And Andrej's death was an accident. If Jayd is indeed dead—"

I snap, "Then someone will certainly take care to make that also appear an accident, though..." I feel ill, thinking of Jayd's ruined shell. "They will have a more difficult task this time."

I lean forward and bury my face in my hands, trying to squeeze out the images that are overwhelming me.

Sasha hesitates, and then speaks carefully. "Donna, let us practice the things I taught you. You cannot be useful to yourself or anyone in this state."

"I can't," I snap.

"Try," Sasha coaxes. "Just try. Sit. Measure your breath."

But I continue angrily stalking the cell. Sasha slips into meditation slowly, without waiting for me. I cannot say how long passes. Hours. I burst into tears a few times, master myself, wash my face, resume pacing. Sasha makes no comment.

Eventually, I grow tired. It must be time, past time, for my sleep cycle. At long last I sit and breathe as Sasha suggested.

Much later I wake up on the cold floor, curled into a ball, my shoulder stiff where it was pinned under me.

Sasha is across the room, leaning against the wall with eir back straight, legs outstretched, hands folded neatly in eir lap.

I turn over and curl in the opposite direction, my face to the wall. I am sick for lack of comfort. I squeeze my eyes shut and try to remember the feel of Anissa's thin arms around me. The smell of her hair. The sound of her relaxed breathing.

I wake again when Sasha wakes and uses the closet.

"It's time for my rotation in Nutri. Will you join me?" I am touched by eir invitation.

"I cannot."

"Are you well?" Sasha asks.

"No," I respond. "I cannot begin to be well. Not until I find who killed Jayd."

"You still believe it was murder?"

"I *know* it was murder. I had no solid proof in Andrej's case but now there can be no doubt. Jayd died of the same wound that was inflicted on Peace-in-the-Sky. That can only mean both injuries were deliberate and both occurred on Station. I've been lied to. Peace-in-the-Sky was gravely injured when Singh sent the pod off to Earth. I spoke to

Shelley just yesterday, but I asked em the wrong question. I need to find em and ask the right questions."

"Donna, I wish you would consider my one observation. That your persistent involvement is making this situation worse. Consider if you had come back from your surface survey and never asked any of these questions."

Although ey is probably right, I cannot find the words to explain why I don't see it that way. "I'm a Records clerk, Sasha. I need to find the truth. And it's too late now." I buzz the door open to go. "I won't stop until I find who killed Jayd."

"Think," Sasha says. "Think, before you decide on a course of action."

Shelley is not in eir cell. Ey is not in Nutri. I see em as I stand at the entrance to Condition, where ey is working eir shell on an elliptical machine.

I wait, ignoring multiple messages in my feed.

When Shelley is done, ey removes eir robe and feeds it through the chute, steps into the booth, rinses eir shell clean, and then dons a fresh folded robe from a cubby. Ey heads for the exit, sees me standing there, and stops.

"Donna."

"Shelley."

Ey waits for a moment. Then says, "What are you doing here?"

"I came to talk to you," I say.

"We talked just recently," Shelley says. "There's nothing more we need to discuss."

"Something crucial has happened in the meantime," I say, trying to keep my voice from shaking. "And I think I now know the right question to ask you."

Shelley focuses briefly on the corridor behind me. I think ey would like to just leave, but I am blocking the way.

"I want to ask about the preparations for my last survey, when I was fitted into the pod. You were there. Was I well?"

"The results of any pre-flight wellness checks are available in Med," Shelley says. "You can ask Marinne to see the Records."

"Marinne?" I can't help but call attention to eir use of Singh's first name. "Never mind about em. You were there. I'm asking what you saw. Just tell me what you saw with your own eyes."

Shelley says nothing. It takes effort not to grab em and shake em.

"Tell me," I say deliberately, "there wasn't a hole in the side of my head when you strapped me into that pod."

Eir eyes flick to the side for just a moment, and I jump into the datalink, too.

"I can see the direct channel you just opened to Singh," I say coldly. "Is this an emergency?"

Shelley pulls back from me without actually stepping back.

"Why won't you lie, Shelley? You refuse to answer, and defer to Singh, and hide behind Med-privilege, but why won't you just *lie*?"

The channel closes with Singh's one word: "Med."

"Well, let's go," I say. "Now ey is expecting us."

Shelley and I walk down the corridor, keeping pace. I worry who else may have seen that direct channel. By now there must be those who are seeking me.

Shelley gives me a quick glance before fixing eir gaze straight ahead.

"Now I am figuring everything out," I say to em, "you may as well admit to me Andrej was murdered."

Shelley's voice is thin and strained. "Autopsy reports are Med-privilege accounts. Med supervisor Dr. Marinne Singh controls access…"

"Who are you?" I interrupt. "Are you Shelley? Or are you just a little tool of Marinne's?"

This time there is steel in eir voice. "I am just a little tool of Marinne's."

I take a few measured breaths to keep my temper in check. I'm not going to get anything useful out of Shelley.

* * *

I'm watching the corridors around Med, and when we step inside I scan quickly for others, but there's no one there but Singh. Ey stands up from eir station when we enter, and there's nothing about em that betrays nervousness or surprise.

"Donna? Are you well?" ey asks.

"No," I say sharply. "Three stationers have been murdered and I'm the only one who seems concerned, so I am not well."

"Shelley, go back to your cell," Singh says, "wait there for my instructions." Ey obeys Singh immediately.

They are close, I think, in the way Jayd and I were. Maybe closer. The thought floods me with anger.

"Is Jayd's shell here?" I ask Singh.

"It is in cold storage awaiting autopsy," Singh answers evenly.

"I can tell you what you're going to find," I say. "Ey was killed by 'discrete penetrating trauma to the upper temporal region of the skull.' Just like I was."

"You live, Donna," ey says.

"I would have died. It was your intention I should die."

"It was never my intention. I am a doctor; I do not take life."

"What did you intend to do, then?" I ask angrily.

Ey reacts to my show of emotion with distaste. "I did not inflict a wound on you, Donna. I sent you to Earth in the state you were delivered to me. Just as protocol dictates."

"Protocol? What protocol calls for sending a dying shell to Earth? That makes no sense, unless you were trying to conceal the fact I was murdered."

I stare at em while my mind works, and ey says nothing. Ey is looking at some point beyond my shoulder.

"You must have watched me be murdered. We were talking before it happened. Why would you cover that up?"

A voice behind me says, "I never can tell what rules you're going to stick at, Donna."

I whirl around, every nerve screaming in alarm, and see a stationer in the doorway. It's Koni.

"I've seen you sidestep direct orders from Guadalupe eirself several times. But when you thought Singh might dispense with some minor Station guidelines, you felt bound to raise an immediate alarm. Does that seem fair? Does that seem the action of an unfaulty mind?"

I don't remember how I might have behaved around Koni in the past. But I know myself. "It doesn't surprise me you can't tell the difference between a rule meant to obstruct and one meant to protect, or why I would choose to ignore one and insist on the other."

A fleeting expression of annoyance crosses Koni's face. "I am always on the cusp of recruiting you, Donna. We work together, but you never come around to agree with me. It's very frustrating. And we can't proceed, not really, without your support. I've always needed either you or Andrej."

"So why would you kill em, then?" I demand.

"I didn't. Why would I? We—you and I—working together, came to the conclusion Wenslow killed Andrej. I still believe that. Ey is very subtle, though. Supplying em with dangerous drugs under some ruse? I'm not so patient. You know my weapon of choice."

It's then I realize ey is standing in an odd pose for a stationer, eir shoulder leaning against the doorway to Med. Eir arm is tucked behind em, concealing something in eir hand behind the hem of eir robe.

I don't move, but Singh takes a step forward. "Koni. You cannot bring that here."

Koni gives Singh a quick glance but locks eyes with me again. "You are already complicit, Singh," ey tells em.

"Both of you," I say, "you loaded me into a pod while I was unconscious and dying." I look at Singh, but I keep Koni in my peripheral vision. "I was *dying*."

"I thought you were beyond resuscitation. Beyond Reforming even. Percussive damage to the brain like that." There's some emotion behind Singh's expression. Fear, I think. But I don't know what ey is afraid of.

"Surveyor shells are tougher than we realized," Koni says. "Stationer shells break so easily."

I look back to Koni.

"Jayd," I choke out.

Red closes in on my vision. I make fists at my sides as my shoulders tense.

"That was a terrible mistake," ey says quickly. "I was in a panic. Wenslow sent me to redirect Jayd to Guadalupe, but Jayd wouldn't be deterred, and I made a snap decision. I regretted it instantly. I am so very sorry."

I was not expecting that response. I am surprised out of my growing rage.

"We can still salvage all of this, Donna," Koni goes on. "Already Wenslow is pulling strings and tightening the knot of suspicion around you. What an unfortunate idea of yours to threaten em and weep in eir office. Ey has video feed in there, you know, just as ey does all over Station. Ey saw you urgently pull Jayd away from Fabrication, knew that you had coerced Jayd to help you and sent em on a mission to recruit others, ey knew you went to Flight to hide. And ey has Guadalupe's ear like no one else."

I hadn't realized how involved Wenslow was. Koni was right to describe em as subtle. Even now, I cannot see what eir aim is.

But Koni is still trying to convince me of something. "Singh is in no position to oppose Guadalupe and Wenslow united, you've seen that. But *I* can hide you. I know where all the video feeds are. I will keep you safe until I send my probes to Earth's surface, and you can ride along. A rough ride, maybe, but it's a solid chance for you. Then you disappear among the humans down there and no one will ever ask after you again."

There is silence while I consider this. I can see Singh is hopeful. Koni is tense.

I say, "More than I want to go to Earth, I want to protect it. If I leave, nothing stops you from ruining it, Singh."

"I will *not* ruin anything, Donna. Your mindless insistence on this one point has cost my project so much—"

Ey wants to say more but Koni interrupts. "Just because your leaving benefits us, doesn't mean it can't benefit you. Ask yourself what is most important to you."

My aching urge to be among people again threatens to drown all other concerns. Anissa. I want to return while she is still living. I want to see Nandi's bright smile. I want to help Rill and his struggling family, I want to help Orco manage the crumbling dome. There is so much to be done.

But I say, "Go to the stars with Wenslow if you want. I don't care. But you can't endanger every living thing on Earth. You can't crash every functioning ecosystem there. It will be another, slower apocalypse. Abandon the horticulture project, or I will continue to fight it on every front."

Singh opens eir mouth, but Koni jumps in with something ey is seeing in the datalink. "Guadalupe is getting impatient, Donna. Ey wants you in eir office with answers, and ey is not going to credit the ones you have to give."

Eir look takes in both Singh and I. "You can have this argument later. But the three of us need to decide on a story that is believable and mutually beneficial. Otherwise Wenslow is going to have all of us declared faulty and strip our privileges."

Singh considers the idea and does appear concerned.

"We need time. I will hide you, Donna, come with me." Koni looks more worried than Singh. I can see em jumping in and out of eir datalink, trying to manage what I'm sure are conflicting demands from different authorities, as ey tries to be useful to everyone.

"How will you explain my sudden absence?" I ask, though I have no intention of letting Koni hide me anywhere. I can think of nothing more dangerous. Ey has already tried to kill me once.

"We can concoct a story for that, too?" Koni suggests, distracted. "A well-developed plan. No more quick decisions. I am not at my best under those circumstances." That's a true statement, I think. Like any stationer, Koni is accustomed to having months to make any decision.

I haven't moved yet, and Koni looks at me pointedly. "Will you come with me?" Ey gestures at the door to Med.

Ey wants me to precede em out the door and ey will follow. I remind myself that ey inhabits a stationer's weak, slow shell. I glance at Koni's arm, the one concealing the weapon. I haven't forgotten who Koni last used that weapon on.

With every bit of my attention focused on Koni, I slowly pass by em.

Sure enough, I hear the sound of skin sliding past fabric and an unobtrusive metallic click.

I pivot and grab eir wrist and slam it against the wall, pinning em with my body. The look of complete and naked surprise on Koni's face is the most gratifying thing I have seen yet.

Singh startles but stays well clear of us.

"I knew you'd think it was easier to just kill me," I say. "Again. That's why you brought this."

I look at the instrument ey is holding. I recognize it. It was hanging on the wall in eir room in Maint. My mind spins into my Survey-privilege datalink and comes back in an instant.

"A bolt gun," I say.

My shoulder is pressing against eir chest. My grip on eir wrist is tightening, tightening.

"Ah!" ey cries out.

"You're causing pain," Singh warns.

"Drop it, then," I say, and I continue squeezing. Koni drops it and it clatters to the floor.

"You couldn't kill me before," I say. "Why would you even try now?"

Through eir teeth ey says, "Because you won't trust me."

I let go of Koni's wrist and ey draws a relieved breath. Then ey wedges arms between us, trying to push me away. I slam em against the wall and ey desists.

"Let Koni go," Singh says with authority. "Ey is disarmed."

"Station is full of things for em to arm emself with." I look to Singh with an accusatory glare. "You never warned me what ey was capable of. You let my murderer loose on station, and you never took steps to protect any of us."

Singh's expression is an unreadable blank.

I turn back to Koni. "The two of us cannot coexist on Station."

Eir eyes search my face frantically, trying to guess what I'm going to do. "Donna, how are you going to get yourself out of this? We have to think of a solution."

"I don't want your help," I say. "You shouldn't have killed Jayd." I feel hot tears in my eyes.

I don't know if it's my words or the tears streaming down my face, but Koni panics. Ey struggles and pushes at my face with both palms.

I slam Koni against the wall, with force this time, and eir head snaps back and strikes the wall. I feel em go limp and let em fall. The smack of eir temple on the floor renders em utterly still.

"Ey is damaged. We must assist immediately." Singh turns back into Med to gather supplies. I don't mistake eir actions for those of someone who cares. Ey is just going through the motions. Singh will revive Jayd's murderer and watch passively as ey takes up eir bolt gun and rejoins other stationers, because stopping killers is not Singh's job, fixing shells is.

Through the tears still coming down my face, I see the scope Shelley was using to read Andrej's slides. I lift it out of its charging station and almost drop it, it's so heavy. I swing it over Koni's head.

And then I do drop it.

Blood and brain matter streak out across the dingy white floor and behind em up the wall.

Singh turns and looks at the ruin of Koni's head with eir mouth hanging open, hands partially outstretched.

I start shaking badly. "That," I manage to say, "that is what a shell looks like when it is beyond resuscitation and Reform."

* * *

I stumble to the sink by the examination table and try to wash my hands. My face, my whole body, feels unnaturally, unbearably hot. I touch my cold wet hands to my burning cheeks. I take deep breaths and lean against the counter.

When I turn around again, I see Singh bent over Koni's dead shell. Beside em is a metal pan with a thin layer of liquid in the bottom. Ey is holding a scalpel over the wound on Koni's head and begins to make a careful cut.

"What are you doing?" I demand numbly.

"Preparing samples for fixation and staining," ey replies evenly.

I feel a wave of heat pass over me, and I worry I may fall. I reach out to the counter again for support.

"So you can investigate eir death?" I ask, too loudly. "You watched Koni die, Singh. You can watch it again on the video feed if you want. Why are you doing that? Stop!"

My voice is rising in a crescendo but eirs is measured and calm as ey says, "It's important to have samples to document the accident. For the Med report to be complete."

"It's not an accident! I murdered em!" I run my hand along the wall to steady my shaky steps. As I pass by Singh, ey is carefully laying thin sections of tissue in the pan.

"Your humanity is dead," I say. "Irretrievably lost."

* * *

In the corridor I stop and take deep breaths, one after the other. The air out here seems cooler, less stifling, though I know that the air all over Station is uniform. I keep a steadying hand on the wall just to be sure of my balance.

I have to think. How soon can I expect Wenslow to know what I've done? What actions will ey take? It doesn't matter, I think to myself. I have to act immediately. It's the only possible advantage I have to exploit.

I have no idea how they may try to restrain or contain me. The only thing I can imagine Guadalupe doing is sealing off whatever section of Station I happen to be in.

So where do I want to be when that happens? Where can I go and cause the most damage to stationers' plans to mine Earth and introduce invasive species? I set off down the corridor at a quick pace.

This won't be gentle. I don't have time for something clean.

Quicker than I expect, a flagged red bulletin runs on our datalink feed. It says: Surveyor Donna Whitacre is under suspicion of unhealthy Reform faults. Direct em to the Council Hall to meet with Commissioner Guadalupe and all division supervisors. Division Supervisors report. Donna Whitacre report.

I increase my pace and watch for other stationers. I'm expecting to encounter Bri answering the summons to Council, so I'm prepared when I see em in the corridor. I slip down a branching corridor to let em pass by. If ey had simply turned eir head ey would have seen me, but stationers don't work that way. When ey is gone I continue on, heading for the Flight command center.

The red bulletin runs twice more at intervals before I reach the room. I stop in the doorway, looking at the banks and banks of terminals, all dark. I fight a sudden feeling of uncertainty.

A direct channel opens to me. It's Guadalupe.

"Surveyor Whitacre, report to the Council Hall."

"Hello, Lisa," I reply.

"Report immediately."

"I'm currently engaged in an important project," I send. "I'll join you as soon as I am available."

I'm counting on it that ey won't reveal details over an open channel. Sure enough, ey sends me a private message, but it's easy to ignore. Wenslow sends me a private message. I'm somewhat more interested in that one, but my best strategy is not to engage. I go to the terminals and wake them, one by one. They are not locked.

Wenslow opens a direct channel. "Donna, we are assembled in Council awaiting your presence. Join us."

"Later," I respond. "You can pass the time by showing em your private video feeds."

"We have all seen your behavior in my office," Wenslow responds. "Please join us to explain yourself."

The terminals in Flight are all humming now, and I choose one at random and query it. The file structure is complicated and not immediately transparent to me. I can barely spare a thought to wonder why Wenslow would ask me about what I did in eir office and not what's just happened in Med.

When I don't respond to Wenslow, ey sends, "Donna, come speak with us."

And after a suitable pause, "Where are you?"

"Don't you know?" I reply.

Guadalupe's direct channel to me lights up immediately. "Whitacre you are disobeying a direct command of your Station Commissioner. Effective immediately I am revoking all privileges. I am instructing other stationers to have no contact with you. You are implicated in the destruction of vital components of Station, tampering with Records, and the death of Fabrication technician Jayd Collins-Brown. I have never levied more serious charges in all my time on Station. Report immediately."

I stand back from the terminal where I'm working, momentarily defeated. I reach into my datalink and find that even my most basic access to Records is blocked. All I have left is communications. I feel a flare of anger.

"I didn't kill Jayd," I fire back on Guadalupe and Wenslow's open channels simultaneously. "Koni did, under Wenslow's orders. Using a bolt gun, the same weapon ey injured me with before I was sent on my last survey..."

The link goes dark. All my links are dark. I wish I could be in the room with Guadalupe to see em mad enough to cut my communications, too. Ey wants to prevent me from spreading my faulty theories to all the other stationers who are by now surely listening in on the link. But how will ey send me instructions now?

In the quiet I can concentrate. I sit down at a different terminal, take a steadying breath, and try again. This time I carefully read any error messages sent up by my commands, and I see that access to shuttle flight sequences is restricted to those with Flight-privilege. That's not unexpected. What I'm hoping to find is instructions on how to physically accomplish an override. Through the bay window before me I see all the entrances to the pods themselves. I am thinking I may have better luck if I go down to the small terminals by the launch chutes themselves when a window opens on my screen and a message scrolls out across it.

It reads, "Donna, Guadalupe has locked down the lower Flight Bay. You are trapped there unless you cooperate."

"Wenslow?" I reply.

"Yes," ey responds. "Come to the forward corridor Blue 5 safety door and you will be let through."

"I'll let you know when I'm ready," I reply.

"No, come now. Come away from those terminals or I will deactivate them, too."

Koni's previous offer to me suggests a good lie, one I hope will convince someone to give me access to the most useful propulsion units aboard Station.

"I just want to go down to the surface," I tell Wenslow. "Why not let me go? It would save us all a lot of trouble."

"Let me discuss it with the assembled members," ey types.

I wait, my mind racing. I might neutralize the shuttle propulsion units, but there's nothing I can do about the food-collection drones. Koni's proposals never mentioned them, I hope because their engines are too small to be really useful. And Jayd thought they weren't suitable for spreading living stuff over the surface. I hope ey was right. Even if they could be modified, it would take time, expertise, and possibly materials that are hard to get.

"We have agreed," Wenslow says, breaking in on my thoughts. "Present yourself at Blue 5 safety lock to be escorted to Med where you will be Reformed into a surveyor shell."

It is a very tempting offer. But frustratingly, it won't work. I need access to the source of engine parts now, before any stationer can use them.

"Am I to trust you won't just let my shell die in Reform when I am helpless?" I reply. "I should just go now. Put Bri on to give me the access codes and launch instructions."

There's a moment before ey replies. "We need time to confer."

I'm surprised this line of negotiations is going so well. But while I wait, a very viable backup plan occurs to me. It hinges on one thing, though, and I can't leave the terminal to investigate it. If I don't reply to Wenslow in a timely fashion, ey will know I am pursuing some other agenda. So it will have to wait.

"Negative Donna. We cannot give you Flight-privileged information. Guadalupe refuses, and ey is not ready to negotiate further."

"What about you?" I type back. "I know things you don't want me to share with Council, I'm sure. Your use of Supervisor Records-privilege, altering Rchive protocols, personally monitoring video feeds around Station. The anticoagulant you gave Andrej, the order you gave Koni which resulted in Jayd's death. It would save you a lot of difficulty if I was simply gone. Why don't you just unlock this terminal and let me go?"

There is a long pause. So long I check several times to see if the terminal is already unlocked with Flight-privilege. But it is not.

"You have no evidence against me, and I have no reason to fear you. Your attempts at covert plans with first Andrej and then Jayd, your performance in my office, your own words over open channels, free for every stationer to witness, have condemned you as completely faulty. No one will believe any argument you make."

I get up from the terminal, frustrated. Just as I turn to leave, another message scrolls out.

"But I will assist you off of Station. It's better, I feel, for every stationer."

I sit quickly, my fingers ready to fly across the screen so we can get this done before Guadalupe moves somehow. I have no doubt Wenslow is operating right now without eir oversight.

"I'm going to send Koni to you, and I'll give em temporary Flight-privilege. Ey will quietly assist you in getting off Station. I expect you to cooperate with em fully. You understand, I think, how very dangerous ey is."

I jump up from the terminal, agitated and feeling too hot all over again. Wenslow is sending Koni to kill me, just as ey sent Koni to intercept Jayd. I should agree. Then I should walk away from this terminal and investigate my other options while Wenslow wastes valuable time trying in vain to locate Koni. Yet after a moment's struggle I find I am completely unable to restrain myself.

"I regret to inform you that Koni is dead. Check the video feeds in Med. Then perhaps you will understand how very dangerous *I am*. Don't send anyone down here to interfere with me. I am only sorry I have to leave before I can get to you, Wenslow."

* * *

I get up from the terminal so angry my hands are shaking, crying over Jayd again. I wish Wenslow had come for me instead of Andrej, I wish ey had sent Koni to confront me instead of Jayd. I really do. But Wenslow left me alive, and that's an oversight I will now make em regret.

I leave the Flight command center and rush through the corridors. I find the door quickly; I've been here often enough.

I pound on the door. I can't buzz without my communications link. I don't know if I'm quarantined down here alone, or if they perhaps forgot about one stationer.

The door slides open. They did forget about one stationer. A very important stationer. A former launch engineer who still has active Flight-privilege. Even if Guadalupe and

Wenslow get wise and cut the link, Sasha will remember how to do the job. I am sure of it.

"Did you decide on a course of action?" Sasha asks.

"Yes. I ran down Jayd's murderer and killed em."

Sasha looks at me blankly.

"Have you checked your feed?" I ask.

"I...don't look at it."

"Check it now if you want to see what I've been up to," I say. "Guadalupe has sealed off this section to contain me and cut all my links and communication."

Sasha gives an almost imperceptible shake of the head. "I don't want to be involved."

"Then I'm sorry. Because I've involved you. Come with me." I start down the corridor.

Sasha does not follow.

I stop and wait. "I need your help in the shuttle bay," I say. "I'm not really giving you a choice."

"No? Will you kill me as well?" Sasha's voice is convincingly neutral.

"No. But I will drag you down the hall if I have to."

"You're hostile."

"I'm in a hurry. Come on, Sasha. I'll explain as we walk." I reach out as if to take hold, and that is threat enough to start em walking.

"Let me tell you what we're fighting about on Station," I say. "Singh wants to terraform the surface of Earth by introducing a nonnative soil microbial community and spreading genetically modified extinct plants across vast swaths of land. Ey has not brought this idea before Council, instead attempting to co-opt survey missions and food-collection drone trips to test formulations without oversight."

I realize I don't strictly know if the last part is true. I never questioned Singh and Koni about it, I was too busy accusing them of murder. But there's plenty to say about Wenslow...

"And Wenslow has taken control of Station systems by granting emself apparently every privilege and using it to alter what is Rchived in Records, to access video and audio feeds on Station, and to learn critical secrets about stationers. Ey killed Andrej, because Andrej was outspoken in opposing eir plans. I wish I could say what Wenslow's objective is, but I don't know. Koni suggested to me ey might wish to explore space, but it's just conjecture. Certainly, whatever ey wants to do requires lots of materials, as ey is pushing hard in Council to mine old cities on Earth for parts to do it."

We have reached Flight Command, and Sasha halts outside the doors, seeing the lights on and all the terminals woken.

"Should I tell you of Guadalupe's part in all this?" I ask.

"No," Sasha says. "You speak so quickly and so...messily that I find it difficult to follow your recitation."

I shake my head, then lead Sasha through Flight and down to the shuttle terminals. I go to stand by the first pod. I speak slowly this time.

"Let me tell you what I believe. It is time for us to let humans on the Earth build their own societies without interference from us. Any resources on Earth belong to them and not to us. I have seen humans are now capable of surviving on their own outside the dome, meaning our Mission Imperatives have been fulfilled and our time as stationers is over."

I open my mouth to continue, but Sasha holds up eir hand.

"If you wish for my cooperation, you should have said that first. Yes. Stationers have long outlasted their usefulness."

I feel a pang in my heart hearing something Jayd would have agreed with. "Will you help me?"

"What do you intend?"

"Koni's plans for sending large collection drones to the surface relied entirely on repurposing propulsion units from these shuttles. So I want to launch them all now."

"Their current navigation modules guide them only to Earth."

"That's fine," I say, relieved, beginning to believe Sasha will help me. "Send them all to Earth. I just want them inaccessible to stationers."

Sasha makes no move to act. I could try more convincing, or more threatening, but for now I just wait.

"Fabrication may be able to manufacture other craft."

I am surprised Sasha is taking an interest in my plan. I don't feel as though I have time to stand talking for long, but I desperately want to explain myself to someone, to have some stationer understand.

"Not without difficulty. Without any way to mine materials from Earth, it is my understanding there is little left aboard Station that's useful to them. Unless they repurpose Station's own engines, which I assume would compromise the whole craft."

Sasha looks at me expressionlessly for a long moment. "I agree stationer time is done. All stationers are faulty, any interaction with them is poisonous to reason and sense."

I don't know if I agree with Sasha. Stationers have lost so much over time, maybe it's true we can't be rehabilitated. But either way human consciousnesses were never meant to be immortal. We cheated death for too long, and now it's time to be done.

Then Sasha says, "But surely non-involvement is the best course," and I feel a wave of frustration.

"The best course *is* non-involvement," I agree, carefully navigating around Sasha's own particular form of faultiness. "But stationers are about to involve themselves very directly with humans on Earth. We have to prevent that."

Sasha lifts a hand, reaching for the terminal. I stand frozen, anticipating. Slowly ey begins pre-flight preparation. The first pod launches, and then the second. My tension ratchets with each one, very sure by now Wenslow can see what I am doing. Knowing ey is watching all eir plans slip out of reach, and certain ey will be desperate to stop me by any means.

When there are only two pods left, I am nearly bouncing on my toes with impatience.

Sasha moves to the last terminal of the last pod, and my hand darts out, blocking the screen.

"Not that one."

"Why?" Sascha asks, though eir voice remains incurious.

"That's for me. I'm going *home*."

The word feels warm and soft on my tongue. How I long for it. I've been years up here on Station awaiting the slow progress of stationer plans, but maybe some of my friends are still there.

And even if it weren't for my selfish impulses, I have to go back and tell them that no Peace-in-the-Sky are coming back. I have to try and convince them to disregard our previous instructions. I have to encourage them to break down the barriers of the dome, to find a way to live as one people, to share the bounty inside the dome and spread its wealth carefully so that all humans are sustained.

And if stationers do manage to get themselves down to the surface, far in the future, long after I'm gone, I have to plant the seeds of caution among human minds. I have to warn them.

"This does not seem in keeping with non-involvement," Sasha comments as ey watches me climb into the pod.

"I won't last long in this shell," I assure em. "Just long enough to explain to them what's happened, so they don't wait for us." I look at Sasha. "Come with me if you want. You could see Earth again before you die."

And now for the first time Sasha reacts. Ey pulls back visibly from me. "Leave Station? Leave?"

I feel a tweak of disappointment. "I didn't think you'd want to come. Stay here, then. I sincerely hope you suffer no consequences for helping me. You must tell them I threatened you, and you feared for your life. I'm sure they will believe that."

And then the lights flicker in the bay and in the command center and all through the corridors.

"Hurry," I cram myself into the seat and start pulling on the harnesses. "They're trying to cut the power to this section."

"They can't," Sasha says, "not without disabling important Station functions running on Flight terminals. We would drop out of orbit."

"I wouldn't be surprised if Wenslow rerouted those functions just so ey could try it."

We finish with the harnesses and Sasha takes the headpiece and shifts it into position. Just before it's lowered over my head, I say, "Head to Blue 5 safety lock and open a direct channel to Guadalupe so you can be let through. Don't just return to your cell. I don't know what they might do to environmental conditions here to try and neutralize me."

"Go, Donna," Sasha says evenly, fitting the mask and headpiece over me.

I feel a rush of pressurized air and my view of the bay disappears.

The pod shifts, rotating into place in the shuttle.

Sasha could choose not to launch me. It would be very easy now to simply walk out and tell Guadalupe I'm harnessed in the pod, and they could all come take me into custody. But the sound within the pod winds up and changes pitch, and I know Sasha will not betray me.

I have a last-minute realization no one ever explicitly accused me of tampering with the food collection system. Do they know? It does seem an odd place for Wenslow to have cameras, perhaps ey does not know what Jayd and I did after conspiring in Fabrication.

If I still had communications, I might at least warn Sasha. But I let it go. They will notice the problem and correct it, or they will all starve. I will not interfere.

"Goodbye to Station," I say into the mask. "Goodbye to stationers."

Countdown sequence initiates within the pod. I close my eyes and breathe deeply from the mask, slipping slowly from consciousness. I'll make the journey in a state of induced semi-torpor.

And then that's all I know. Everything fades away.

Epilogue

I'm aware first of a headache. A very strong and unpleasant headache.

I open my eyes. The pod within the shuttle has opened itself, as it should, and the shuttle door remains sealed. I unlatch the harnesses and try to pull myself free.

There's a jolt of pain from my left shoulder. I extract that arm carefully and hold the limb against me as I disengage and lean over to peer out the very small portal in the hatch. It's dark.

I maneuver around and unlock the hatch, allowing it to hiss open. Dry, cool night air hits me. I breathe deep.

There's nothing around me but empty arid land. Scraggly dark brush. Orange rock outcroppings. Dust and chalk swirl by when a breeze stirs.

Cradling my arm, I pull my legs from the pod and step out onto the sand. I feel the shape of every jagged pebble through my thin Station slippers.

I smile.

Among the dark dunes I see a cloud of dust rising. I narrow my eyes in the dark to peer into the distance and see the two camels whose progress generates it. Someone must have seen my shuttle streaking through the atmosphere and come to investigate.

I realize, unhappily, that I will not be able to speak their language and have nothing to help me learn it. But maybe I will recall some from my previous trip. I climb on top of my vessel, slipping over the slick surface, and balance precariously on top.

And I wave.

ACKNOWLEDGEMENTS

I would not be a writer without my writers' group. They nurtured and encouraged me, and I'm so grateful to have found a community with them where I could grow and learn. Special thanks to K.D. Edwards, Paige Nguyen, Scott Reintgen, and Jennifer Perez, who helped *Peace in the Sky* take its final form.

Between the first and second books, I moved halfway around the world and lost that support. I struggled to find time and make space for my creativity. Without Mary Robinette Kowal's amazing Patreon and Sandra Tayler's *Structuring Life to Support Creativity* talks, I would have foundered. I'm also grateful to the many authors who freely share their writing and publishing advice online. *Station in the Sky* could never have launched without those resources.

William C. Tracy, Heather Tracy, and XM Moon take credit for helping me navigate the editing, publishing, and promotional side of being an author. I learned so much with their generous guidance.

And finally, special thank you to all those who order, review, share, or talk about books you enjoy. You help authors reach readers, which is what we are all here for.

ABOUT THE AUTHOR

Caye Marsh is a former biologist writing Sci-Fi and Fantasy. She cherishes the unbroken quiet of wild places and the true dark of night, so please keep it down and remember to extinguish all outdoor lights. You can find her at cayemarsh.com.

Please take a moment to review this book at your favorite retailer's website, Goodreads, or simply tell your friends!

9 781960 247360